A LADY'S HEART OF GOLD

A LADY'S HEART OF GOLD

HEARTS OF ARIZONA BOOK 3

SALLY BRITTON

Published by Pink Citrus Books
Edited by Jenny Proctor of Midnight Owl Editors
Cover design by Blue Water Books
Illustrations by Melanie Bateman

Sally Britton
www.authorsallybritton.com

First Printing: September 2022

CONTENT WARNING: Chapter Nine of this book includes historically accurate descriptions of Native American children removed from their homes. We now know many of those children died while at so-called "Indian Schools" and never returned home. There is also mention of abusive practices in the training of horses.

For Those Who Fight for Equality, Justice, Love, and Beauty. May You Continue to Change the World.

AUTHOR'S PRE-READ NOTE

The term "Indian" for Native American and First Nations people is inappropriate. However, it was applied here with historical accuracy in mind. The term was used sparingly, and in reference to the characters' understanding of the Native peoples of North America.

As the author of this book, I spent several months researching the history of Native Americans, especially in regards to the 1890's in the United States of America and its Territories. This is a gentle love story and does *not* delve deeply into all the things that were *wrong* about treatment of Native people and People of Color. Please do not mistake this for an accurate account of how things were. Please read the historical notes at the end of the book for more information.

I believe the United States Government owes more than apologies to those who lost so much, including their lives, their children, their homes, and their culture. The Native Americans of the United States of America still fight against racism, cultural appropriation, poverty, and the loss of their ancestral identity.

There is content in Chapter Nine that may be disturbing for some readers. Please see the content warning on the copyright page for more information.

CHAPTER 1

LONDON, ENGLAND

NOVEMBER 1895

I f the right combination of doors opened all at the same time, the noise from the presses in the basement traveled all the way to the rooftops of the publishing district. But since most people considered the click-clack and thrum of machinery deafening, the doors of *The London Guardian* all stayed firmly shut during business hours. Which made the fact that Molly McKinney could hear the editor-in-chief shouting inside his office while she remained in the waiting room quite a feat.

Molly kept her shoulders back, her chin up, and her gloved hands folded tightly over her portfolio of clippings. She made brief eye contact with Mr. Gilchrist's secretary, who winced sympathetically when the editor's voice rose still higher. Really, it was quite impossible to miss what he shouted at the half-dozen journalists inside the room with him.

"You're all writing fluff that any street urchin'd do a better job reportin'." Several words unfit for print followed as he continued to describe the quality of the stories the men had submitted. "We need somethin' better. Somethin' different. We're fighting against cheap novels, sensational headlines, and you give me more stories about wharf-murders and society parties? We need stories better than that if we're goin' to capture our readers. We need somethin' they come back for, week after week, that they can't get anywhere else."

Someone else in the room spoke, too low for Molly or the secretary—whose neck had disappeared into her shoulders—to hear. Whatever that person said, the editor didn't like it.

"Get out of here! All of you, get out of here and bring me back something worth the paper and ink I waste on you!"

The first man out flung the door open and rushed through the room, clapping a hat on his head as he went, his face pale. The other five men who'd sat through that tongue lashing hurried out, too. Some of them red in the face, others white as sheets, but all looking as though they'd eaten something that disagreed with them.

The secretary stood and picked up a small notebook. She swallowed, then walked on shaky legs to the door. "M-M-Mr. Gilchrist?"

"What is it now?" he snarled.

Molly pulled her leather portfolio tight against her chest. The clock on the wall opposite showed the exact time she had scheduled her meeting with the editor. And while she had no intention of letting his temper get the better of her, an impatient man was unlikely to give her a fair interview.

"Your next appointment is here. A M-M-Miss McKinney?"

"The lady journalist?" He sounded as irritable as ever as he said, "Show her in. And bring us some tea."

Nothing else could have relaxed Molly the way the mention of tea did. Tea was a civilized drink. A drink that people took time to consume. Tea meant at least a quarter hour of Mr. Gilchrist's time.

She rose at the same moment the secretary reappeared in the doorway. The older woman offered Molly a tremulous smile. "Mr. Gilchrist will see you now, miss."

"Thank you." Molly adjusted the purse at her wrist, briefly touched the locket resting against her chest, lifted her chin, and pasted on a confident smile. She knew she wasn't much to look at, but a smile went a long way to making a plain person attractive. At least, that's what her schoolteachers had told her.

Molly entered the office to find Mr. Gilchrist already on his feet, standing beside his desk. Had she not heard the man's shouting moments before, she wouldn't have guessed that he had a temper at all. He was her same height, which wasn't overly impressive for a man even if it was unfashionable for a woman to be five foot six in her stockings. And Molly wore heeled boots that gave her two more inches on the man. But he was built like a bull, with wide shoulders and forearms that made the sleeves of his jacket strain against them. He had dark hair and a large handlebar mustache. He wore a lemon-yellow bowtie and a kind smile.

"Miss McKinney. A pleasure to meet you." He held his hand out, and Molly offered her own. She never knew whether to expect a firm handshake or a bow, and most men didn't seem to know which was best when greeting a female reporter. Mr. Gilchrist went up in her estimation with his offer of a handshake. "Please, have a seat."

Molly thanked him and took a seat on the leather chair across from his desk while he made his way back to his own chair. "Thank you for agreeing to see me, Mr. Gilchrist."

"How could I say no when you included an introductory letter from J.S. Wood?" Gilchrist folded his hands on his desk. "He called you a promising young mind, you know."

The letter of introduction Molly had obtained from Mr. Wood had been sealed. She hadn't any idea what he had said of her, but the glowing praise gave her courage another boost. "That is most kind of him."

"He's a good fellow, of course. A man with more of a mind for helping people around him than helping himself. I've noticed he has a real eye for people. I've read articles and editorials written by him for years, and my wife and daughters read aloud from his *Gentlewoman* magazine every time it comes into our house." He shook his head slightly, and in a single blink,

Molly could imagine him sitting in a room before a fire with a wife reading to him. "But I imagine you didn't come to talk about Wood."

Molly curled her gloved fingers around the portfolio in her lap. "No, sir. I actually came to see about a job with your newspaper."

His broad shoulders sank. "Oh?" His smile faded. "Ah, I see. Of course. May I ask what sort of job you were hoping for?"

Her hope of a fair hearing lessened. Whatever the man had expected her to say, this clearly wasn't it. "I would like a position on your staff as a reporter. I am an accomplished journalist. I brought samples of my work to show you." She held the portfolio up but hesitated to place it on the desk. "I have written a few pieces for *The Gentlewoman*."

"Very well. Let's have a look." He held his hand out and she surrendered her work to him. He appeared no more cheerful than before. "I must warn you." He put her portfolio down in front of him. "I have a full staff of reporters and several who work freelance and send things in from time to time. I'm not in great need of more journalists at present." He flipped open the portfolio, and Molly held her breath.

She had put her best piece first. The one that meant the most to her. At the beginning of that year, she had visited Octavia Hill and interviewed the social reformer about her organization, the National Trust for Places of Historic Interest or Natural Beauty. Molly had spent an entire day with the woman who many called a troublemaker even while others thought her a saint.

The interview had changed Molly's life. The hours speaking to a woman with such a love for nature and people had shifted Molly's perspective. Working for a woman's publication had been a safe start for her. But she could do so much more.

And she wanted to see the world in all of its natural beauty.

The secretary came in and quietly put the tea tray on a table near Mr. Gilchrist's desk. She made a cup for him, setting it at his elbow. She softly inquired after Molly's tastes before handing her a cup, too. The woman gave Molly an encouraging smile before closing the door, which Molly returned with tightened lips.

"I read this when *The Gentlewoman* published it," Mr. Gilchrist said quietly, as though to himself. Then he turned that article and went to the next without another word. Molly's heart sank. Her best work, and he'd already read it and had nothing to say about it.

The teacup rattled in the saucer, so she lifted it off the plate to stop the noise. She sipped at the warm drink, letting it soothe her anxiety as much as warm leaf-water possibly could. Why had she let herself hope for more than what she already had? The world of newspapers and journals hadn't opened to women until recently, and she still found herself elbowed out of the way by her male peers. If she didn't ask for private meetings with the interesting people of the day, she didn't get to ask questions at all.

Her kind-hearted teachers had warned her when she left school at seventeen. They'd showered her with gifts—beautiful writing pens, reams of paper, notebooks, and letters of recommendation—but they had not given her much hope regarding her prospects. Indeed, it had taken her three years to find a newspaper willing to print her, and even then they'd only allowed her to comment on fashion.

The Gentlewoman had been a dream come true when they'd hired her the day she turned twenty-two. Now, at twenty-five years of age, five years of journalistic experience in her hat, Molly hoped for so much more.

"I notice you use initials in all your work," Mr. Gilchrist said, turning another article over. "M.E. McKinney. Why is that?"

She returned her teacup to its saucer. "That was under Mr. Wood's advisement. Even while writing for a publication meant for women, the thought is that using my initials will make readers take me more seriously. Most assume I am a man when they read my work."

Mr. Gilchrist snorted. Then he picked up his teacup and sipped, his large mustache twitching the whole time. "I told you I have daughters. Two of them. Their mother was a governess before we met. A dying breed, I'm told. She's well educated, and so are our girls. They're thirteen and eleven. The eleven-year-old fancies herself a newspaper woman. Mrs. Gilchrist and I often wonder what we should tell her. Do we encourage her, because we can see women making steps in the world of newspapers—there's even that lady editor now. I'm sure you've heard of her. Or do we tell her to become a teacher? Or a nurse?" He gave Molly a sad sort of smile. A commiserating smile. It finished off the last of her hope that the day would end as she wished it.

Still, she addressed his question with a sympathetic tone. "I imagine it is difficult as a parent. My teachers walked that line, too. They all told me I had a great talent for writing, but everyone stopped short of encouraging me to make a living from it."

"What do your parents think of your work?" He put his cup down and tidied up her portfolio. A precursor to him closing it and handing it back.

"I hope they're proud of me. Though I don't know what they would think. They passed away when I was quite young." She forced a smile, the one that told people it was an old wound that didn't quite hurt anymore.

Mr. Gilchrist's mustache stopped twitching. "Oh. I am sorry to hear that."

She placed her saucer on his desk, the cup rattling until the moment she released it. She wouldn't cry. She refused to cry. How many times had men sneered at her vocation and told her a woman was far too delicate, too emotional, for such work? Crying only proved them right. Men certainly didn't cry on the job. At least, not that she had seen.

And Mr. Gilchrist was being exceptionally kind. Somehow, though, that made it hurt even more.

The editor closed her portfolio and held it out to her. "Your article on the National Trust was interesting. I thought so the first time I read it, too. My wife thought I should have one of my men cover the story after she read what you said, about the responsibility we hold to safeguard natural beauty for our children. We were both quite moved."

Molly nodded her thanks and held the portfolio close again, feeling rather like a child clutching a favorite doll for comfort. Would Mr. Wood be disappointed when she returned to her desk at the magazine with the news that she was unwanted elsewhere? Perhaps he would second-guess her place with his staff of writers, too.

"I wonder." Mr. Gilchrist tipped his head to the side, his bushy eyebrows coming together as he studied her. "If you worked at this paper, what would you hope to write? Society pieces? Fashion advice? Or perhaps a column for women's suffrage?"

"If that was what my editor wanted." She smiled, then laughed at herself. Why not confess her dream? She wasn't going to get it. "If I could do anything I wanted, I would ask for a position as a traveling reporter. I would love to go places that most in London, or in England itself, will never see and write about those places. That way, everyone might know what Niagara Falls in Canada looks like, or whether there really are alligators the size of trams in the swamps of Florida. Perhaps I would write a piece on the American West—about the cowboys and Indians that fill our novels here. Do they still exist? Are they still at war, as our fiction would have us believe?"

"Fascinating ideas." Mr. Gilchrist stood, and Molly did the same. "But I'm not certain our readers would care for those things."

Molly reached for his hand when he offered it, knowing the interview was over. "You have a fine paper, Mr. Gilchrist. I hope you find what you need for those readers. The thing they come back for, week after week, that they can't get anywhere else."

He blinked at her, perhaps surprised she remembered what he had said to his staff or that she had heard him at all. "Yes. Thank you."

Molly stepped away from his desk, promising herself not to

shed a single tear. Not until she made it outside to the pavement. She had only gone a few steps, however, when Mr. Gilchrist called her back.

"Miss McKinney? I beg your pardon, but I wonder—what does M.E. stand for?"

She looked over her shoulder at him, one hand on the door-frame of his office. "Mary Elizabeth." There had been so many Marys, Elizabeths, Beths, Pollys, and so forth in the school for girls where she'd ended up that her teachers had settled on calling her Molly, and so she had been from the time she was nine years old.

Mr. Gilchrist held his hand out to her. "Wait a moment, Miss McKinney. Please."

She stood frozen, half in and half out of his office. "Sir?"

He came around his desk. "Perhaps I was too hasty before. You see, I'm not a superstitious man. But I do believe in signs. That's why I asked Mrs. Gilchrist to marry me, you see. A sign. And it proved a good choice." He tugged on the lapels of his coat. "Our daughters are called Mary and Elizabeth."

Molly blinked at him, hardly believing that a man in his position would give heed to something so simple as a coincidence in names. "How lovely." What else could she say?

The editor smiled, and his mustache turned up at the corners, too. "Maybe you better sit down again, Miss McKinney. Tell me more about this idea of yours. A traveling reporter, you say? How would such a thing work?" He gestured to the chair, and Molly's hope rose like a phoenix from the ashes.

Her dream hadn't died yet.

CHAPTER 2

ARIZONA TERRITORY, USA

AUGUST 1896

F ort Huachuca was quiet at one o'clock in the afternoon. Though not as warm as Phoenix or even Tucson, the sun hanging high in the sky still made people lazy. Ed stayed in the shade, which had to be ten degrees cooler than the packed earth parade in the middle of the fort's four walls. Most of the barrack windows were open, letting in whatever breeze they could catch coming down from the mountains at their back.

A couple of soldiers sat in the shade of a building across from where Ed stood, a table with checkers between them, their weapons leaning against the wall behind them. They had stopped their game in favor of staring at Ed, gesturing his way and occasionally laughing. He didn't need to guess what they spoke of, because he'd heard it all before.

Eduardo Enoli Ramirez Byrd thought little about the opinions of others. He'd long since given up trying to win anyone's approval. That's what came of growing up beneath the umbrellas of two vastly different cultures. Someone would always be unhappy with his choices, and the only person he could really count on pleasing was himself.

Because of this, Ed ignored slurs and insults sent his way with practiced ease. The people trying to get a rise out of him were usually unhappy about something in their own life, and they hoped rattling someone like him would restore whatever strength or joy they'd lost. His mother called people like that *lost souls*, and she'd tell him to light candles for them at church. His father would say those people deserved silence and nothing more.

Instead of focusing on those who hated themselves enough to take shots at him, Ed found his place among people who respected his abilities regardless of the color of his skin. For the last six years, that place had been KB Ranch. He worked circles around most cowboys and *vaqueros,* too, because he'd taken a true risk and put his money back into the ranch as an investor. That was why, when most men packed it up after a cattle drive and moved along to the next place, Ed stayed put.

At the moment, Ed held a notebook in his hand and the stub of a pencil. He was writing. Something he did when there wasn't anyone else around to see. He described the men across the parade ground, from their faded hats to their mud-splattered boots. Maybe he could use the idea they'd given him later. Maybe not.

In the room behind Ed, his two closest friends negotiated with an officer for cattle the army wanted and KB Ranch would supply. Duke and Frosty, both attached to the ranch for as long as they lived—along with their wives—were good at negotiating. They'd settle on a price fair to the ranch and satisfying to Uncle Sam.

Ed had come mostly to get a change of scenery. He hadn't left the ranch in over a month. He'd used the excuse that they needed him to help drive the twenty head of cattle that two of their other cowboys waited with outside the fort. But he'd seen the look Duke and Frosty had exchanged. He knew what they thought.

He'd heard it called many things over the years, but "Itchy-Feet" was what they said most often at the ranch. They worried he'd grown restless at last, that he wanted to move on.

Let 'em worry like a couple of fluffed up hens over their brood. He wasn't going anywhere. Not until he could afford a spread of his own.

Even then, he didn't mean to go far. KB Ranch sat in the best valley in the whole territory. He was sure of it. Not to mention that there were a couple of families in the area who'd look kindly upon Ed when he eventually settled down.

A door on the second floor of the bunkhouse opened, and the men playing checkers stopped mid-laugh to look that way. Then they both stood, tugging at jackets and adjusting hats.

Ed let his eyes travel lazily to the subject of their fuss, and he couldn't keep back his smile. A woman had appeared in the doorway, outlined by the shadows at her back. She shut the door behind her and stepped into the edge of sunshine peeking beneath the porch. She made her way down the walkway and then the stairs leading to the ground floor, her shoes clipping along at a business-like pace.

"Good afternoon, Miss McKinney," the sergeant greeted her when her boots hit the boardwalk on the ground floor, his words a drawl that sounded like he'd come straight from Louisiana to his post. "Did you enjoy your rest?"

The woman's gaze skimmed across the quiet parade grounds. "Thank you, Sergeant Tompkins. It was adequate."

A chuckle almost escaped Ed's throat. To someone else, her accent might've been hard to place. But he'd spent almost a year listening to two people who sounded remarkably like Miss McKinney. The woman seemed as out of place in the barracks as a cat at a coyote sing-along.

Greenhorns were one thing in Arizona Territory. British greenhorns were another.

Ed tucked his notebook into his back pocket, then watched from beneath the brim of his hat as the woman exchanged pleasantries with the two men. Their commanding officer must've placed them on the floor beneath her borrowed room to guard her. She seemed ready to dismiss them and walk across the dusty stretch of ground between her quarters and the major's office where Ed stood. But the two men picked up their weapons and fell into step on either side of her.

Were they worried someone would attack the *señorita*? Or that she meant to wander off? Either way, the picture of a woman in long skirts and a straw hat marching between two calvary men in blue made Ed smile. As the odd group drew closer, the woman's expression was one his mother wore when she'd grown tired of men and their antics.

Miss MicKinney's voice pierced the stillness in the air the same way her pointed boots dented the dry dirt. "Is it really necessary for you two to follow me everywhere? I am certain I am quite safe."

The man she'd identified as Sergeant Tompkins answered. "Ma'am, it's our honor to escort you wherever you need to go. A lady like you don't know much about the dangers of the Territory."

The other man, a corporal by his stripes, added with an eagerness possessed by the young, "That's right, Miss McKinney. It's not like it is back east. This here's still wild land."

Ed tipped his hat up on his brow, watching the woman come closer. He wore his hair shorter than his grandfather's people, most of the time, but had recently taken to growing it out again. His straight black hair brushed the tops of his shoulders, he'd inherited his father's sharp and wide cheekbones, and the bend of his nose would tell just about anyone with sense that he wasn't White. A quarter of his blood came from somewhere else.

The woman had drawn close enough to notice him, and to look him in the eye. Though several feet still separated them, her step faltered.

Ed heard his mother's voice in his mind.

"When I looked into your father's eyes, I saw my soul within them. That is when I knew everything would change."

12

She'd told him the story a hundred times. Every time his grandfather's people pretended she did not exist. When letters came from her family, disapproval in each stroke of the pen. Ed's mother used those words to explain why she and his father had altered the course of their lives for one another.

Why her words came to him in that moment, when the pretty Englishwoman stared at him with widened eyes and parted lips, he didn't want to know. Because he didn't believe in fairy tales. Not the kind his mother told, not the myths and legends his grandfather's people spun around smoky fires. Fiction was all well and good. But it was still just a pretty pack of lies. He ought to know, even if his particular brand of fiction hadn't ever been published.

He kept his face blank and lowered his gaze to the dust underfoot. He ground his teeth together and didn't look up again.

It took a moment for the Englishwoman's escorts to realize the reason for her hesitation. The soldiers were used to Apache, Navajo, and the Pima. They had scouts living within their walls with tribal heritage. Ed didn't give them any more pause than a piece of furniture.

"Oh, don't worry about him, ma'am," the corporal said. "He's just here with the ranchers. He's a *vaquero*. Aren't you, fella?"

"He's an Indian," the sergeant corrected. "Sure as shootin'. Oh, pardon my language, ma'am."

A soft cluck came from the woman. "I have heard courser words from fishmonger's wives, I assure you." She came forward.

Ed heard each step she took on the dirt, and then the clip of her boots on the wood walkway. "Good afternoon, sir."

There was no one she could mean but him. Ed tried not to sigh too loudly. Might as well give them what they expected. There was usually less trouble that way. "*Buenas tardes, señorita.*"

"See?" the corporal spouted, a note of smugness in his voice. "He's Mexican. Not an Indian."

The Englishwoman took a step closer to him and away from

13

the men on either side of her. "I beg your pardon, sir. Do you speak English?"

This time, he didn't bother to hide his irritation. "Yes. Better than some Americans do." His first language, learned at his mother's knee, was the beautiful lilting Spanish from her family. They had come from Texas. Her father had fought in the Texas War of Independence, a thing she had taught Ed with pride.

"So you're not an American?" the corporal asked, sounding still more confused.

"You are named for my father, Eduardo. Never forget that he fought for his freedom, the same as the Americans."

"I'm from Oklahoma Territory," Ed corrected quietly.

"Like I said. An Indian," the sergeant said, wrinkling his nose, though in confusion rather than derision. "Right?"

Ed didn't owe them an explanation, but he made a gesture with his hand and answered in Spanish, "*Más o menos.*" More or less. He didn't fit in their clearly defined categories of the world. And that was fine with him. The two soldiers looked at one another behind the woman's back with expressions that Ed might have found comical on another occasion.

His grandfather was full Cherokee. But he'd married a Mexican woman who hadn't given up her faith or culture, and their son had married a Hispanic Texan not long after the War Between the States had ended. Which made Ed mostly one thing, partly another, and entirely himself.

Ed met Miss McKinney's gaze again, mentally fortifying himself. "Do you need something from me, miss?"

The woman wore a chocolate-colored traveling gown, and her hat matched. She had to be hot in her get-up. He couldn't imagine wearing that much tight-fitting wool and standing in the sun.

"Actually, I would like to interview you. If you have a moment. I am a journalist from London, you see. I am collecting interesting stories from people who live in the American West for my newspaper."

Sounded like a busy-body way to live life to him. But he'd humor her. "Why?"

She blinked, and he realized her dark lashes were gold at the tips. "Why what?"

"Why does anyone in England care about people in Arizona?" He didn't care about anyone living overseas. It didn't concern him what people in England did or didn't do with their time. Interesting stories or not.

"Why does anyone care about anything, outside of food and shelter?" she asked, keeping him pinned with her gaze. She wasn't about to be cowed by his short answers. "Curiosity. An adventurous spirit. The desire to know more about the world. Entertainment. Boredom. Take your pick of reasons. None is more valid than the other. So. Will you let me?"

He liked her. He liked the way she tilted her chin up, showing a hint of stubbornness. Liked the way her brown eyes darkened and flashed. But he wasn't about to let her win.

"Let you what?"

The woman's lips curved upward, as though she liked him, too. Or at least recognized an opponent in the game she played.

But the men on either side of her didn't understand more was at work than the mere words they exchanged. The corporal's chest puffed out, and the sergeant's eyes narrowed in his reddening face.

"Now you look here, *vaquero*," the sergeant said. "The lady asked you nice. You show her some manners, or we'll have to show you out of this here fort."

The lady looked irritated. She sounded it, too. "That won't be necessary, gentlemen." She gave Ed a look of extreme annoyance. "I do apologize. It seems my guards take their job quite seriously."

Now both soldiers had flushed, and Ed had to chuckle. If he wasn't leaving with his friends, he might've worried a little more about the ornery set to the corporal's shoulders. Fights started over less than a man's embarrassment.

There was no use stirring up trouble when the ranch bene-fitted from selling beef to the fort. So he pushed away from where he'd leaned against the wall. "As they should. They are not wrong when they warn you Arizona is harsh and still wild. And you are a lady of some refinement. These men must keep you safe."

He didn't have a chance to see how his words impacted the soldiers, because the woman in front of him took a charged step forward. "I beg your pardon. Do you mean to imply that my *refinement* or that my being a lady is some kind of weakness out here?"

They were now standing close enough that he couldn't bend over without their heads crashing together. She'd riled quicker than he thought possible. "Neither," he said. "Because I know ladies who sit a horse better than most men, and I know refined folk who are making their mark on the Territory."

Her eyes narrowed. "Then what in heaven's name did you mean?"

He didn't get to answer her challenge, because the door behind him opened and men's voices burst through.

"Thank you for your business, Captain." Frosty's even tone was usually as soothing on people as it was on the stock. He was tall and lanky. The man with him, Duke, was tall and broad-shouldered. The two of them together looked like they could take on an army all by themselves. Just so long as Duke didn't open his mouth. The moment he did, people tended to doubt he could hold his own in a fight.

Ed finished their trio at a closer-to-average height, and he probably appeared the least threatening of the three. But appear-ances could be deceiving.

"It was a pleasure, sir," Duke added, his accent revealing his birthplace was a heck of a lot closer to Miss McKinney's than his faded hat and banged-up boots let on.

The lady journalist picked up on it immediately. "Oh, how extraordinary. A fellow Englishman."

The commanding officer had followed them out, without his

hat on. He extended his hand toward the woman. "Ah, yes. Nearly slipped my mind in all our talk of cattle. Gentlemen, this is Miss Molly McKinney. She comes to us by way of England, New York, and Missouri, and for some reason thought to add a stop at our fort to her journey. Ma'am, allow me to introduce Mr. Morgan and Mr. Rounsevell."

She latched on to Duke's family name immediately. "Rounsevell? Are you related to the Marquis of Rothwell? I recently interviewed his daughter-in-law."

"That would be my father and my sister-in-law," Duke admitted, then held his hand out to shake hers. Ed silently chuckled. It had taken Duke a while to get used to that custom being as much for women as men in these parts. "It's a pleasure to meet you, Miss McKinney."

Her mouth popped open as she shook his hand. "You're the son who disappeared into the wilds of America. Oh, goodness. The gossip columnists had a great deal of fun inventing reasons for your disappearance. Why on earth are you here?"

Duke's smile appeared, friendly as ever, as though he didn't mind someone prodding into his private business. Ed had believed the English were generally standoffish until he met Duke. "I fell in love."

"With the deserts of Arizona?" The way she asked, Ed could already imagine the story she'd write about the romantic lord turning cowboy to ride off into the sunset. The woman had no idea what the realities of their lives were like. She'd wind up spinning fantastical yarns if people let her wander around, unchecked.

"Partly. Mostly, it was a rancher's daughter." Duke glanced to his left and grabbed Frosty by the shoulder, dragging him forward. "This gentleman, my very good friend Mr. Morgan, married nearly as well as I did. He wed a widowed countess."

Frosty, who'd rather slink off to a corner to observe social situations than find himself in the middle, gave Duke a look that would melt iron. "Yep. It seems a lot of you Brits keep showing up around here."

"Fascinating. I hadn't any idea I would find any of my countrymen when I ventured this far west."

Ed cleared his throat and took a meaningful step off the officer's porch. Duke shot him a look that accused Ed of rudeness. Frosty sighed. They all knew they weren't going anywhere just yet.

"Maybe you'd all like to come back in my office for a drink," the captain said. "You can swap stories for a bit before the gentlemen get on their way. Not for long, mind you. Wouldn't want them traveling after dark, of course."

Molly McKinney beamed at them. "That sounds lovely, thank you." Then she walked into the office without looking back.

Frosty's shoulders fell. "And here I thought we'd get home early," he muttered. He wasn't usually an impatient man, but his wife was expecting. Though they had three other children running around their house, Frosty hadn't fathered any of them in the traditional sense. He adored the children. He had two adopted kids, orphaned when their parents passed of illness, and a stepdaughter from his wife's first marriage. This new little one was all his, and the first he'd see come into the world. Which explained why the usually confident ranch foreman seemed rattled most of the time. Possibly even more than he let on.

"Teresa and the children will be fine, Frosty." Duke chuckled and followed Miss McKinney into the shadowed office. Duke's wife was likewise ready, or nearly so, to deliver their first child, but he remained as collected and proper as ever.

The ranch's owner, Duke's father-in-law, had just welcomed a daughter into the world, too. The ranch was full of babies, and Ed wasn't all that used to the two-legged variety of offspring. But he could see the tenderness and care the other men lavished on their families and admired it. Sometimes, it made him miss his own relatives. He couldn't begrudge his friends their eagerness to set their sights and their horses on the path home.

He clapped Frosty on the back. "The sooner you answer the lady's questions, the quicker you get home."

Frosty grumbled something Ed didn't quite catch and walked in, then reached back and grabbed Ed. "Oh, no. If I'm having a tea party with the British, you're coming with me."

CHAPTER 3

The United States of America stretched farther than Molly had expected. From her first weeks in New York City, she had felt it much the same as London. Perhaps people were a bit ruder, and certainly a great deal louder, but the city had divisions of class and society that she understood. Poor people lived in parks and on streets. Some buildings looked too old to stand, while at the same time, there was a mania for buildings called skyscrapers.

She had also wound her way through places the Americans deemed historically significant in Philadelphia. They lavished that city, old by their standards, with praise and importance. Everyone seemed especially pleased to gloat about the consequence of that city when they realized she was British, and she heard several quips asking whether she came by land or sea. While their war of independence happened more than a century before, people took great pride in lording it over her.

"I hope you do not mind our appearance, Miss McKinney. Had I any way of knowing I'd be having tea with a lady, I would have tried to keep the dust off."

Yes, speaking to another English citizen was quite refreshing.

Lord Evan Rounsevell, though dressed in the same type of

work clothing as his companions, held himself with the same stiff-backed posture as other members of British nobility she had met.

"I wouldn't expect such a thing is possible out here, even with the frequent rain I've observed. I understand it is the monsoon season."

This time, the taller of the two other cowboys answered. They had introduced him to her as Mr. Morgan, but his friends both called him Frosty. "Yes, ma'am. We get almost regular showers through the summer. Some years, there's more rain than others. This year, some fella in Tucson says we're approaching a record number of rainy days."

The one called Ed, or Mr. Byrd, snorted. When both his companions sent puzzled glances his way, he folded his arms over his chest. "My apologies. I just think it's strange you traveled across an ocean and half our country to talk about the weather."

She'd never met a man so near her age with such a cantankerous spirit. When she'd first made eye contact with him, before they'd spoken a word to each other, she had formed a completely different opinion of him. Normally, she was an excellent judge of character. Her editor had called it her *female intuition*, but Molly preferred to think of her sixth sense as a gift.

Apparently, an imperfect one.

"It's called small-talk, Mr. Byrd," she said, keeping her tone amused. One caught more flies with honey than vinegar. And a sweet smile took her a greater distance in her interviews than a quick quip. "And the weather here is fascinating. I'm certain Lord Evan felt the same when he experienced his first monsoon season." She turned pointedly away from the grumpy cowboy. "Am I right?"

"Absolutely. The change the land undertook, not to mention the way people themselves adjusted, was incredible. I think people live the rest of the year anticipating these storms. It isn't unusual for the first rain of the season to bring people out of doors to dance in it." A soft look stole over the man's features, and Molly sensed a story behind the glimmer in his eyes.

She caught herself glancing again at Mr. Byrd, watching his reaction to his friend's story. Nothing about his exterior changed. He didn't shift or blink.

Why, when she'd approached him on the dusty parade grounds, had she experienced such an odd tickling sensation in her stomach? An increase of speed in her pulse? She'd felt momentarily giddy when he'd spoken, too. Admiring the texture of his voice. The slant to his cheekbones and the dark lashes framing his deep brown eyes.

His gaze flicked up to hers and caught. His lips turned upward.

Molly looked away quickly, trying to listen to whatever it was the other American was saying. How long had he been talking? How much time had she lost, staring at a man who didn't seem the least bit interested in her or her work? She hadn't been caught staring at someone like that since…well…ever.

"—but that was the last time Duke here tried to get that particular chore done in the rain." The tall cowboy laughed along with the Englishman, and Molly forced a chuckle, too. Though she hadn't the least idea what they were all finding humorous.

Thank goodness her cheeks had sunburned during her ride around the fort the day before. Her blush would remain unseen by the men.

After their talk of the weather, she shared her hopes for finding stories that would interest readers in London. "Stories about Indian tribes, for example," she said, trying not to look directly at the man her escorts had called both a Mexican and an Indian. She caught the way one corner of his mouth briefly turned up anyway. Perhaps if she approached the topic from a different direction, he would have something to say. "Or perhaps about the way Mexicans and Americans live out west. Is it harmonious? Difficult? Are there still language barriers?"

The men didn't answer her questions directly. "It sounds as

though you have a lot of ground to cover while you're in our territory," Mr. Morgan said. "It's not an easy place to get answers to all those questions. Not too long ago, people mostly came west to escape their pasts. Not everyone will be eager to speak to you."

Including the three men sitting in that room with her, it would seem. When a natural pause occurred a short time later, the men rose.

"Miss McKinney, it has been a pleasure." Lord Evans, at least, had kept his voice cordial the entire time.

"Thank you for taking tea with me."

"Absolutely a delight, ma'am," Mr. Morgan said before replacing his hat on his head.

She walked with them out the door and found her guards had relocated their checkers game to sit outside their captain's office and wait for her. Had they nothing better to do with their time than trail behind her? She'd learned as much as she could about the fort. Now, she needed something different.

"Do you think I might visit your ranch?" For a woman, inviting herself anywhere was bold. But for a journalist, however, the request was perfectly normal.

Lord Evan hesitated and looked to Mr. Morgan, who in turn looked to Mr. Byrd and then shrugged.

"If you ever make it out our way, you'd be welcome," Mr. Morgan said. "We've never turned good company away before."

"Indeed." Lord Evan offered her a small bow. "Best of luck to you in your quest for stories."

She'd hoped they'd offer to escort her themselves. Or that the invitation would be a little more specific. Not everyone was eager to be a news story, she supposed. Or to chaperone strange women across a desert.

As the two taller men walked away, Mr. Byrd stayed where he was, his stance relaxed, his head tilted to one side. His warm brown eyes regarded her with curiosity.

"I hope you are careful, Miss McKinney, as you gather your stories. Not everyone in these parts tell the truth, and even if they do, most stretch it near to the breaking point. Especially when it comes to making themselves look favorable." He touched the brim of his hat to her in a farewell salute she'd seen a few times since making her way westward.

She wasn't about to let him leave on that note. "Thank you for the advice, Mr. Byrd. Though as I am a professional newswoman, I hardly need you to remind me how to find the truth."

He smirked, nodded to her, and walked away with a peculiar swagger to his step. He didn't look back. She folded her arms before her, ire stirred by his easy dismissal of her.

To think. She'd actually thought him attractive. *Interesting*, even, with the clever way he talked to the soldiers. He had hardly said a word during tea. She'd done her best not to look at him after he'd caught her staring, but she had certainly slipped more than once.

Such a shame that he hadn't returned the interest. It might have helped her get a story out of him, which would have been nice. Ah well. Obviously, those men didn't wish her to step foot on their ranch anyway. She would have to find something else to write about in Arizona.

Perhaps it was time for her to go elsewhere. Fort Huachuca was quite dull. All the stories about the fort that were even remotely interesting had occurred a decade before. The army didn't even seem to know what they were doing in the middle of the desert. The only thing she'd written about was the unit known as the Buffalo Soldiers. Unfortunately for her, the day after she'd arrived, the unit had gone out into the wilds for training.

She had no intention of sitting around the dusty, quiet fort waiting for them to return. Perhaps she could circle back later. In the meantime...

Molly turned to her overly attentive guards. "Do you think the two of you might gain permission to escort me to Tombstone? I have a marvelous idea for a story, and it would be lovely to visit that town."

The men exchanged a glance, and she could practically see the disappointment descend on them like the summer rain that had fallen the day before. Getting to Tombstone wouldn't be a problem. The captain had already said he'd be happy to take her all the way to Tucson, which was at a greater distance, to see her onto the next part of her journey. These men were likely just sad to see her go.

But that was none of her concern. She had stories to find.

She could only hope Tombstone would prove more interesting than the tired old fort.

ED DIDN'T LOOK BACK UNTIL THEY'D RIDDEN OUT OF THE FORT'S gates, even though he'd wanted to. Forcing himself not to turn until he was sure the English lady was out of sight hadn't been easy. But he had a feeling, deep in his gut, that staring too long or too often at Miss McKinney would lead him down a path he had no desire to walk.

"I've never been in a situation when Frosty talks more than you do." Duke had come up beside him, his gaze trained ahead. "Have you something against journalists?"

Frosty came along Ed's other side. "I could've sworn you didn't have a shy bone in your body, Ed."

This is what came of having friends, Ed reflected with a wry grin. They wound up being nosy about things. And noticing what he'd rather they didn't notice. "I'm not sure what either of you are talking about. The two of you did enough talking for all of us."

"Did we?" Frosty pushed his hat up on his forehead. "When she started askin' about the Mexico border, I thought for sure you'd have something to say."

"Why?" Ed shrugged. "I was born in Oklahoma Territory."

"You mean Indian Territory?" Duke asked with false innocence. "So when Miss McKinney specifically mentioned her interest in meeting with local tribes, you didn't think it time to say anything then, either?"

"I'm not local." Ed dropped his chin. He had half a mind to ride ahead of them both, kicking up enough dust to fill their mouths with something other than questions.

"But you have a great deal to say on the subject of how they're treated." Duke's tone changed from teasing to something more cautious. "I have heard you make insightful arguments about the way the Territory's litigation is harming the native people—"

"It's just one man's opinion, Duke. A man without much say in the matter." Ed looked sideways at Frosty. "As far as either of you are concerned, I'm just a cowboy from Oklahoma. Not an Indian. Not a Mexican." Though in his heart he was both, it was easier to lay claim to nothing more than his vocation. At least, that's what he told himself instead of feeling guilty about it.

"Well. You're a bit more than that." Frosty's tone turned serious, too. "You're one of the best men I know."

"Agreed," Duke added. "I apologize if I offended you."

"Takes a lot more than friendly questions to offend me. I've built up a good-sized defense against what people say." Ed pulled his bandana up to cover his nose as wind whipped across their path, ahead of a storm most likely, sending dirt into the air and their faces. "I suggest you two stop jawing and focus on getting home to your ladies before the clouds get there first."

Mentioning their wives had both men focused on moving across the desert rather than talking about nonsense. Ed didn't have anything against chewing on politics every once in a while, but there wasn't any use getting riled up about things he couldn't control. Many a man had driven himself to the brink of ruin trying to change things. And thinking about that woman, writing for a British newspaper...well. She had even less say on the American public's opinion than he did.

Molly McKinney. He liked the name, though he couldn't say why. It didn't roll off the tongue, but it made an impression, and in far fewer syllables than his own name.

The way she talked, he'd found himself intrigued by the way her vowels came out somehow rounder and softer than his own. And she hadn't sounded quite like Evelyn—Frosty's wife—but that was probably the same as saying a lady from Tennessee didn't sound like a lady from Illinois. Regional differences. He'd never given much thought to the fact that English people could sound that different when they were all from the same island.

He could've happily listened to her all day, enjoying the cadence of her speech and the spark of intelligence in her eyes. Eyes that had made him wonder—if only for a moment—if there wasn't something to his mother's story of finding the other half of one's soul in another person.

Good thing he didn't believe in fairy tales. Or he might feel more than mild regret that he'd never see that Englishwoman again. Why was he wasting so much thought on the journalist anyway?

Ed looked westward, where the sky was still blue. They had a chance of beating out the afternoon's monsoon storm before it arrived. If it meant to rain that day. The rainfall had been pretty steady this year.

Whiskers and Dominó, the cowboy and the vaquero who'd joined them to bring the cattle to the fort, rode along at an easy pace behind, letting Frosty and Duke take the lead. Ed drifted there between the two groups for a time before Whiskers rode up alongside him.

"You goin' to church this Sunday, Ed?" The cowboy had earned his nickname because of his patchy black beard. He couldn't be more than twenty. Whiskers had an easy smile and a kind way about him that the ranch bosses liked.

"The circuit preacher won't be in town," Ed answered, and he mentally calculated if he wanted to make the ride out to the Catholic church he'd visited on several occasions. He didn't hold too close with religion. But he loved his mother, and she'd made him promise to attend services "regularly."

"Men need to rely on more than themselves, mi hijo." She'd

wrapped her black and red shawl tightly around her shoulders as she'd admonished him from the ground, while he'd sat on the back of a mule. He'd been sixteen when he left home the first time, and he could still picture his mother perfectly in his mind. Her black eyebrows drawn tightly together, her long dark hair in a looped braid at the back of her head. "Go with God, no matter what paths you tread."

He sighed. "I suppose I'll make time to visit San Xavier."

"Skip that," Whiskers said with an easy shrug. "Come with us to Tombstone. Dominó here is coming. And he's as Catholic as you are."

Dominó had ridden up close enough to chat, though he hadn't pulled even with them. "I am going to Tombstone, yes. But I will not skip services." The *vaquero* was from a small village in Mexico, and he'd ridden for ranch bosses across the border for years. Duke had hired him a year previous, to help with the slowly growing ranch. "Have you not been to the Sacred Heart Church yet, Ed? It's Catholic. Mostly."

San Xavier's mission had stood since the Spanish owned the land in Arizona Territory, turning wild horses and cattle loose to populate the area. The little chapel was hundreds of years old. The people of Tombstone had built Sacred Heart a little over a decade before.

"Never been inside," Ed admitted. "It looks like a big white box with a roof on top."

Dominó chuckled. "It's pretty enough on the inside. Come with us. We will go to church, then we will have some fun." Young as he was, Dominó didn't yet have the self-restraint age usually provided. The people of Tombstone were an upstanding lot; most went to church on Sundays, and they even had one of the best theaters in Arizona Territory. But there were still many ways a *vaquero* could get himself in trouble.

Even though it wasn't Ed's job to keep the hands in line, he found himself saying, "Fine. I'll go with you. When are you planning to leave?"

"Saturday morning." Dominó grinned hugely. "We'll spend the night at a hotel. Do the whole thing right. Church on Sunday. Then back to the ranch before nightfall."

And that was that. A few days more of work, then Ed would be on his way to Tombstone. Ah well. He didn't have much to do around the ranch on his off days except find a place to be alone with one of his notebooks. Maybe he ought to spend some of that time with people instead. A trip into Tombstone might be the break from routine he needed to perk back up. Feel like his old self again.

Because lately...maybe things *had* started to feel a little off.

CHAPTER 4

A woman in Molly's position couldn't trust everyone. Besides the fact that being a female made her vulnerable in a male-dominated world, as a journalist promising to publish stories, she found people absurdly willing to tell her tales that stretched the imagination. Especially when the teller made themselves the modern equivalent of Herakles.

"Truly, Miss McKinney. There I stood, a perfect hole from the bullet shot directly through my hat. An inch lower, and I certainly would not be here to tell you the tale." The gentleman expounding on the danger of traveling through bandit-riddled canyons, Mr. Shafer, tapped the elegant, rounded-top hat sitting on the table between them.

To appease the man who had joined her at her breakfast table, without invitation, Molly pretended to write shorthand notes of the story in a notebook on the table before her. The reality was, her notes had nothing to do with him and everything to do with the delicious breakfast before her.

Steak and eggs for breakfast, with fried tomatoes and cornbread. Lemonade, too. Part powder, part tea. Sweetened with local honey. Why not write a story about local cuisine and send that to her editor? Even if they put it in a different section of the paper than the rest of her work, or sold it to a magazine dedicated to food, someone might find it of interest. There wasn't much else to be said about Tombstone. The town was small. Many of the business buildings were empty—she'd been told about a mining mishap several years before that had meant a mass exodus of the once vibrant city.

"Say what you will of civilization and progress, it has yet to find its way to Arizona," Mr. Shafer said, almost echoing her thoughts. He had a large mustache, almost as impressive as her English editor's, that looked rather like a horse brush. He wore a dark gray suit with pinstripes of bright marigold.

He looked like he belonged in a city somewhere, selling second-hand carriages and mules, rather than in Tombstone at her table. She'd left her room at San Jose house with the goal of avoiding the man, who also had a room at the boarding house, by having her morning repast at the Palace Hotel. One of the few two-story buildings in town, the owner dedicated half of it to gaming tables and a saloon. The other half held a dentist's office, the small restaurant, and rooms to rent upstairs.

"After visiting New York City and Philadelphia, I understand what you mean." She lifted her teacup and sipped at the lemonade. Delightful. It almost made the pompous man's company bearable. "Where are you from originally, sir?"

"Charleston, South Carolina." He puffed his chest out as though this detail ought to mean something to her.

"How fascinating. That is along the eastern coast, is it not?" She'd studied maps and geography for weeks leading up to her trip, on her sea crossing, and she possessed an atlas full of maps for her reference as she wrote and interacted with Americans. But she still knew little about cities she had no plan to visit. Charleston meant nothing to her.

He began expounding on the old southern wealth of the city, its beauty, the nearness to the ocean, and how the city had a dignity and charm no place in the west could ever hope to achieve.

Molly wanted to close her eyes and sink into her seat, sipping at her lemonade in peace. Instead, she nodded. Smiled. Asked more questions. She had already tried to disentangle herself from Mr. Shafer, but he'd proved barnacle-like in his attentions. He'd come to Tombstone to see about purchasing land cheaply. He called himself a property investor.

Until he left for an appointment, she feared he would follow her about.

"—that isn't even the worst part," he was saying when she finished her drink. "The Indians are notorious for making deals in bad-faith."

A snort from behind her made Molly startle. She turned, looking up and over her shoulder, and then up a little farther to meet the gaze of the man almost directly behind her chair. A man she instantly recognized by his loose, comfortable way of standing, the tightness of his jaw, and the annoyance in his dark brown eyes.

When had he come into the restaurant?

"Mr. Byrd." She stood, her nerves making the motion jittery. "I didn't see you come inside."

His glare momentarily left her to settle on her companion, who had risen much slower than she had and with far grumpier an expression.

"Miss McKinney." He touched the brim of his hat to her. She noticed the men didn't remove their hats in public buildings. They were simply part of their attire. Though plenty of hats were doffed on the street when friends met to speak. "I came in for some breakfast. When I saw you, I thought I should pay my respects." His gaze shifted back to hers and turned friendlier at last. "I see you slipped your guards at the fort."

"Indeed. Their enthusiasm for my presence there was rather sweet, though I found it somewhat stifling to my purpose. Please, won't you join me? This is Mr. Shafer." She looked to the bristle-brush mustached man. "Mr. Shafer, this is Mr. Byrd, another recent acquaintance."

Mr. Shafer's eyes had narrowed and his lips disappeared beneath the edge of his mustache. "Mr. Byrd? First name Flying or Singing or some such thing?"

Molly's lips parted, but the man's rudeness shocked her too much for her to form a quick-witted reply.

"Nope. It's just Ed. Not that you need worry about that." His arms stayed relaxed, and his tone light. "Only my friends call me Ed."

"You've a good handle on English."

"As do you." Ed's smile didn't reach his eyes. "But neither of us speak it as well as our British friend. Miss McKinney. Thank you for the invitation." He turned his eyes onto her again. "But I think I'll have my breakfast elsewhere today."

How awful. She'd hoped he'd rescue her from more of Shafer's unbelievable rambling. Instead, she'd exposed him to insulting remarks. Maybe she could still use Mr. Byrd's appearance to her advantage. She gathered up her notebook. "Oh, dear. Does that mean we must postpone our interview once again?"

His eyebrows raised. "Again?"

"I could come with you, if you plan to dine elsewhere. I promise I won't be a bother. I have a handful of questions about your life on the ranch."

"Ranch?" Mr. Shafer said. "If it's ranchers you want to talk to, I can introduce you to a few."

Molly forced a wide, false smile as she nodded to the businessman. "Thank you, Mr. Shafer. That won't be necessary. The U.S. Army already made introductions to Mr. Byrd and his associates." Then she turned away from Shafer enough that he wouldn't see the change of her expression from painful politeness to pleading. "Mr. Byrd? Shall we be on our way?"

Mr. Shafer's chest puffed up, as though he would protest as soon as he found the right words to bluster.

Ed Byrd studied her, expression inscrutable for a long, silent moment. Then he sighed and extended his hand to gesture to the sunlight flooding through the open door. "After you, ma'am."

The tension in her shoulders didn't ease until they'd gone down the boardwalk to another little storefront promising coffee, eggs, and biscuits for a nickel. Mr. Byrd walked along a half step behind, on the outside of the boardwalk. He said nothing. Just nodded to the broad window of the tiny place and in they went.

Though tempted to prattle, filling the uncomfortable silence between them, Molly followed his example and remained quiet. No use annoying the man who had helped her exit an uncomfortable conversation with a far-too talkative companion. They stepped out of the morning sun and into the shadows of the business, and the scent of fresh-baked bread immediately engulfed them.

"Oh, it's a bakery." She looked about with pleasure at the shelves with round loaves, stacks of tortillas, and twisted pastries decorated with shining crystals of sugar. "I haven't visited this place yet."

"*Panadería.*"

Upon hearing the softly spoken word, Molly looked over her shoulder at Ed. "Panad—? What was that word?"

"I said *panadería.* A Mexican bakery." He stepped forward and took hold of a chair. He pulled it out from the table. "Do you wish to sit? Or now that you've broken free of Shafer, have you somewhere else you need to be?"

She felt her cheeks heat. He didn't sound the least bit pleased that she used him as the means of her escape. "About that. I really must thank you for playing along. It was most kind of you. And if you don't mind the company, I'd enjoy speaking with you again."

His dark eyebrows raised, doubt drawn upon his features. He nodded again to the chair. "Have a seat, then."

MAYBE ED WASN'T ACTING THE BEST PART OF A GENTLEMAN. HE could practically hear Duke groaning that "one doesn't tell a lady to have a seat." But Ed doubted *a lady* normally used one man to escape another the way Miss McKinney had. He didn't mind coming to a lady's aid, but he wasn't about to let her make a habit of using him that way.

In fact, the sooner they parted ways, the better.

He'd not intended to eat at the Palace. He'd glanced through the window as he passed. And then he'd looked twice when he recognized the profile of the English reporter. He'd stood still for some time, watching as she sipped from a dainty cup. He hadn't even realized she sat with someone until his boots had dragged him inside.

Would meeting her gaze have the same effect it had before? His mother's words about seeing his father for the first time hadn't left him, not since he'd laid eyes on the Englishwoman. And he hated that he was curious about her. Surely, speaking with her one more time would remove her from his thoughts. After he confirmed what he'd felt before had been nothing more than a passing, fanciful notion.

Except it had happened again, the moment his gaze collided with hers. That strange heat had grown in his chest. He'd wanted to sway toward her like a flower reaching for the sun.

She sat in the chair he'd pulled out for her, fussing with her skirts the way women did to make sure everything laid right.

"I am grateful you came along when you did," she said, her gaze lowered to the table. He sat down across from her. "Mr. Shafer is harmless enough, but he's rather slow to take a hint."

"Maybe you'd have better luck being direct with him." Ed looked up as the daughter of the shop's owner came over. She was dressed in a white blouse and embroidered skirt, her black hair pulled up high in twin buns, and she had a brightly colored shawl wrapped around her waist.

"*Señor* Byrd, welcome back."

She was as American as he was, speaking English effortlessly, accented lightly enough that English speakers would understand. But she dressed as she would if she lived in Mexico City. And she spoke Spanish fluently, too. She was only fifteen but interacted with the customers more often than her father, who kept to the back and his baking.

"Mercedes. This is Miss McKinney, from England." He tried to recall if he'd seen her plate before leaving the other restaurant. "Are you hungry, Miss McKinney? I pulled you away from your breakfast."

"Oh." Her cheeks pinked. She divided her smile between him and Mercedes. "I'm not especially hungry."

Ed narrowed his eyes at her. "Then perhaps a dessert. Mercedes, if you please. A cup of hot chocolate and your favorite pastry for my guest. Coffee and empanadas for me."

"Of course, Señor." The young woman disappeared through the swinging doors to the back to see to their order.

"Hot chocolate? In the middle of summer?" Miss McKinney raised her eyebrows.

"Mexican hot chocolate is different. You'll see." He folded his arms and leaned back in his chair, studying her. Why had this woman made him feel as though he had to approach her? Had to speak to her? A tightness between his shoulders knotted, and he shifted his arms to try to stretch it away.

She put her notebook on the table in front of her, then folded her hands on top of it. "Mr. Byrd, perhaps you will consent to an interview *now*? We can speak of whatever you wish. I thought I might write an article on the experiences of different cowboys in Arizona territory. I would include more opinions than your own, so you needn't feel overly exposed."

"I'm not interested." He didn't have any reason to share the details of his life with her. Even if he found her alluring. "I think you'll find around here that the people who *are* willing to share that much about themselves tend to tell stories just shy of the truth."

"Is that so?" She smiled at him, as though perfectly content with him thwarting her plans.

"I heard what Shafer was saying when I came to pay my respects." Ed had wanted to knock the man over to wipe the smug smile from his face. "Bad faith deals with the tribes are common, but it's not the tribes that go back on their word. Not at first."

"Really? And how would you know?" she said, her little pointed chin coming up, challenging him.

"Experience. Family history." He shrugged. "Having a head on my shoulders that does more than look pretty."

"Did you think Shafer pretty?" she asked, widening her eyes in mock-innocence. "Because you cannot mean to compare yourself to me."

He chuckled despite himself. She had him, unless he was quick. "Wasn't comparing. Merely acknowledging that I'm pretty."

She pursed her lips, perhaps to keep from laughing at him. Mercedes returned with their drinks and food on a tray. She served them, happily explaining the contents of the hot chocolate to Miss McKinney. "We use brown sugar in our chocolate here, Señorita McKinney. Then there is cinnamon and a pinch of chili powder. My father also recommends vanilla, which I added to yours. We import all our vanilla from Veracruz. There is nothing else like it in the whole world."

"Thank you, Mercedes. It sounds delicious." The English-woman held the steaming cup in both hands and inhaled deeply. "We make it quite differently in England."

Mercedes nodded politely to them both and withdrew to help a new customer at the bakery counter.

Ed sipped his coffee, letting the bitterness coat his tongue and warm his throat slowly. Normally, he'd wrap his empanadas in a clean bandana and leave. The meat-pastry was made to be eaten that way, hot or cooled. But with company, he took up the fork and knife beside his plate. It was hot. He wanted food. No reason to shock the foreign woman at his table with poor manners.

"Oh. This is divine." She had tried the chocolate. Eyes closed, she hummed with pleasure. Her expression was soft, her eyebrows pulled together as though she puzzled something out. She took another sip, not cracking an eyelid, and made another satisfied sound that made heat creep up the back of Ed's neck. Then she licked her lips.

He averted his eyes. What was the woman doing? It was only chocolate.

"How do I begin to describe this?" she muttered aloud, certainly not to him. She opened her eyes and put down the cup, then started taking notes. She wrote rapidly, and Ed leaned forward to peer at her paper. Curious. But the letters she wrote formed no words he'd ever seen before.

She glanced up at him and smiled. "It's my own personal form of shorthand. I can write faster this way, then I type it out later to send to England."

Shorthand. He'd never considered using it himself. When he wrote, it was every letter and syllable of the words he came up with. Her writing didn't even look like the same language as his.

Pretending disinterest, he leaned back in his chair and focused on his food again.

"What do you have against reporters, Mr. Byrd?" she asked suddenly. "Or is it me you object to?"

He dropped his fork. "What?"

The woman's eyes were focused completely on him, the look sharp and searching. "I cannot determine what sort of man you are. At the fort, you mocked the soldiers and then effortlessly diffused their anger. Your friends think highly of you. I could tell by the way they spoke to you during our tea. Yet you kept your mouth closed as though you'd rather be tortured than spend a quarter of an hour in my company." She took off her gloves and reached for her pastry with a bare hand, her long fingers pale and her nails trimmed short. "Then this morning, you made a point to greet me. You even let me use you as an excuse to escape Mr. Shafer. But you seemed quite disagreeable up until the moment you ordered my hot chocolate."

"Just trying to be sociable," he muttered, picking up his coffee again.

She tilted her head to one side. "You cannot hide behind that mug, Mr. Byrd. I know you think yourself clever, cautioning me as you did against those who like to stretch the truth. Or outright lie, I suppose. Would it interest you to know I have been a reporter for seven years? Since my eighteenth birthday. Nor have I been pampered and spoiled to the point that I think the world exists for my pleasure. I am not a naïve little girl."

"Didn't say you were." He wanted to squirm, as uncomfortable under her gaze as he'd once been under his mother's when she caught him misbehaving.

"Yet you don't seem to accept that I am capable of doing my job. So. Which is it? Is it me you object to, or all reporters?"

Did he owe her an honest answer? He couldn't admit that it was less about objecting to her and more about being confused by her. So confused, he didn't know whether he hoped to see her again or wanted to high-tail it out of Tombstone as fast as his horse could get him gone.

"Neither." The one-word answer made the woman's eyes narrow. How rude would it be if he just walked out of the building and didn't look back? The women of the ranch would never let him hear the end of it if they ever found out he'd behaved that way. So he released a long, drawn-out sigh as he tried to find the right words. "I don't object to you, Miss McKinney. I don't even know you. And I figure reporters are just doing their job, trying to find a good story to tell. But sometimes, being interesting is more important than being accurate. I've seen that a time or two in local papers, and back home in Oklahoma Territory."

"So you disapprove of me because I might—*might*—twist facts to make my readers happy?"

"Maybe. You're interviewing people here in Tombstone about living in Arizona. Fact is, the people who live in town rarely know what goes on elsewhere. You look in the paper, you'll see advertisements for California hotels and Colorado schools. They come and go, easy as you please, or only know what they see here in town and in the mines. That's not Arizona.

And when you ask these folks about cowboys and Indians, they're going to talk like they know what's going on in the mountains and desert, when they have no idea or experience with the matter. It'd be like asking a banker about being a shepherd." He stabbed at his food again. "Men like Shafer talk big, but if it didn't come out of a carpet bag, he's probably never seen it."

It frustrated Ed to no end when people acted like they understood part of the world they'd never experienced. When Ed wrote his stories, they never left the pages of his notebooks. But if they did, people would find accurate descriptions of the world in which Ed lived. And they'd know which bits were fiction, too. Not fiction masquerading as truth.

Her dark eyes glowed across the table at him, and she leaned forward eagerly to whisper, "Then let me interview you."

"That's not going to help much." Ed looked away from her face before her expression melted fully into disappointment. "Not because I don't want to tell you about me, Miss McKinney. But because I don't have the words you need. I could tell you all about the sunsets, about the rustlers we caught last year, about the long nights spent in the desert listening to coyotes sing. What I say might be true, but it doesn't give you the whole picture. Not like living it does."

Her hand appeared on his wrist, the pressure light, her soft fingertips warm on his skin. He swallowed and looked up, ignoring the way his heart's rhythm sped up like a horse kicked into a gallop.

"I can understand that concern. There is only so much words can do. Believe me, I am well aware of how short they fall. My whole life is words." She released him, her posture more relaxed. Her gaze dropped to the notebook. She tapped it with one finger. "Taking pieces of life and translating them to black and white on a page is a difficult endeavor, but I have devoted my life to it. I wish you could trust that I would do your words justice."

"My words wouldn't be enough." Ed put down his coffee.

"You'd need to talk to more people. Or you'd need to experience it all for yourself."

Her shoulders fell. "I so often feel that way when I'm writing. It was easier in New York City, you know." She flipped her notebook closed. "I could wander about and write down everything I saw. But here, the towns are so small. And no one is willing to take me beyond them to see more."

He almost volunteered right then and there. But Frosty and Duke hadn't issued any invitations to the Englishwoman when they met her. It wasn't his place to ask her out to the ranch, surely. He lived in the bunkhouse with half a dozen other men. That meant he had no business having a guest. Especially a pretty guest like her.

"Would you like to come to church with me tomorrow?" he asked, then he clamped his jaw shut. What was he thinking? The woman wouldn't want to sit in a chapel next to him, a stranger, for no reason at all.

Except she immediately answered, "Yes, that would be lovely." Her smile returned. Smaller than he'd seen it so far, but still genuine. His insides twisted. She seemed like a good person. She'd taken the time to explain herself to him when she could've stormed out, offended. "Where do you attend in town?"

He told her, of course. Then they finished their breakfast with relatively little else said. She told him where she was staying. She thanked him for breakfast. He stood when she excused herself. Then he sat again, alone and wondering what he'd done.

Mercedes approached his table to gather Miss McKinney's dishes and cutlery. She raised her eyebrows at him. "She's a very pretty lady, Señor."

"Yep." Ed rubbed at his eyes. "I think I must be plum loco, Mercedes. I asked her to come to church with me."

She giggled. "Not any more *loco* than most boys when they like a girl. You should see how the *vaqueros* fall over themselves trying to talk to me." She winked at him. "Good luck, Señor."

He already knew he'd need it. Because he hadn't asked the

Englishwoman to church just to be neighborly. Nope. He had every intention of asking her to come out to the ranch. He just needed to figure out how he'd justify it to his bosses and where she'd stay.

If she wanted to write about Arizona, she needed to get it right.

At least, that was the excuse he put in his mind. Thinking past that reasoning wasn't something he intended to do, either.

Ed left a few extra coins on the table when he left, his problem still unsolved. At least he could distract himself by heading to the Western Union office to see about any mail for the ranch. They had a farmer in Sonoita who regularly brought out the mail to everyone, but no one minded if folks picked up their own correspondence in town.

Ed received a packet of letters tied together with twine. After he stepped back out into the sunshine, he flipped through them, checking the addresses.

Tucked midway in the stack, he found a letter from his mother. He recognized her handwriting immediately. She wrote with a precise, tiny print when she put his name on an envelope: Eduardo Enoli Ramirez Byrd. Always, she used his full name.

Inside, he'd find larger, looping letters in her usual handwriting. The handwriting his own most resembled, since she had been his first and most attentive penmanship teacher.

He tugged the envelope out of the stack without untying the twine, then found a bench outside a barbershop where he could sit undisturbed to read it.

Dearest Eduardo. She wrote in a mix of Spanish and English. Something that might frustrate others, but Ed had come to enjoy it. His mind slipped easily between the two languages. *It has been a long time since your last visit. Our family is healthy. Your sister had her third daughter, and she named her Carmen. That means I now have seven grandchildren. You should come home to see your nieces and nephews. There are three now you have never met. We all miss you. Me, most of all. Hijo, with your grandfather growing older, he wants to speak to you. Your father, too. They have words they would say to all their children. Please, write back, and perhaps set a date for a visit?*

Ed read the rest of the letter with news from his family but went back to that first paragraph again after finishing the whole.

His mother had never requested a visit before. She always said she missed him, but this felt different. Her reassurance that all his family was healthy made her request odd. What did his grandfather and father want from him? Perhaps they wanted to pull him into yet another one of their arguments.

Folding up the letter, Ed tried to put his mother's request from his mind. There had been no urgency in her words. He had time to think on it before responding. And he already had plenty on his mind. He'd worry about the letter another time. Right now, he had an Englishwoman occupying his thoughts.

CHAPTER 5

Molly had a trunk the size of a small wardrobe in her possession, with clothing suited for every occasion she could think of. Including church. Her yellow dress trimmed in pink ribbon seemed like a good choice for attending services that morning, completed by her heart-shaped locket. When Mr. Byrd arrived at the hotel doorstep to escort her the short distance to the church, his wide-eyed appreciation didn't go unnoticed.

He wore clean clothing, but not a suit. Instead, his choice of church-wear suited his way of life: a white shirt, gray vest and matching trousers, black boots, and the same hat he'd had on the day before. A dark blue bandana took the place of a necktie. He'd brushed his black hair into a tidy knot at the back of his head.

He didn't dress or look like any gentleman who had ever escorted her before. Yet she couldn't deny finding him quite handsome. Sitting next to him during the Catholic service wasn't difficult. In fact, she stolen several glances at the attractive figure he cut.

The congregants of Sacred Heart varied in age and appearance, as well as in ethnicity. The service, led by a priest with red hair and freckles, she found pleasantly short. After the homily, the priest mentioned those who needed help by name. He read a text that reminded everyone present to show love to their neighbor. He spoke in lightly accented English, his voice lilting so subtly, she could think of no other tongue that had that feeling to it than Irish.

She leaned closer to her cowboy escort. "I didn't expect to find an Irish Catholic priest in Tombstone."

Ed shifted to lean closer to her, and she caught the scent of pine. "It was an Irish woman who raised the money to build the church in the first place."

The priest repeated himself in Spanish, too. A thoughtful thing to do. She couldn't imagine anyone being so accommodating in England.

By the time mass ended, and they left the cool shade of the building for the sunlight and dusty street, a peace had settled in Molly's heart. One she hadn't felt in some time. Relaxed, she looped her hand through the crook of Ed's arm without invitation. He stiffened up momentarily, but when he gave her a questioning glance, she smiled at him as though they'd been in that position a dozen times before. Indeed, once he relaxed, it felt quite natural to walk arm-in-arm with him.

"Now, Mr. Byrd, we have had tea together, breakfasted yesterday, and you have escorted me to Sunday services. I think that must make us friends of a sort, don't you?"

His expression remained still as stone. "I s'pose."

"Lovely." Molly flashed him her most winning smile. She wasn't completely beyond using her feminine charms to further her work. "Then might you reconsider telling me more about yourself? I should like to know how you found yourself a cowboy on a ranch. A ranch that people in Tombstone tell me is one of the largest in the territory."

His shoulders came up briefly, but he changed the nervous motion into a shrug so swiftly she wondered if she imagined the defensive movement. "How does any cowboy find himself working out west? We wander around, work where we can find work, and stick if the place is worth sticking to."

Her intuition was almost never wrong. Ed had a story worthy of telling. She felt it. But it would take more than a smile and shared breakfast to get it from him. Before Molly could try a new strategy, he cleared his throat as a preface to speaking.

"I've been thinking about what you've said, about people in England wanting to know more about the Territory. Because it's so different. I don't think you're going to get those stories by interviewing folks. Especially if you're in towns like Tombstone."

"Really? I thought Tombstone the perfect place for my venture." A stray dog flopped onto the boardwalk a few feet ahead of them and released a huge puff of air before closing its eyes to sleep, as uninterested in their approach as it would be a passing cloud. Ed looked from the hound to Molly with raised eyebrows.

"Yes. The whole town is brimming with excitement," he said, tone as dry as the dust on the ground.

Molly had to laugh. And skirt around the dog in their path. "I was given to believe a town called Tombstone would be a bit livelier. I've had several people tell me all about the shootouts, thefts, and Indian raids of a decade before."

"Tombstone's lost its teeth since then." He chuckled. "That would be disappointing for a journalist. But that's not exactly what I meant." He tilted his head toward the small green square —a park of sorts, though no one in Britain would ever deign call it such—and she nodded her agreement to him leading her across the street.

Molly looked down at her shoes, noting the coat of dust changing them from black to gray. "You suggest I not conduct interviews, Mr. Byrd. How should I go about finding stories if not that way?" She raised her free hand to touch the locket resting above her collar bone, but lowered her hand again swiftly.

He stared ahead, the slightest curl of his lips making her stomach twist in anticipation of what he would say next. Which was quite a juvenile response for her. "Maybe living your own adventure would be best."

She didn't bother tempering her tone as she scoffed. "Yes, of course. I could become a sharpshooting cowgirl and perhaps rob a few trains as well. Perhaps I will even dig for silver in the mountains. That sounds lovely and not at all difficult. Hm. Let me just find a good pair of boots, and you can point me toward the desert."

Ed stopped them both and tipped his hat back on his forehead. "You've got a quick mind, Miss McKinney."

She withdrew her arm from his and folded her hands before her. "And a sharp tongue from time to time. Yes, so I've been told."

The handsome cowboy mirrored her stance, head tilt and all. "As much fun as it would be to watch you attempt all of that on your own, I thought maybe you'd like to come out to the ranch. I think you hinted at it before, but it sounded like you'd be asking a lot of questions. Which is why no one was all too keen on the idea. But if you come out to learn, to try things for yourself, maybe you'd find the story you're looking for." He shrugged and looked across the street, back toward where they'd come from. "I'm not the boss, which means inviting you like this isn't exactly my right. But I think, maybe, if we approach it from this angle, the Boltons and foreman won't mind so much."

"Why, Mr. Byrd." Molly halved the space between them with one small step, looking up into his eyes. "It seems we *are* friends after all."

He tugged his hat back down into place and shrugged. "You might change your mind if you wind up rounding up a bunch of ornery cattle." He turned on his heel. "I'm leaving for the ranch at four o'clock. If you don't mind riding in a buckboard wagon, you can come too."

"I will ready my things, sir."

He turned and walked backward a few steps. "Call me Ed. Everyone does."

She couldn't help the grin that burst across her face. She'd won him over, and she'd get a story out of him, sooner or later. She had a good feeling about it. "You must call me Molly, then."

He gave a quick head-jerk in agreement, then turned. "Well, c'mon then, Molly. I'll escort you back to your hotel so you can get packed."

She quickened her steps to catch up to him, not saying another word in case she somehow spoiled her luck and made him change his mind.

WHISKERS DIDN'T GREET THE IDEA OF SHARING HIS WAGON BENCH with enthusiasm. Especially since it meant his close proximity to a female stranger. He tended toward shyness but sounded irritable when he spoke. "What d'ya mean, your newspaper gal is coming back with us?"

"She isn't *my* gal." Ed threw the heavy saddlebags he'd brought with him over his shoulder. Whiskers and Dominó sat at the round tables in the saloon, their belongings in piles beside their chairs, and their hands clasping the handles of thick, glass mugs. They'd spent their morning lazily playing cards and swapping gossip with cowboys from nearby spreads.

"You went to church with her, yes?" Dominó shuffled his deck of cards. "And you said she is pretty."

They were focusing on the wrong parts of Ed's conversation with them. He needed to rope them back into order. He crossed his arms and lazily leaned against the pillar beside their table. "I barely know her. But I think the boss will be interested in what she's doing out here."

"He is always reading books and newspapers. I guess he'd find a lady writer interestin'."

It took an extra shot of patience for Ed to correct Whiskers in an even tone. "I meant that King wouldn't mind being involved if someone's writing about Arizona Territory. On account of him wanting to make statehood."

Dominó tucked his cards into his vest pocket. "I am wondering, Ed. Why do *you* want her to come to the ranch? You are the one that asked. Not the boss." The *vaquero's* eyes gleamed with amusement.

"It doesn't hurt to be friendly to folks," Ed said, leaning heavily on his American English. Every time he started arguing with Dominó, or even engaged in more friendly chatter, he heard his accent returning and fought against it. He'd worked hard and long to diminish the influence of his mother's language. He didn't need one more thing separating him from the friends and community he'd chosen.

"Especially when they are pretty," Dominó added for him.

Whiskers grumbled. "I don't see why we need more females on the ranch." The man always got tongue-tied around females. Even the littler ones. Sure, he was polite and respectful, but he never spent more than a few minutes in company with a woman if he could help it.

"It does not matter what we say. Our friend has invited her, and the English *señorita* accepted. That is that." Dominó stood, hefting his saddle bag with him at the same time. "We should get the horses and wagon from the livery, so we can meet the lady on time."

Finally, Ed relaxed. "Thanks."

Dominó shrugged, and his grin returned. "You are practically a second foreman. We can hardly say no to you, can we? But I am interested to see what Frosty and King have to say about it when we get back."

Whiskers, still muttering to himself about females, followed Dominó out the door. Ed trailed behind them, already rehearsing what he'd say to his foreman and his boss when the time came to introduce the English journalist and admit he'd extended an invitation he had no right to give. Everyone at the ranch might be easy-going most of the time, but Ed hadn't ever stepped out of place like this before. His role was to act as second-in-command to Frosty. He was a cowboy, a drover, not someone who should make big decisions about cattle drives or ranch guests.

When the men arrived at the hotel where Molly McKinney was staying, Ed nearly regretted the invitation all over again.

A steamer trunk nearly half the size of the wagon, and painted a brilliant shade of blue, waited on the boardwalk.

"What in tarnation is that?" Whiskers said, glaring down from his buckboard wagon bench. "Looks like a da—" He swallowed the four-letter word as one of the hotel doors opened and revealed Molly McKinney herself.

She was adjusting a leather glove on one hand, and the fringe of her matching vest swung cheerfully as she stepped into the sunlight. A bright white straw hat with a blue band around its brim set nestled atop her dark hair. She flashed a bright smile at all of them and walked forward in her split skirt, the ends of that garment barely reaching her boot-tops. "Gentlemen. It's a lovely day for a ride, isn't it?"

Ed rubbed at his forehead, then his chin, looking from the lovely woman to the giant box next to her. "Is that—" He was afraid to ask, to be truthful. "—your luggage?"

She put her hand atop the flat surface of the trunk and gave it a smart rap. "Indeed, it is. But you needn't fear. It isn't all that heavy. I emptied the whole thing of my winter clothing and quite a few evening gowns when I left Independence, Missouri. The heaviest thing inside is my typewriter."

"A typewriter?" Ed repeated, failing to mask his curiosity. The loud, mechanical things had fascinated him ever since he saw one at work in Tucson at the newspaper office. He'd gone with King to place an advertisement in the paper for people needing local beef. How did anyone think well enough to write when those machines made as much noise as a box of horseshoes thrown down a staircase?

He eyed the trunk from the back of his horse. It would fit in the wagon, but only because they hadn't needed a full supply run this time around.

"Yes. A Remington." Her chin came up, her shoulders went back, and the pride in her voice couldn't be missed. Not even by Whiskers.

The shy cowboy blurted, "You've got a rifle in there, too?"

"A rifle? Heavens, no. I wouldn't know what to do with a weapon of that sort." She looked at Whiskers in confusion, and the cowboy blushed before ducking his head and muttering something unintelligible.

"Remington makes rifles," Dominó said, swinging down from his horse.

"Ah. That explains the misunderstanding." Miss McKinney's bright smile returned, and she directed the full force of it at Whiskers, who turned even redder beneath his patchy black beard. "My typewriter is a Remington Standard, model number six. Quite new to the market still." She went to the mule tied up at one of the hotel rails. "I was thinking of naming my new mule after my typewriter, actually. But perhaps it would be better to give him a writer's name. Byron, perhaps. Or Chaucer. I rather like Chaucer."

Ed's boots had just hit the dirt, and he stared over the back of his horse at the woman's mount. "You bought yourself a mule?"

"Of course. A woman ought to have transportation of her own when she can manage it." Molly patted the animal's neck. "And the livery agent assured me that a mule was perfectly acceptable. Harder working than a horse, not as stubborn as a donkey, and certainly less expensive." She lowered her voice. "Don't tell poor Chaucer, but his new mistress only has a reporter's salary. It isn't enough to keep him as spoiled as he deserves."

Ed looked at the mule in some shock, then back at the Englishwoman. Mules were decent enough mounts, he knew. A man wouldn't ever ride one if he meant to be a cowboy, but they pulled wagons and transported people well enough. This particular mule had the body of a fine enough horse, passed on to it from one of its parents. But it had the long face and large ears of a donkey, which was pretty typical of the hybrid creatures.

The animal already wore a saddle and had been decked out well enough to keep his rider comfortable.

"He is a sweet creature, isn't he?" Miss McKinney scratched the mule's chin, and darned if the animal didn't close his eyes like a big cat enjoying the attention of his mistress.

"If you say so." Ed shook himself free of his thoughts and went to help Dominó lift the trunk—which was lighter than he expected, as promised—into the back of the wagon. Whiskers stayed in his seat with his head down and his hat pulled low over his eyes. Apparently, his short conversation with the British woman had been too much for him.

Dominó said nothing else as he retook his seat in the saddle. Which left it up to Ed to approach their guest. "Do you need help getting into the saddle, Miss McKinney?"

"I'm certain we agreed you could call me Molly," she said. She peered up at him, squinting against the afternoon light. "It's more efficient. And yes, if you don't mind. Tombstone is frightfully short of mounting blocks."

He bent and cupped his hands together, and she stepped into them. He had a moment to realize her boots were new—and stitched with a cactus flower print—before he tossed her upward into her saddle. She landed well and took up the reins with confidence.

At least she knew how to ride.

"This is quite exciting." Molly McKinney nudged her mule onto the road. "I do hope you will be willing to answer more questions for me as we ride, Mr. Byrd."

"Ed," he corrected, his horse coming alongside her. "And that's Dominó." He pointed to the vaquero ahead of them, and his friend turned to tip his hat. "And Whiskers is in the wagon."

She waved over her shoulder at Whiskers, who hunched his shoulders and tried—failing, of course—to look smaller. That made Molly frown and lower her voice as she asked, "Is he upset about something?"

"Nope. Just a bit on the shy side." Ed kept them moving

forward. "We don't have much call for spending time around ladies. Except for the women on the ranch, and all of them are married to our bosses."

"Tell me about the women on the ranch, please. I would like to know something of them. I think there are any number of ladies in England who would be interested in what it would be like to live in the desert."

"I don't know that I should say much. You'll meet them for yourself soon enough."

She settled back in her saddle with a dissatisfied frown. "Then perhaps you will tell me more about the community as a whole. There must be a settlement of some sort out near the ranch."

Though he hadn't counted on the woman wanting to conduct a horseback interview, he probably should've guessed she wouldn't ride in silence to KB Ranch. Ed released a heavy sigh, then explained Sonoita—the small town that barely merited the name—to a woman who had walked the largest streets in England and the United States.

"There's a road that goes through Sonoita. A church, and a trading post, but not much else. A few people built their houses there, to be near one another instead of all spread out on their ranches and farms. There really isn't much to see."

"Why do you think people choose to live like that?" The question didn't sound as though she expected an answer, but he did his best to give one anyway.

"The answer is probably different for everyone. For a lot of folks, they want the room. Or the quiet. It means something, too, to own your own land as far as your eyes can see. And if they want company, they get together with neighbors. People who actually care about them. Instead of losing themselves in a crowd of strangers."

The woman's alert brown eyes focused on him, and Ed didn't mind in the least being under her gaze. "But you were in Tombstone, looking to spend time with other people, I would presume."

He shrugged. "Sometimes, it's nice to get away from what's become ordinary."

Apparently, Dominó had been listening in. "It is good for him to take time away. Ed has not been himself."

Molly gave him a quizzical look, and Ed forced a smile. "Don't pay him any mind." He'd heard the talk, when he wasn't meant to, between Frosty and Duke. Duke and Dannie, his wife. Even King and Abram. Lately, everyone had been looking at him like he'd sprouted a new head.

Maybe he had been a touch withdrawn lately. But it had nothing to do with living on the ranch. His hand twitched, and he brushed at the subject like he would a fly. Waving it away. "We've got more to worry about right now than usual, is all. Storms will be over soon. Then we'll have the fall cattle drive. Should be plenty for you to learn about ranch life at this time of year."

"That is good to hear." She didn't appear too concerned about his response.

"The trail's a bit dusty," he said, looking over her outfit one more time. Ed reached into his vest pocket and withdrew a tightly folded square of blue cloth. His spare bandana. "Here. It's clean. Tie it around your face to cover your nose and mouth once we get out of down. No sense eating dirt while you ride."

"Oh, how very kind of you. Thank you." She followed his instruction, her eyes bright above the makeshift mask. "How do I look?"

Prettier than a cactus flower. Ed swallowed the compliment and offered a nod of approval. "Like a cowgirl."

She laughed as she touched her heels to the mule's sides and rode ahead next to the *vaquero*. "Excuse me, Dominó. Won't you tell me something of yourself? What brought you to this particular place in the wide world?"

Ed stayed back, between the other riders and the wagon, alone with his thoughts. He watched the woman in front of him, watched the way she gestured with her hand when she asked questions. Listened to her laugh when Dominó said something clever. And he wondered, not for the first time, why he'd felt the need to invite her out to the ranch at all.

Maybe he had gone *loco*.

CHAPTER 6

E d's small party reached the foothills prior to wending their way up the path between mountains and canyons both to get to the ranch. The Mustang Mountains were to the north, Canelos to the southwest, and they'd just passed through the lowest point of Wayne Canyon when Ed called for a break.

Thunderclouds had gathered on the horizon to the west and north. The columns of gray connecting the clouds to the land predicted a heavy deluge, and it would be better for them to sit and wait for it to pass instead of trying to push through with a greenhorn reporter on an untested mule.

When Ed explained his reasoning, Molly protested. "I'm certain Chaucer and I can handle an afternoon storm. We had the monsoon rains at the fort, too. They never lasted long."

"It's not so much about how long they last as it is about lightning sending animals into a panic," Ed said, dismounting. "Look, we've got some good cover here." He gestured to the spindly pine trees and large boulders. "We'll tie the horses and mule to the wagon, make a fire and stretch out a tarp over those boulders to keep dry. If it's over soon, then it won't be a big delay. If the storm lasts a while, you'll thank me when it's over and you're still dry."

She opened her mouth to protest again when Dominó interrupted. "We always break when there is a big storm coming, Molly. It is the safest thing to do."

Her forehead wrinkled as she looked between the two of them, then she sighed helplessly. "Very well. I will defer to your experience and judgment, gentlemen." She dismounted and patted her mule along his neck. "Do you hear that, Chaucer? You must conduct yourself perfectly during the rain. Thunder or no thunder."

The mule's ears pricked forward, and he moved his long face around to nudge her shoulder. The woman laughed and laid her cheek against the animal's, and Ed's heart stuttered unexpectedly. Even with a mule cheek-to-cheek, the woman was prettier than a meadow in spring.

Ed turned away quickly and mounted his horse again, ignoring the way his neck and ears turned warm. He needed to get hold of himself. A little distance would help. "I'm going to ride up the hill to see if I can get a better fix on the storm's direction. The wind will be stronger up there."

Whiskers grunted, and Dominó waved him away. "Go on. We will have everything settled before you get back."

Ed glanced once in Molly's direction to see her frowning up at him again, but before she could ask a question or even invite herself along, he put heels to his horse and cantered away. The last thing he heard was her asking Dominó, "What is a *tarp*?"

Uphill he went, through a few scraggly pines, to the top wall of the canyon. It didn't take long, but he was far enough away from the others that he couldn't hear them or see them through the trees and desert brush. Ed looked down the eighteen-foot slope to the dry wash below. They'd crossed at the shallowest point of the wash, and the ground had been dry and dusty. The washes weren't much to worry about, unless the storms were bad. Then they'd funnel all the extra rain from the mountains down to the valleys, the water sweeping away just about anything that got in its way.

He looked northwest, his eyes taking in the heavy gray clouds.

A rumble of thunder closely followed a flash of lightning. The storm would be on them soon. It'd been the right call to wait it out.

Ed's horse danced impatiently beneath him, and he soothed the animal with a low murmur and gentle brush along its neck. "We'll get back to the others soon. The storm's blowing right at us."

Which meant he'd be stuck under that tarp and between those boulders with Molly McKinney. The fact that he didn't at all mind the idea worried him. He barely knew the woman, yet he'd offered to escort her to the ranch. A ranch he didn't have any right to bring guests to visit. What was wrong with him? Why did her bright brown eyes make him want to say yes to anything she might ask him to do? It had been difficult to deny her as he had more than once.

At least he had enough presence of mind to avoid her interview questions. Those he could say no to with a clear conscience. He didn't have anything special to say about his life on the ranch, and he wasn't about to go telling all his personal details to someone who possessed the ability to share them with a broad audience full of strangers.

Ed shifted in the saddle again, taking more time than he needed to survey the land around him. Keeping his past to himself was just about the only thing he could think of to keep a wall up between him and the Englishwoman. Because he wasn't about to act like a fool over a woman he'd barely met. His mother's story of *knowing* her life would change after meeting his father's gaze was true. But Ed had no intention of letting himself fall for a woman based on nothing more than sight.

It might work in fairy tales and folk stories, but Ed couldn't even begin to imagine how an English reporter and an American cowboy could have anything in common.

Thunder cracked again, and Ed looked upward, surprised he'd missed the lightning.

He blinked up at the graying sky when the sound continued,

changing to the splitting sounds of tree branches snapping, and accompanied by a loud rush. He looked down instead, and into the distance, where a wide swatch of water spilled from what had once been a trickle of stream into the canyon.

It wasn't a stream anymore. It was a river. The storm in the mountains ahead of them had caused a flash flood.

Good thing they'd already crossed the wash. After a few twists and turns, that water and the rotten logs it carried would sweep right across where they'd crossed dry ground.

He'd waited long enough. He needed to help make their temporary camp.

Ed rode his horse back, quicker than he'd left. The others would be relieved to know they'd missed the oncoming water. Except when he rode up, he realized right away that someone was missing. Whiskers was putting rocks on either side of the wagon wheels to keep it in one place. Dominó hammered the last stake into the ground to keep the tarp from blowing away.

But the reporter was missing.

Ed's heart stuttered and stumbled. "Where's the lady?" he asked, voice cracking like a whip over the heads of his friends.

"She had to use the necessary," Whiskers muttered and jerked his head in the direction Molly had presumably gone.

Right back where they'd come from.

Where they'd crossed the dry wash.

Ed's blood went cold, and he jerked his horse around, snarling out curses in Spanish and English both, as he rode fast as he could toward the wash. Hoping he'd see Molly before he made it that far. Mentally, he traced the route of the canyon and prayed to all the saints in heaven that he'd find the woman before it was too late.

After Dominó informed Molly that a *tarp* was just the cowboys' lazy way of saying tarpaulin, there wasn't much else for her to do. The men refused her help with the animals and the temporary shelter. She dragged her toe through the dirt, noting the way dust picked up in even the slightest wind.

The men had also worn bandanas on their ride from Tombstone, and the thick feeling of dirt coating her skin made her grateful for Ed's thoughtful loan of the blue bandana. Did everyone in the desert battle a constant swirl of dust? She'd heard at least one person mention the terrible storms that could arise occasionally, coating entire towns in the red, orange, and brown dirt and making it impossible to see more than a few feet in front of their own eyes.

The weather patterns were quite odd. Dust storms, rainstorms, and more sun than she'd ever experienced in her life.

"We will be stuck together for a time, won't we?" she asked Whiskers where he stood in the back of the wagon, covering up their supplies. He turned red and nodded once but said nothing. "Very well. If it is all right with you, I have need of the necessary."

He turned redder still and pointed back the way they had come, where the ground sloped downward toward the canyon. Yes, that little mound of dirt would be the only place she could see to her needs and be out of sight. Without going in the same direction Ed had ridden, anyway, and who knew when he would return.

"Thank you. I won't be long." She brushed her hands against her skirt and went off in that direction. She kept her eyes open, looking about herself with interest. Though there were evergreens growing along the slopes of the mountains, there wasn't much more than grass, cactus, and dried-out looking bushes where they were at present. She walked into the dip of what was likely a stream during wetter times, then looked left and right. If she turned around, she could still see the tops of the cowboys' hats as they worked.

Molly ended up walking several feet farther, until the side of the little dry bed was higher than her head. She could no longer see or hear the men. After she performed one of the most basic needs of humankind, she glanced at the opposite, lower bank. Cactus and tall, prickly plants lined the area as efficiently as a garden wall. Movement caught her eye closer to the ground, and she held perfectly still.

A mouse scampered out from the protection of the plants. It had short round ears and long hind legs, with short arms tucked up close to its chest. It rose up on its feet to look at her, holding its hands together.

"Aren't you adorable?" Molly whispered, staring in fascination at the animal. Its tail was more than twice the length of its body, with a tuft of hair at the end that looked as brittle as horsehair. The creature sniffed the air, its whiskers wiggling, and then it made itself more adorable still. It *hopped*. Like a rabbit. Not toward her, but not back into hiding, either. Just to the left. Then it stood up on its hind legs and looked at her again.

The tiny creature was as curious about her appearance as she was of his. Had she held the animal in her hand, it would fit snuggly in her palm. Not that she intended to do such a thing. But she rather wished she had her sketchbook to better capture the look of the odd rodent.

Suddenly, the mouse stretched taller still. Its ears went forward and its body froze. Molly hadn't moved, but the animal sprang away from her as though terrified. It scrambled into the brush, uncaring of wiggling stems, but disappearing from her sight with a speed that startled her. "Dear me."

Perhaps it had scented a predator.

A strange sound reached Molly's ears. Loud. Rushing. Rather like waves upon a beach, actually, but continuous instead of ending with a crack. Strange. The rumble and whoosh grew louder still. She looked toward the mouth of the canyon, listening harder.

A trickle of water appeared in the distance, turning the earth from light brown to a darker color.

"Molly," a shout came from just above her head. She turned, startled, to see Ed above her. He jumped from the back of his horse and laid down, his shoulders above the line of the short canyon wall. "Jump!"

Though it was the only instruction he shouted, Molly obeyed. The urgency in his voice, coupled with an expression of wide-eyed fear, kept her from asking the dozens of questions running through her head.

She trusted him. And she jumped, hands reaching for his. He caught her around the wrists at the same moment she heard what sounded like a dozen trees felled at the same moment. Her head whipped to see the source of the sound at the same moment a river full of mud and debris hurtled around the bend straight for her.

Before she could so much as gasp or scream, Ed pulled her up and back with the kind of strength born from desperation. He dragged Molly's body over the lip of the canyon, pulling her atop him as he collapsed backward. His hat fell off when he hit the ground. Molly landed atop his chest, forcing all the air out of him and her with a grunt.

A deafening sound, a cacophony of snapping wood and rushing water, made it too loud to even hear her own thoughts. The ground beneath them vibrated, and Ed turned to the side to let her roll off him. With her back against the ground, she could feel the power of the water hurtling down the previously dry canyon.

Molly pushed herself up, leaning back against the heels of her hands, and watched as the sudden flood overtook everything lower than where they were. The wall of prickly plants had disappeared completely beneath the churning mud.

She scrambled to her feet and backed farther away.

"Flash flood," Ed said, his voice raised to carry over the sound of snapping and groaning. "Five years cowboying in this territory, and this is only the third one I've seen." He chuckled without humor. "And you had to be right in the middle of it."

Her whole body shivered. "Merciful heavens."

"ED!" A shout that sounded dull and soft compared to the

water came from behind Molly, and she turned to see Dominó and Whiskers hurtling toward them on foot. Whiskers grabbed the horse, his eyes hugely round as he surveyed the flooding. Dominó skidded to a stop beside Molly. "You are not hurt?"

She shook her head mutely, but he didn't wait before kneeling beside Ed's still prone form. He spoke rapidly in Spanish, gesturing at the river and then Ed. She didn't understand a word of what he said, but Ed shook his head slowly and replied in the same language. Then he let Dominó give him a hand up.

At that moment, the clouds above them broke. The rain had reached them at last.

Molly came closer and grasped at Ed's arm with both hands. "You saved me," she shouted. There was no doubt the water would've killed her. If not by drowning, than by being crushed beneath the debris.

He gently pulled away from her grasp, only to wrap his arm around her shoulder and pull her close. Molly didn't resist burying her face tightly against his chest. She shuddered, and then the shock became too much. She started sobbing into his shirt.

Never in her life had she come so close to death.

"We need to get under cover," Whiskers yelled. "Get her on the horse."

Ed tugged her toward the animal, and she sniffled. Someone gave her a boost. Maybe it was Ed. Maybe Whiskers. But a moment later, Ed was behind her on the tall animal. "You two hurry up," he shouted, then they turned and rode back to the wagon.

Chaucer's ears were laid back, but he stood as still as the other horse while the rain poured down. Ed slid from the back of his horse, tied its lead loosely around a ring on the side of the buckboard, then reached up to Molly. He had his hands on her waist and tugged her down before she could try to move on her own.

He pulled her beneath the tarpaulin. A low-burning fire

already sent smoke up the back of the boulders and warmed the small space. Ed tugged her to the ground beside him and pulled her close again. Only then did Molly realize she was shivering.

When Whiskers and Dominó came back, someone wrapped a scratchy blanket around Molly's shoulders. It was probably meant for a horse to wear beneath its saddle. But she accepted it with gratitude, drawing her knees up close and wrapping her arms around herself.

It took some time for her to realize the low, gentle murmurs of sound were coming from Ed and Dominó as the two talked about the flood. And about her.

"She is lucky you were there." Dominó's words seemed more thickly accented than before.

"Have you ever been that close to one before?" Ed was still beside her, though they were no longer touching.

"Not since I was a small boy." Dominó sat on her other side, almost as close as Ed. She blinked and turned to look for Whiskers, only to find him leaning against the boulder, as close to the edge of cover as he could get and remain dry. He watched the sky, his eyebrows drawn close together.

"It seems I do have some luck," she said. Her voice trembled more than she liked. "To experience such a rare thing firsthand."

Ed looked down at her. "This hasn't changed your mind about your time here? The desert isn't for the faint of heart, Miss McKinney."

Molly forced a smile. "It will take more than a little water to frighten me away." He raised his eyebrows at her, but she caught an approving tilt to his lips before he looked away. Though the danger had passed, her heart picked up its pace again. She snuggled deeper into her rough blanket before she said, "Thank you for saving my life, Mr. Byrd."

His eyes darted to hers and then away again. "I'm glad I made it on time. It was a near thing."

"That it was," she murmured, letting her gaze drop to the fire. She'd seen the fear in his eyes as he'd reached for her. She would remember that moment the rest of her life. As she would remember his hands gripping her tightly and bringing her to safety. He'd held her close, perhaps to reassure himself she was out of danger. Despite the terror of what had happened, she'd never forget the relief she'd felt the moment she realized she was safe in Ed's arms.

CHAPTER 7

The mule that Molly had christened after an English author behaved himself quite prettily on their ride to the ranch. A ride that took several hours due to their brief stop after the flash flood. The ground soaked up the water quickly, though, leaving it cracked and dry in next to no time at all.

They went uphill the rest of the way, between a set of mountains, and before Molly was aware of it, the landscape had changed. Wild grasses grew in abundance, the cactus plants she had seen littering the desert were gone, and the air was different, too. Cooler. Softer. Barbed wire fences lined the road on either side.

Birds darted through the air, trilling songs she had never heard before. Occasionally, she'd see a twitch in the grass that revealed a tall, thin rabbit.

"Jackrabbits," Dominó informed her. "Tall and thin creatures, with ears nearly as long as their bodies."

A hawk circled in the sky high above them, and the sun dropped in the west.

If she were a painter, she'd have a difficult time transferring the beauty of browns, greens, and blues to canvas. But as a writer, she had a full stock of words at her disposal. Not that they'd let her use all that many in the newspaper. Her editor wouldn't hesitate to cut a descriptive line or two if it meant giving more room on the news-sheets for paid advertisements or more sensational stories.

Since stepping foot on American soil, Molly had toyed with the idea of writing a book. Perhaps a travel log, or a fictionalized version of her journey across the United States. Then she could send the snippets of her adventures to the newspaper with the knowledge she would tell her story in full later.

Ed stayed behind her, and she heard his voice when he made an occasional comment to Whiskers, the nearly mute man driving the wagon. She kept hoping he'd join her and Dominó again. A silly thing to wish for. She barely knew the man, and he'd probably had his fill of her when he'd had to save her life. At least he hadn't blamed her for the near-miss and wandering off. He'd said it could have happened to anybody. Still, since he was the one who had invited her out to the ranch, she'd thought that would mean a little more conversation with him.

Instead, Dominó was left to answer her questions about the weather, the plants, the animals, and anything else she could think to ask. He met all her queries with patience. And with more than single-syllable responses.

Perhaps Ed Byrd regretted asking her to visit the ranch. Molly didn't like how much this disappointed her. How intrigued she was by him despite his tight-lipped replies whenever they spoke.

She looked over her shoulder at him, and immediately caught him staring at her. How long had he been watching her?

Silly woman, she thought to herself. *He has nowhere to look but forward. You are directly in his path. Where else would he look?*

As though in answer to her silent question, Ed leaned a bit in his saddle, as though to peer around her.

Molly faced forward again, and she noted dust rising from behind a bend in the road.

Another wagon approached from the opposite direction. This one was driven by a man with a woman at his side, and a collection of blond children of varying sizes in the back. Whiskers took his wagon a little off to the side of the narrow road, leaving the family room to pass. Dominó guided his horse to do the same, and Molly followed suit.

"Mr. Harper," Ed shouted when the family's wagon drew nearly even with them. "Good evening, sir."

"Ed." Their wagon didn't slow, but the man said, "It's a fine Sunday afternoon. Where're you men coming from?"

"Tombstone. All's well with your folks?" Ed tipped his hat to the wagon when it drew even.

This time, the woman answered. "We're all doing fine, thanks for asking." The woman made eye contact with Molly. "You'uns have a guest?" This seemed to be a signal for her husband to stop the wagon, which he did with a sigh.

Whiskers kept right on driving, but Dominó and Ed kept their horses aside. The animals paced a bit anxiously, likely sensing they were close to home. Chaucer the Mule merely flicked an ear at them.

To his credit, Ed didn't sound as impatient as Mr. Harper looked. "Yes, ma'am. This is Miss Molly McKinney. Miss McKinney, this is Mrs. Harper, Mr. Harper, and their kids."

"It is a pleasure to meet you, Mr. and Mrs. Harper." Molly's answer was nothing unusual, but both husband and wife started and exchanged a glance of surprise.

"Landsakes, Miss McKinney. Nice to meet you, too," the woman said, a smile appearing on her face. "Are you a friend of Mrs. Morgan? Or maybe Duke? Seems like you English will outnumber the rest of us pretty soon with how often your countrymen show up."

Mr. Harper chuckled. "Seems like an invasion, sometimes." He winked, softening the words. "I can't say we mind. Folks from your place seem mighty nice."

"I'm afraid I have no real acquaintance with my fellow citizens, though I have met Mr. Morgan and Mr. Rounsevell." Molly adjusted her hold on her reins and looked to Ed, who seemed perfectly content to stand in the road as long as it took for their polite exchange. "I hope to come to know them better, though I have no intention of taking part in an invasion. I am here only temporarily."

The couple chuckled, then one of their children whined from the back of the wagon, "Ma, I'm hungry."

Mrs. Harper huffed and shook her finger at the little boy. "Mind your manners, child. We'll get on home to supper soon enough." She shared a commiserating look with her husband. "We best be on our way. It was nice to meet you, Miss McKinney. I hope we'll see you again soon."

"Sure. We don't get enough new faces around here." Mr. Harper tipped his hat, then gave his team a slap with the leather leads. "H'yup, boys. Let's get on home."

"Goodbye," Molly called after them. Dominó started forward again, and Ed's horse came alongside her as Chaucer picked up his feet. "They seemed pleasant."

"They're good folks." Ed shrugged, not looking at her. "They're close friends with the Bolton family. Their oldest daughter is sweet on King's son, Travis. He's in Texas, at Baylor University."

Intrigued by that, Molly nearly asked a question, but remembered in time that Ed hadn't been all that keen on talking about others. Or himself. Which made his invitation out to the ranch where he lived and worked strange. She pressed her lips together and smiled at him instead.

They went around the turn that had concealed the Harpers' wagon from view, and Molly got her first glimpse of the KB Ranch's entrance. Hanging above the gate that Whiskers had left open for them was an iron archway that looked a bit like a vine. The sign, which swung from the vine, said KB Ranch, with a three-pointed crown above the initials.

"KB with a crown is the ranch's brand," Ed said as they passed beneath, and she craned her neck to admire the iron-work. "Every ranch has to have one and register it. King's is hard to brand over, which is s'posed to cut down on cattle theft."

"Does it work?"

"Most of the time."

Dominó had picked up his pace and had crested a small hill ahead of them. Molly let her gaze travel across the hills she could see, the mountains in the distance, and took a deep breath of the warm air. The sky had turned purple and orange, and stars appeared in the darkest patches of oncoming night.

"Do you like living out here?" she asked as a gust of wind made the grasses wave like water around them. She caught Ed's shrug from the corner of her eyes and gave her attention fully to him. "Is it much different from where you grew up?"

"Oklahoma Territory?" He chuckled. "Very different. Where I grew up, I was surrounded by trees and streams. It rained and thundered most of the year, seemed like. You couldn't look in any direction without trees hemming in the view." He shrugged. "I miss it sometimes. But this is home for now."

"I went through Tulsa by train to get to Texas." They were nearly at the top of the hill. "I cannot say I recall much about that city."

"I've only been there once myself. I lived farther east, within the Indian Territory."

He hadn't been this talkative since they left the church together. She nearly asked him another question, but then they were at the top of the rise and the ranch stretched out in front of her. Cattle dotted the landscape between them and at least half a dozen buildings. Houses, barns, and smaller sheds. Fences, too. People milled about. A dog barked in the distance.

This ranch appeared busier than Sonoita itself had. It could be its own village.

Ed spoke at her side, his voice warmer than she'd yet heard it. "Welcome to KB Ranch, Molly."

She looked at him, catching his smile, before he put his heels to his horse and cantered down the hill. She urged Chaucer to do the same, and her mule gamely stretched his legs to catch up. She saw Dominó ahead, but the wagon had disappeared from sight.

Ed led her directly to a long adobe-brick building, riding through it with her alongside. The corridor was cool and dark, and when they emerged on the other side they were in a stable yard of sorts. More men were unloading things from the buckboard wagon, Whiskers giving them direction. Dominó had dismounted and walked his horse toward a barn.

The largest of the houses had a porch facing the busy area, and the porch door swung open to reveal a young man, still gangly and not full grown. He tromped down the steps, a grin stretching across his face.

"Howdy, Ed. Mom wants to know if you brought the sugar she asked for."

"I've never let Mrs. Bolton down before. Don't intend to start anytime soon." Ed swung down from his horse, and at the same time Molly caught the young man's curious glance, he introduced her. "I've brought a guest. Clark Bolton, this here is Miss Molly McKinney, from England. Think your mom has a minute to meet her?"

"You know she likes guests." The boy came to Molly's side and held out his hand. "May I help you down, Miss McKinney?"

"What fine manners." Molly accepted his hand as she put her leg over the side and dismounted. "Your mother must be a lovely woman."

"She's the best," the boy agreed. "I'll let Ed bring in the sugar, if you don't mind me takin' you inside, ma'am."

Delighted by his charm, Molly agreed, but stopped after a single step. "Oh, but I need to see to Chaucer. And my things."

"We will take care of it for you," Dominó said, appearing suddenly at her side with a wide smile. "You are our guest, Molly."

She glanced at Ed in time to catch him scowling at Dominó. Perhaps he didn't like the reminder that he'd invited her without permission from his employers. She'd known it was a risk to accept, but she couldn't turn down this opportunity to *really* see the wild west. Which wasn't as wild as she'd hoped, truth be told.

"Thank you," she murmured to the *vaquero*. Then she turned her smile to Clark. "Shall we?"

He led her up the porch steps and opened the door, releasing her arm and gesturing for her to enter the house first. She didn't look back, though she could have sworn she felt Ed's eyes on her with every step she took.

It took a moment for her vision to adjust to the shaded room in which she stood, but she realized it was a kitchen. Well. Half kitchen, half dining room, given the long table on one side. She removed her straw hat and followed after the young man as he walked through the open doorway and into a short hallway.

"Everyone's still in the parlor," he explained. "The last of our visitors left just before you arrived. Which means it'll be easy to introduce you around."

Oh dear. Perhaps she should have waited for Ed. She hadn't thought through the introductions, beyond meeting Mrs. Bolton. How was she to explain she'd been invited to stay at the ranch when the person who had extended the invitation wasn't with her?

They entered a parlor as fine as anything she'd seen in the middle-classes of England. The room was well-furnished, papered in blue and white stripes, with artwork upon the walls. Several men stood upon her entrance, and she saw two familiar faces right away. Mr. Morgan and Mr. Rounsevell, dressed in finer clothing than they'd worn when they'd visited Fort Huachuca.

An older, taller man stood, too. He had a sturdy look to him, and a confident stance that made her think at once that he must be the King Bolton she had heard so much about. A Black man who sat near him, with hair turning white above his temples, also stood, his posture easier and nonchalant.

"Who do you have here, Clark?" a woman asked, and Molly's eyes darted to the speaker. She was in her late thirties or early forties, with light-colored hair and a babe in her arms. The woman smiled kindly, though her eyes remained curious.

"Miss McKinney." Mr. Rounsevell stepped forward and offered her a slight bow. "We meet again."

"Oh, the English reporter," a woman who'd been sitting in a chair next to his said, coming awkwardly to her feet with one hand on her midsection. She looked close to Molly's age and as though she might go into labor at any moment. "I'm so glad you found your way here. I told Evan he should've brought you home when he met you." She approached and held out her hand, which Molly took with some amusement. "I'm Mrs. Rounsevell. Everyone calls me Dannie. It's a pleasure to meet you."

Another woman, also with child, approached too. She had red hair half down, and an easy grace that was explained the moment she spoke in a refined British accent. "I said the very same thing to Chris. I'm Mrs. Morgan. I cannot believe our husbands left you at that dusty fort rather than bring you home to us, Miss McKinney." She cast a somewhat reproving look at the foreman, who'd hunched his shoulders somewhat sheepishly.

Molly's nervous stomach settled with the warm welcome. "It seems I was fated to meet you both. It is a true pleasure. Your husbands are lovely gentlemen, I assure you. I think they were both merely anxious to return home and didn't want to bother with a strange woman slowing them down."

"But how did you manage to arrive here at last?" Mrs. Morgan asked, taking a step back after they'd shaken hands. Her husband hovered at her side.

A throat cleared behind Molly, and she looked over her shoulder to find Ed in the doorway. "That'd be my doing," he said, twisting the brim of his hat in his hand. "I invited Miss McKinney to come for a visit."

"Did you now?" King Bolton himself asked, his deep voice coming out in a low drawl. "That was mighty forthright of you, Ed."

Oh dear. Molly took a step back, putting herself nearer to the cowboy. "Mr. Byrd had the most wonderful suggestion for my work. Of course, he insisted I come to speak to you about it directly, Mr. King." She looked at Ed, smiling brightly. "Do you wish to tell them your idea, Ed, or shall I?"

Those who had stood at her entrance had retaken their seats. Curiosity hummed through the room, though no one made a sound as they looked from her to the cowboy nervously turning his hat through his hand like a wheel.

EACH GAZE RESTING UPON ED WEIGHED AS MUCH AS A LONGHORN steer. Here it came. The reckoning for overstepping his bounds. Assuming he had more pull as a cowboy than he had any right to suppose. He cleared his throat and glanced at Molly. The Englishwoman offered him a tentative smile, and for some reason, it sent warmth echoing from his chest to just about everywhere else.

He spoke with more confidence than he felt. "Miss McKinney wants to write about life on a cattle ranch, since that's not something folks back in England will know much about. I suggested that she'd have a better perspective on the subject if she lived on a ranch for a bit, rather than confine herself to interviews. Given that her work will be published, it might be good publicity for the Territory, too. That is, if you think it's all right, boss."

King Bolton didn't flinch or give away his thoughts by any change of expression. His eyes rested on Ed for a long moment, then went to Molly's. "You want to write about our ranch?"

To her credit, she didn't shy away from his matter-of-fact question or stare. Her shoulders stayed squared up, and she answered in as even a tone as he'd used. "I think it would make an excellent subject for a series of columns. Perhaps a magazine article, too."

King turned his attention to his son-in-law and daughter.

"What do y'all think? You weigh in too, Frosty. Can we handle a guest at this time of year?"

"I wouldn't be underfoot." Molly sounded somewhat offended, and King's gaze swung back to her. Ed tightened his grip on his hat. "I have been in many dangerous circumstances during my time as a journalist. Why, I traveled all the way out here on my own, which is something of a feat for a woman."

Frosty's wife, Evelyn, tilted her head to the side. "It is a rather daunting journey for a woman alone. I made it myself. With my daughter." She offered Molly an encouraging smile.

"Well. Would you be a guest or a hand, Miss McKinney?" King asked, tapping the arm of his chair. "Sounds like you want to experience what it's really like out here. Does that mean roping heifers or baking cornbread?"

The journalist lifted her chin. "Both, I should think. And I am happy to act as a hired hand, if that will cover my room and board."

The ranch owner released a long sigh. "It isn't an easy life. And you say you won't be in the way, but I have to consider the safety of you, my family, my men, and whether you'll be a distraction to the cowboys."

Mrs. Bolton chuckled. "If our cowboys can't do their job with a lady reporter riding around, then we might need new cowboys."

"I'll keep an eye on her, too," Ed volunteered quickly, cutting Molly a sideways glance. She gave him a grateful tip of the chin. "And train her up as best I can while she's here."

Abram Steele, part-owner and retired drover, cook, and Buffalo Soldier, gave his old friend a shrug when King looked to him for an opinion. "Couldn't hurt to have another pair of hands. And you never know. Might get some English tourists or investors out of it."

The old cowboy drummed his fingers along the chair again. Once. Twice. Three times. Then he slapped his hand against the arm. "All right. We can give it a try. Though you can't stay in the bunkhouse, Miss McKinney. Even if you are actin' the part of a hired hand."

"Miss McKinney is welcome to our spare room," Evelyn hastened to say, as though she wanted to beat the others to extending her invitation. She smiled brightly at the journalist. "We have three children, and they will love having a guest. I have to say, they're quite good at teaching people about life in America, too."

"Sounds like a mighty fine plan," Frosty added, his arm going around his wife's shoulders. "I can make certain you're up at the crack of dawn for work, and Evelyn will keep you from feeling too homesick."

"And hers is the only house not about to experience the joys of a crying infant," Dannie put in, her hand resting on her midsection.

The baby girl in Mrs. Bolton's arms took that opportunity to start up a fuss, prompting her mama to stand and rock in place to soothe her. "That's probably the best of reasons to stay with the Morgans," she said, a grin overtaking her pleasant face. "Little Samantha hasn't quite learned the difference between night and day yet. No reason for you to have to listen to her figure it out, Miss McKinney."

King stood and held his arms out for his daughter, and as he settled the fussy youngster against his shoulder, he made his decision. "Sounds like we've got ourselves a plan. I hope you enjoy your time here, Miss McKinney."

Ed watched as a grin overtook the woman's face, making her even prettier than before. Her eyes crinkled at the corners, her cheeks turned rosy, and his stomach completely flipped backward and forward again as she said, "Please, call me Molly."

They invited her to have a seat in the parlor, while Frosty left his place next to his wife. As he passed by Ed, he used a jerk of his chin to get the cowboy to follow him. They made it all the way to the kitchen before Frosty stopped and turned, arms crossed over his chest.

He gave Ed a hard look. "What's this really about?"

Ed put on the most innocent expression he could. "I ran into Miss McKinney in Tombstone. She was looking for a good story to tell. We got to talking. I figured, why not let her come out here and tell the ranch's story? There's no better place in the Territory for a writer to stay."

The older man raised his eyebrows, his cool blue eyes full of skepticism. "So it didn't have anything to do with her being as pretty as a fawn in a flowerbed?"

Try as he might, Ed could never come up with phrases half so colorful as Frosty's. He couldn't help chuckling at that comparison. "It didn't hurt," he admitted. "But I probably would've let a male reporter come out, too."

"Right." Frosty sighed and ran his hand through his hair. "Listen. I've got a lot on my mind right now. We're getting close to the fall cattle drive. Evie's a month shy of having our baby. I'm keeping track of three kids and a passel of cowboys and cattle. Duke's a bundle of nerves with his baby on the way. Everyone's got something going on to keep them busy. This lady, if she's going to be out here, she'll need as much looking after as any other greenhorn. You've gotta keep an eye on her, Ed. For her well-being."

His friend's serious attitude sobered Ed. He answered with full sincerity. "I know, boss. I promise I'll keep her safe."

"That means safe from you too," Frosty added sternly, and Ed nearly choked. "She's got a job to do, just like you. And she's going back to England when she's done. I can't see a lady like her hanging around here. So don't let her get attached, and you don't go getting attached, either. I don't want to lose my best cowboy to heartbreak."

What did Ed say to that? He wasn't sweet on her. Not at all. Even if he was having a strange reaction to her voice. And her smile. He could ignore those things like he did with other pretty women. "My heart's going to be just fine."

Frosty gave a curt nod. "Good. Go ahead and get done whatever you need to for the evening. I'll make sure Miss McKinney is up and fed early so she can go with you on some fence checks and repairs. Might as well show her the scope of the ranch first thing."

Though he knew it wasn't his place to sit in the parlor with the boss, his family, and the foreman, Ed couldn't deny the stitch of disappointment in his chest at the dismissal. He left with a "yes, boss," and went out the door, shoving his hat back on his head. The buckboard wagon was gone. The horses already seen to. He made his way to the bunkhouse, feeling a bit like a cat put out for the night.

Dominó stood outside the entrance to the bunkhouse, at the opening of the zaguán corridor. He smoked a cigarette, the tip glowing as he took in a puff. Ed had tried the common cowboy habit years back. His father smoked. His grandfather, too. But Ed hadn't really taken to it, even if it did warm a body up on a cold night watching cattle.

"So?" Dominó blew a puff of smoke into the night air. "Your señorita. Does she stay?"

Ed tried not to smile, but a bit of his relief leaked out in his answer. "Yep. She stays. As long as she keeps from being underfoot. I've volunteered to mind her."

"You will keep her out of trouble, eh?" Dominó's grin turned sly. "And who will keep you out of trouble, *amigo*?"

"Frosty seemed to think I'd have trouble keeping impartial, too." Ed sighed dramatically. "When have I ever mooned over a female? I'm not about to get any more attached to her than you are."

"There is a first time for everything, Eduardo." Dominó dropped his cigarette and ground it beneath his heel, then clapped Ed on the back. "Come. Let's tell the others about the guest, and we can all lay bets as to who will fall in love first. You or the lady."

Ed groaned but followed his friend into the bunkhouse. But he didn't deny the danger of such a thing a second time. If he protested too much, that would just make it more fun for the men to needle him about their guest.

And it was already going to be a heap of work to keep his word to Frosty and avoid forming an attachment to the pretty Englishwoman. But Ed would manage it. He had to. Because whether or not he liked it, she couldn't stick around forever.

CHAPTER 8

A loud thump made Molly's eyes blink open, and she lay still, trying to recall where she was. There had been many strange beds lately, with her travels. It always took a moment to remember where she'd last laid her head.

She looked up at a white-washed ceiling that slanted overhead, but everything in the room around her was tinted the blue-gray that preceded dawn. She shifted in her bed, the soft feathers beneath her at odds with the sound of something pricklier. Dry grass?

Oh. Her mattress was stuffed with straw. Evelyn Morgan had explained the bed to her the night before. Straw made up most of her bedding, but a thin feather mattress went atop that to make the bed softer.

Molly stretched, reaching her arms over her head then back until her knuckles brushed the wall behind her simple headboard. She threw back the blankets and put her feet on the woven rug beneath her feet, then slipped across the room to the curtained window. She pushed aside the thin material covering the glass and looked out at the ranch in the pre-dawn light.

She saw someone walking from the bunkhouse to one of the outbuildings, carrying a lit lantern. The bunkhouse itself only had a few small windows, but they flickered with light. She had to angle herself differently to look toward the main house, and she saw a light in the kitchen window there, too.

The day started early on the ranch. But what had woken her?

A door downstairs closed, hard, and then a flurry of hissed commands followed.

"You're going to wake the lady," a young voice said.

"Sorry. I had to get eggs for Mama. I forgot."

Even the children were up before the sun.

Molly wasn't about to get herself labeled as lazy. She hurried to the basin and pitcher of water left for her needs the night before. She was in the midst of poking pins in her hair when a soft knock sounded at her door. She crossed the short distance and flung it open, cheerfully greeting Mrs. Morgan on the other side.

"Good morning! I am nearly ready."

Evelyn Morgan blinked once in surprise, and then she smiled back as she rested her hand atop her protruding stomach. "Wonderful. Do you need any help?"

"None at all. Is there something I can do to help you this morning?"

"While you are in my house, you are a guest." The red-haired woman gestured to the stairs. "Once you step out the door, you are at the ranch's mercy." The gleam in her eyes gave Molly confidence Mrs. Morgan hadn't meant it as a terrible fate. "May I make a suggestion?"

"Please. I can use all the advice you have." She put her hands up to her coil of hair, pins still in her fingers.

Mrs. Morgan tugged at a curl of her own red hair. "The style you're wearing isn't the best idea for the work you'll be doing. You will regret every one of those pins before long. I suggest a braid instead. As few pins as you can manage, too."

Though not usually a vain woman, Molly touched the crown of dark hair atop her head and frowned. "It seemed all right yesterday."

"You rode here directly from Tombstone. Today, you will be hard at work. Bending, lifting, riding, and sweating, if you'll excuse the indelicacy of me saying so. There's also the matter of your hair getting caught in the brush. A braid is easier to slip out of thorns than hair coiled tightly and littered with pins. Dannie taught me that before I learned it the hard way."

"Oh." Molly's shoulders fell. She clutched the pins tighter in her hands. "I suppose if Mrs. Rounsevell suggests such a thing, we all ought to listen."

The older woman's gaze softened. "Would you like help? I've had a lot of practice with plaiting hair, thanks to the two little girls running about."

Self-sufficiency had brought Molly too far in life for her to give it up now. "I can manage, thank you. I will be downstairs the moment I am finished."

"Take your time." Mrs. Morgan turned around and walked in that careful way expectant mothers had, all the way to the stairs. Molly turned away before the woman disappeared from sight, her fingers already searching out the pins she'd secured in her hair.

Once she replaced the familiar hairstyle with a long braid, she pushed the rope of hair over her shoulder and picked up her hat from the bureau. She left her room, closing the door behind her, and kept her step light.

She'd spent much of the night lying awake, thinking of how she would sell this series of columns to her editor. Molly needed to convince him to print her words in a series about Arizona Territory itself. Her mind hummed with ideas, which made it easy for her to smile happily as she sat at the table and accepted tea, cornbread, eggs, and a helping of beans.

Molly ate every bite with gratitude. Though she hadn't done much physical labor in her life, she appreciated the notion of beginning the day with a full stomach.

The back door opened as she took one last sip of her tea. Mr.

Morgan stuck his head inside, a wide smile on his face. "You ready to go, Molly?"

"Absolutely." She darted up from her chair and called to the other woman, who had already started helping one of her daughters with the dishes. "Thank you for breakfast, Mrs. Morgan."

"Call me Evelyn." She dried her hands on her apron, then darted a look at her husband. "Don't let her work too hard, love."

The lanky foreman grinned at his wife and winked. "I'll pass your advice on to Ed. He's the one in charge of our new hand."

"Ed?" Evelyn repeated, then put her hands on her hips. "Really? No one thought it might be best for her to learn from the foreman? Or even her own countryman?"

"Duke's nearly a greenhorn himself." Mr. Morgan didn't seem the slightest bit perturbed that his wife questioned his decision on the matter. "And Ed doesn't mind."

That was something of a relief, Molly supposed. Ed had invited her in the first place, so it stood to reason they had selected him to educate her on the finer points of ranch life. She followed Mr. Morgan out the back door and around the little house. The two of them made their way down a well-trod dirt path toward the main house and yard.

"You'll be repairing fences with Ed and Clark today," he told her. "You'll take a wagon around the perimeter of the ranch, covering as much territory as you can. You'll check for breaks. Wires that need to be replaced or stretched, or posts that are falling over."

The same wagon that had brought her trunk to the ranch waited at the barn, with two mules attached and facing toward the adobe building, ready to walk through the tunnel-like corridor. Clark Bolton, hat and crooked smile in place, nodded politely to her as he dropped a box of tools in the wagon bed.

"'Morning, Miss McKinney."

"Good morning, Clark."

She peered into the back of the wagon. Large, rope-like coils of wire waited in the back, along with several wooden poles. As she studied the materials, a crate landed heavily in the wagon and made her jump. Ed had walked up beside her without her knowing.

"Molly," he said, voice a bit gravelly as though he hadn't used it much yet that day. "Ready?"

Apparently, some people at the ranch didn't think it necessary to speak in full sentences. Perhaps he wasn't the sort of person who started the day off cheerfully. She knew a lot of people like that, actually.

"I am, thank you."

He pointed to the wagon bench. "Climb on up."

At least he didn't assume she needed help. The split skirt she'd obtained in Tombstone made it easy for her to maneuver her way up the wheel spokes and into the seat. She patted the vest pocket where she'd stowed a couple of short pencils and a notebook, reassuring herself of their presence, then checked the other small pocket for her leather gloves and handkerchief.

Clark stood at the back of the wagon and whistled. One of the dogs Molly had seen ran and jumped onto the wagon. The animal had a mottled coat of tan, black, and gray fur that almost appeared blue, with darker patches of fur over his eyes. He was a stunning creature.

"This here is Tex. He's learning how to be a lookout." The boy scratched the dog behind the ears.

"He's adorable."

Ed appeared on the opposite side of the wagon and hauled himself up and onto the bench beside her. "Get your horse, Clark. We're picking up where Duke and Dannie left off."

"Sure." The boy closed the back of the wagon. "I'm right behind you both."

With a click of his tongue, Ed had the mules and the wagon moving. They drove through the shaded corridor and out into the early morning sunlight. They went eastward, and Molly briefly regretted not purchasing the tinted spectacles she had found in a Tombstone shop. The darkened glasses would've made it easier to travel into morning light. As it was, she tugged the brim of her hat down as much as she could and looked to the side to avoid facing the sun head on.

"Did the Morgans treat you well?" Ed asked, bringing her mind back to the present.

She turned to face him, which also kept the sun out of her eyes. "Yes. They are lovely people. Their children are sweet, too."

He nodded once, but didn't say another word. So, she took it upon herself to continue the conversation. "What about you? Is everything all right? You didn't get into any trouble for bringing me here, did you?"

"No. No trouble." But his gruff answer struck her as somewhat subdued. He still hadn't looked directly at her, either.

"Perhaps you were teased?" she dared to suggest. "Dominó seems like the sort to make jokes."

"He is."

She waited, but he didn't elaborate. It seemed the tight-lipped cowboy she'd first met had returned. What a shame. She turned away again, and caught sight of a beautiful animal jumping from the brush, springing away from the wagon. "Goodness. Is that an antelope?"

"That's what folks call 'em." Ed didn't sound overly interested in the creature. "Some scientist who came through a few years ago said we'd do better to call them pronghorns."

"A less elegant name, for certain."

"That's what I thought, too."

She turned quickly to catch his expression, but it was as set and still as before. "I suppose there isn't much that is elegant about the desert."

At last, his expression changed. He tilted his head to the side and looked at her, his eyes narrow in the sunlight, but she read the skepticism in them anyway. "I know you've been in the Territory for a while now, ma'am. But you can't judge our *elegance*, as you call it, by what you've seen at forts and mining towns. Life on the land itself is something altogether different."

"I hope you'll show me what you mean." She crossed her arms over her chest and leaned toward him. "And please, Ed. We're friends. Call me Molly. Not ma'am."

Eᴅ ᴛᴡɪsᴛᴇᴅ ᴛʜᴇ ᴘʟɪᴇʀs ɪɴ ʜɪs ʜᴀɴᴅs, ᴡʀᴀᴘᴘɪɴɢ ᴀ sɴᴀᴘᴘᴇᴅ ᴇɴᴅ ᴏғ barbed wire around a new strand of metal. He explained the process as he went. Winding the fence wire away from himself on one side of the repair, and then toward him on the other. The resulting twists of old and new wire together fixed a three-foot break in one fence.

Molly stood near him and asked questions he answered as simply as he could.

The reminder of her purpose, given by Frosty the evening before, had quelled Ed's desire to make more conversation than necessary. Maybe he'd fallen under her spell in Tombstone. Or even before that, at the fort.

Something about her big brown eyes, the curve of her smile, had pulled him in.

No. That wasn't fair. It wasn't her fault he'd lost his good sense.

Tex sat nearby, watching their surroundings with all the enthusiasm of a pup. The type of dogs they had at the ranch had been bred by a sheep farmer, originally, but they were just as handy with beeves as they were with the fluffier livestock. And they were excellent guard dogs. Tex's sire, Gus, protected people by alerting them to rattlesnakes, cougars, and even varmints of the two-legged variety. The more experienced dog spent more of his time on the Morgans' porch these days, meaning it was time to train up the next generation of ranch dogs.

Farther down the fence line, Clark whistled to himself as he tightened a wire that had too much slack in it. He used a more pliable metal, twisted it with the pliers, and wound the whole line that way, tighter and tighter.

"Next break we find," Ed said to the woman standing at his elbow, "you'll do the repair. It takes a little muscle, but the pliers do most of the work."

"I am certain I can manage." She grinned at him, then straightened her posture and stared down the fence into the distance. "How long does it take to repair the whole fence?"

"If we did it all at once? Days. Weeks, even." Ed shoved the pliers in his back pocket and took off his gloves, then used the bandana around his neck to swipe at the thin line of sweat on his forehead. "We take it in turns to check the fence. We mark off where we've been in a book that Frosty keeps for us. The next one sent out will check a different section of fence. We keep track of breaks we see when we're out checking on the herd, too."

"It sounds as though the job is never finished."

"That's how most things on a ranch are." He looked up at the sky. "Looks like we've got a warm day ahead."

"Would you like some water?" Molly's eyes went round, and she went to retrieve it for him before he answered. He'd stored his canteen beneath the wagon bench, where it would stay cool in the small pocket of shade. She had to stand on the tip of her toes to reach it. He tried hard not to notice how adorable that made her look.

Ed accepted the canteen with a sincere thanks but didn't say much else. Which was difficult. It wasn't like him. Frosty had always said Ed was mouthy. He talked too much. Acted too cheerful, even on hot days. He wanted to tease her. Wanted to ask more about her life. But it felt risky to act as he normally did around her.

Why?

How had a petite English lady thrown him for such a loop?

"Have you ever come across any sort of danger while doing these routine chores?" Her eyes flashed with interest, and her tone shifted to something stiffer. Almost formal.

He fought back a grin. This was her journalist tone. He'd heard it at the fort, and when she'd tried to ask him questions in

Tombstone. At least it was easy to tell which questions were for her own interest and which were for the story she would tell.

"It's always dangerous out here, if you're not prepared." He shook the canteen so the water sloshed against the inside. "Even something so simple as leaving the ranch without enough water can doom a man to illness or death."

"That sounds ominous," Clark said as he approached, a crooked smile on his face. "But it's true. If you got caught out in the sun for longer than you expected, and tired yourself out, heat exhaustion is a dangerous risk."

"That isn't something I'd considered." Molly reached into the small pocket of her vest and drew out a stubby pencil and small notebook. She flipped open the cover and scribbled at the paper while Ed put his extra wire back in the wagon. He climbed up and waited for her to join him. This time, he offered her a hand as she approached.

"Have you ever had heat exhaustion?" Molly studied his ungloved hand for a moment, then accepted it. When her slim, warm fingers slid against his to accept his grip, an electric current shot through his hand and straight to his heart, then fizzled about in his bloodstream while he pulled her up. He released her as quickly as he could, but the sensation didn't abate. He half expected his hair would stand on end and spark like lightning if he wasn't wearing his hat.

What was wrong with him?

"Nope. But I've seen it plenty." Ed cleared his throat but didn't follow up with so much as a hum. He picked up the leads, hunched over just enough to avoid eye contact with Molly, and slapped the leather against the mules to get them moving.

"What are the symptoms?"

"Dizziness. Nausea. Weakness in your limbs and in your pulse." Actually, some of the same symptoms he'd had while drinking plenty of water but being near her. "Heat stroke is worse," he added. "Everyone used to call both of 'em heat sickness. But Ruthie read that some doctor in Tucson says heat stroke is when your body gives up.

It's too hot. It stops sweating. You black out. Everything stops working the way it should, and it's harder to bring a person back from that."

Molly kept making notes in her little book, clearly unperturbed by both the subject under conversation and the way their shoulders touched. That told him the strange sensations he felt were one-sided, or maybe all in Ed's head. He needed to shake free of them before he did something stupid. Like flirt with her.

"Apart from carrying water with you, how do you protect against such a thing?" She looked up at him, her head tilted so the brim of her hat didn't interfere with her curious gaze.

"You avoid being out during the hottest hours of the day. It's not as bad up here, in the mountains and valleys, as it is in the flatter places in the desert. But we take a break in the middle of the afternoon, anyway. We find a patch of shade, if we're not back at the ranch, and rest."

"Will we need to do that today?" The way her eyes brightened meant she thought the idea exciting rather than a bother. How would she feel about it if she had to sit still in a gulch next to him for two hours? A mind as quick and busy as hers couldn't be happy that way.

How long would she truly last on the ranch? Not long, he reckoned. As soon as she had enough to write a passable story, she'd take off. No doubt about it. And he'd have to say goodbye before he'd even had a chance to get to know her.

His chest tightened unpleasantly.

"Nah. Not today. We're heading back around the same time we'd normally stop and rest. We'll cool down the team back at the ranch, do some indoor chores, and give you time to rest."

"Me?" Molly tossed her braid over her shoulder. "I assure you, I am perfectly capable of keeping up the pace."

"We'll see." She had drive and gumption, but that didn't mean she had the strength and stamina to back it up. A little thing like her. She'd be lucky to do more than a few repairs before her arms shook with fatigue. Then again, greenhorns had surprised him before. Duke was a prime example of that. He'd started as a soft-handed lord and ended up one of the hardest workers Ed had ever seen.

They stopped at another line of busted fence. Clark, already off his horse, held up a jagged piece of wood.

"Not sure what did this pole in." He dropped it in the wagon. Wood was in short supply on their side of the mountains. They had to haul in lumber from a mill when they had serious building to do. Broken up, wooden posts could be used back at the ranch for firewood, if nothing else.

Ed pulled on his gloves and then jumped down from the wagon. He helped the boy find a likely replacement pole from the back. Then he got pliers and held them out to Molly as her boots hit the dirt.

"Once the pole is up, we'll need to splice up the wires together. Get your gloves on."

She accepted the pliers with an eager smile.

After they had the wooden post in place, Ed looped the loose wires over it. They had three lines going from post-to-post all across the ranch. Bottom, middle, top. Simple. And every foot or so there was a sharp-twisted barb to discourage cattle from knocking over the fencing for the fun of it. Of course, any bull or cow that wanted through bad enough wouldn't hesitate to tear up even the prickliest of fencing. But this kept the casual wanderer where they belonged.

"I'll head north a bit more." Clark gave a whistle and Tex jumped down from the wagon, ready to follow the boy and his horse. "Just a few hundred yards, probably. If I don't find anything, I'll wait on y'all to catch up." He mounted with the ease of someone who'd ridden since infancy. Then he glanced over Ed's head to Molly, and his eyes widened. "Um. You might want to give her a hand."

He rode off as Ed swiveled on his heel to see Molly attempting the trick he'd shown her for pulling together two broken pieces of barbed wire. Except she wore a pair of gloves more suitable for church-going than any kind of work.

"Molly." He got on over to her quick and put a hand atop hers where she gripped the pliers. "Lady, these gloves won't protect you from so much as a mean-spirited fly."

She blinked up at him. "I beg your pardon?"

"Take those off." He tugged at his own. "Wear mine, unless you want to scar up those pretty hands of yours."

She looked down at her gloves, then up at him. "You think my *hands* are pretty?"

"Figure of speech. But I s'pose they're a sight prettier than mine." He briefly held up the back of his right hand to show off a long, thin scar stretching from knuckle to wrist. He ignored the heat creeping up his neck with her surprised stare. And he held out his thick leather gloves. "Here."

She pulled off her own carefully and tucked them into the belt of her split skirt. Then she held out a hand to accept his. He slapped them into her palm, making sure she felt the difference in the weight and quality of the material.

Molly pursed her lips as she pulled on the gloves, which were a little too large for her hands. "Very well. Now that I have the appropriate accessories: pliers, please." She held her hand out to him.

He chuckled and handed them to her.

She brought the two broken ends of the wire so they were side-by-side, then pulled the ends on either side up a smidge. She held the wires together with the pliers, then used her gloved hand to twist one broken end under and over the stronger wire. She grunted toward the end, when she had less wire to work with. Considering she'd never done anything like it before, she attacked the chore with a determination that impressed Ed. Maybe she took longer to do it than he would've, but she got the job done.

She released the pliers and backed up, scrutinizing her work carefully before looking to Ed, clearly looking for his approval. He folded his arms and stared hard, waiting unnecessary seconds before saying, "That looks good. Like you've been doing this all your life."

She laughed. "Flattery isn't necessary, so long as the job is done correctly."

"Better do a good job of checking then." He gave the wire a little shake. It barely budged. "Well, look at that. Steady as a rock."

"Good." She handed him the pliers, then went to the wagon to climb up. Ed followed close on her heels, tossing the pliers in the wagon bed and using the same motion to catch her by the waist and lift her onto the seat. Molly gasped, then turned and glared at him.

He affected an innocent expression. He hadn't any better an idea what had gotten into him than she did. Especially since he'd held off teasing her a dozen times already. He shrugged, then hauled himself up into the wagon beside her.

"Trying to hurry things along," he said, by way of excuse.

"Are you saying I am too slow for you?" She scoffed. "I will have you know that I've won every footrace I've ever taken part in."

"Really?" Ed feigned disbelief. "How many of those have there been?"

She pursed her lips, then pretended to count on her fingers, before declaring with great pomp, "Perhaps eight."

He tried not to laugh. "Impressive."

"Indeed."

He didn't mean to flirt with her. And maybe this didn't count as flirting. Maybe it was merely fun. It felt more natural than hemming and hawing, treating her like she'd break, or avoiding saying over two words at a time. He'd exhausted himself trying to act business-like. And she didn't seem to mind. Maybe he could afford to loosen the reins a little without worrying about letting his feelings run wild.

"Who do you think would win if it was the two of us?" he

asked, sitting back and propping one leg up on the footboard. "Me or you?"

She sniffed daintily. "Why, me. Of course."

"Should we put that theory to the test?"

"I see no reason why that's necessary." She calmly stripped off his gloves, then went about examining them. They were newer, but there were still a few cracks along the knuckles.

"I won't take hold of you and throw you in any more wagons if you win."

"You say that as though you think it bothered me." She glanced at him from the corner of her eye. "So long as you don't sling me around like a sack of beans, I don't mind the extra help into this rickety old thing."

"Rickety old thing? I'll have you know this wagon is the best of its kind." He gave the buckboard seat a pat, then yelped and looked at his hand. "See. Only got two splinters instead of half a dozen."

She laughed, dropping his gloves into her lap. She held out her hand. "Let me see those splinters."

Whoops. He didn't have any intention of letting her hold his hand. "I was joking. Not a splinter in sight."

"I'll be the judge of that." She snatched his right hand away from the leads, and he let her take it into her own without a fight. She pretended to examine his palm, then turned his wrist and studied his knuckles instead. "Dear me. I can see why you decided I need the gloves. All these scars cannot be from fences, surely."

He cleared his throat and tried to keep his eyes on the mules. He saw Clark in the distance. If the boy caught sight of Molly holding his hand, it might well lead to the sort of gossip in the bunkroom that would earn a lecture from Frosty about how to treat women on the ranch. A lecture that Ed hadn't ever needed before.

"Nope. There are lots of things in this line of work that'll leave their mark on a man." He pulled his hand away gently. "Cactus. Rocks. Ornery horses. Cattle. Ropes."

"Wagons with dangerous splinters," she added. "Thank you for loaning me your gloves."

"Yes, ma'am. Any time."

They were out of the wagon again in no time. Molly fixed several broken fences, wiping away sweat on her forehead on the third fix. Ed took his gloves back and handled the next several.

They set aside the tools long enough for lunch, and Clark took over the conversation. He talked about growing up on the isolated ranch, where his only real friend was his brother, and his schoolroom was beneath the wide-open blue sky of the Territory. The boy didn't have any trouble talking to her, and the reporter seemed to eat up every word. She even laughed a time or two, and Ed's defenses slipped a little more each time she did.

He could spend a lot of time listening to that laugh. But did he dare allow himself to enjoy it, and Molly's company, when she'd be on her way soon enough?

CHAPTER 9

(Please See Content Warning on Copyright Page)

T he second day of ranch life, Molly woke later than the first. She only knew that because someone had to knock on her door to wake her.

"I'm up," she called, then groaned as every muscle in her arms and back protested her attempt to get out of bed. Repairing fences hadn't been as easy as she'd pretended.

Sitting up in bed proved equally painful to her backside. Bouncing along on a hard wagon seat two days in a row hadn't been the best for her...constitution. She approached the mirror hanging over her small chest of drawers and smirked at her reflection. She lifted her chin and examined the red ring around her throat. The taut feel of her skin confirmed that her hat and bandana hadn't protected her from the sun completely.

Molly dipped her hand towel in the basin of cool water and bathed her sunburned neck, patting gently at the skin. She winced at the feel of cloth and wondered how it'd feel to have a shirt-collar rubbing the same spot all day long.

"This isn't the worst thing I've done for a story," she reminded herself. "I stood in the rain for three days to speak to the Prime

Minister." She'd never actually spoken to the man. He'd never looked at her. Just rushed from the front door of his house out to the carriage, holding an umbrella tilted to block out the rain and Molly McKinney. "Not that it matters. The story his housekeeper gave me was better, anyway."

Even though two newspaper editors passed on it before a women's magazine agreed to run it.

She pressed the cool, wet cloth against her eyes. Then she hung it on the rack built onto the side of the dresser, squared her shoulders, and hurried through the rest of her morning routine. She walked down the stairs in her socks. She'd left her boots on the front porch the night before, after she'd had to clean them off. Unfortunately, she'd been so busy asking Clark questions that she'd stepped in cow-leavings. The boy had proven himself a gentleman by not laughing at her.

"Good morning, everyone," she sang out to the kitchen as she descended the steps.

This morning, the three children in the family sat at the table with slates before them. Their breakfast things were already cleared away.

Frosty sat at the head of the table, a mug in one hand and a book in the other. He glanced up as she hopped from the last step to the floorboards. "Good morning, Miss Molly. You're in time for our spelling review. Last week we learned the word *gargantuan*."

"An excellent word. It is both unusual and evocative." She went to the stove where Evelyn waited with a plate of eggs, corn-bread, bacon, and sliced tomatoes. She accepted the plate with thanks and settled at the table, watching as the children wrote out three of their most difficult words from the week before.

A knock on the back door interrupted their studious attitudes, as all three children looked up to see who had come when Evelyn opened it wide. "Ed, how lovely to see you today. Won't you come in for some coffee?"

For no explainable reason, Molly's cheeks warmed.

Perhaps an effect of having a sunburn. Didn't those cause

strange fluctuations in temperature? She had read that somewhere, hadn't she? Though, sunburn didn't explain her sudden
urge to smooth back her hair or straighten her blouse.

"I don't mean to disturb your morning." He slipped inside,
staying near the door, hat in hand. "It's horse-shoeing day for a
few of the mounts. I thought I'd bring Molly to watch."

"Come on in and sit a spell first," Frosty offered, tapping the
back of the empty chair at his right—the chair directly across
from Molly's. "Molly's finishing breakfast."

"And we're finishing our spelling," the little boy, Ben, said
with enthusiasm. "Check my work, Papa." Though the boy was
American through and through, he pronounced both his parents'
names with an English accent.

Molly had learned the night before that Evelyn and Frosty
had married a year ago. Madeline, the blonde little girl, had come
from Evelyn's first marriage. The other two children, Laura and
Ben, were relatives placed under Frosty's guardianship. Together,
they made a family, with a fourth child to join them within the
next month.

Though she hadn't yet learned all the details, Molly could tell
their story was one filled with affection. It sounded like the sort of
romance people wrote novels about and then sighed over quite
dreamily while hoping to never go through such things
themselves.

Ed settled into his chair with a mug of coffee. He smiled when
they made eye contact. Molly raised her mug slightly toward him
and said, "Good Morning."

Frosty checked the children's slates, announced everyone had
spelled the words correctly, then looked at Molly. "Would you
care to suggest a couple of words for this week?"

She swallowed her last bite of eggs. "Oh, yes. I have two
favorites. *Fascinating* and *irresistible.* I nearly always spell the latter
word incorrectly."

"Can you use the words in sentences?" Laura asked, her chalk
hovering over the slate.

"Certainly." Molly clasped her hands on the table before her. "I find the desert *fascinating*. It means the desert has captured my interest and imagination. It intrigues me. Makes me curious."

"A good word." Frosty spelled it for the children, and they copied it onto their slates with care. "All right. And the other one?"

"*Irresistible*. Chocolate is irresistible." She grinned at Madeline, whose nose wrinkled. "I cannot help eating chocolate when I come upon it. The desire to taste it is too strong."

"I feel that way about watermelon," Ben said with a tilt of his chin, looking pointedly at his mother. "When will we have some?"

Evelyn brushed her hands against her apron as she approached the table. "We should harvest the last of them this week." She spelled the word for the children. Correctly. Then she took Molly's plate. As much as she'd tried, Molly had been forbidden from helping with household duties. Evelyn wouldn't let her lift a finger.

"After the horses are shoed, maybe you should keep our new hand in the shade," Frosty said, directing his comment to Ed. "She's looking a little pink around the edges."

Putting a hand on her neck, Molly smiled somewhat sheepishly. "It's not that terrible, surely."

"Stop making her self-conscious," Evelyn said from the sink. "A little calamine lotion will set you right up, Molly."

"That stuff will leave you pinker than before." Ed's teasing tone accompanied a grin before he sipped at his coffee.

"But it works," Evelyn argued. She opened a cabinet and withdrew a large pink bottle. "Here. This will stop it from itching and protect you from burning more. You can keep it up in your room."

Molly sighed. Walking around the ranch with a bright pink neck wasn't much better than the sunburn, but she excused herself from the table and went up to her room to dab the lotion on. When she came down again, Ed stood by the door, hat in hand, ready to leave. She had her boots on and hat atop her head as quick as she could. Molly followed him out the kitchen door.

"Fascinating and irresistible," Ed said aloud as they walked around the house, toward the main ranch buildings. He looked at her from the corner of his eye, the shadow of his hat making him appear sly.

"They are good words," she pointed out, uncertain why she needed to defend her choices.

"Descriptive words." His tone suggested his mind had followed another track altogether. Which made the back of her neck prickle and her stomach flutter.

Was he flirting with her? Not many men bothered, once they realized she had a career she cared about. Still. She had entertained callers at her boarding house before. Male reporters, mostly. And one kind-hearted but severely disappointing accountant a friend had introduced to her.

But why was she thinking on her romantic misadventures?

She'd caught glimpses of a playful nature in Ed, but his character shifted back to a more serious demeanor every time she glimpsed that side of him. Almost like he wanted to act crossly when around her. Molly kept pace with him, thinking far too much about the cowboy at her side when she ought to start mentally composing her first article about ranch life.

"Will you ever give me an interview about *you*, Ed?"

"Maybe."

"Ah. I see. Will it be an interview consisting entirely of one-word answers?"

His step slowed, then stopped. He hooked his thumbs on his belt and studied her. "I've answered a lot of your questions already. Using more than one word at a time."

"When it comes to things like fence repair and the weather, yes." She mirrored his stance, thumbs in belt and chin raised. "Not when I ask questions about *you*. Anything personal gets me no more than a single word at a time. Perhaps if I asked enough questions over the course of a month, I'd have enough to write an entire paragraph."

He tipped his hat back on his forehead and appeared perplexed. "Huh. You think I'm that close-mouthed?"

"As I said, when it comes to talking about yourself." She tipped her hat back, too.

Ed took a step closer to her. "Is there something wrong with wanting to keep personal details private?"

"No." She stepped closer too. "But it makes it harder to form a friendship."

"Friendship? You mean with you?"

"Hm." She tapped her lip with one finger. "I suppose we could consider ourselves friends already, by virtue of you saving my life. If that doesn't make for a fast friendship, I'm not sure what else would. Unless you have something against making friends with women." Every time she thought of that moment, when he'd grasped her arms and pulled her to safety, a feeling part fear and part something-else-entirely made her stomach twist.

He made a show of looking at the distance between them—which was about two feet. She hadn't realized how near they stood until that moment, but she wasn't about to step back. That would look too much like a retreat.

"I would've done the same for anyone else," he said, his tone dry. "But you could argue it creates a unique bond between us." Ed shrugged. "Maybe I don't want what I tell a reporter *as a friend* to make it into any newspapers."

"Oh." Understanding lit her mind like a photographer's flash powder. "Ed, I would never publish a friend's words—or anyone else's—without their permission. If I interviewed you for the paper, that would be entirely different. But just the two of us, talking? Nothing you say will go into my stories. I promise."

He eyed her carefully, a hint of distrust still in his deep brown eyes. This close, she could practically count his eyelashes. Why did men always have the most beautiful, thick, black eyelashes?

"All right. Ask me a question. As a friend."

Molly pulled in a fortifying breath and took the last step between them, their boot-tips almost touching. "What do you find fascinating about the desert?" she asked the cowboy.

His eyes searched hers carefully before he said, "Everything."

Molly bit back a smile. Another one-word answer. "You still don't trust me?"

When his grin broke free, his handsome face became even more appealing. "It's not that. We've got work to do, and we're going to be late. C'mon, Miss Molly. Let's shoe some horses." He walked away, and Molly had to walk twice as fast to catch up with him.

Despite the way he dodged another question, she sensed a change had occurred. Ed might not be ready to give her an interview, but chances were good he was ready to talk. Like one friend to another.

And a very handsome friend, at that.

SHOEING HORSES LED TO A CONVERSATION ABOUT THE DIFFERENT types of animals on the ranch. They walked along the fence line of the horse paddock and Ed pointed out what made a horse good at its job. Cutting horses. Horses for riding herd. Pack horses and mules.

They toured the stables, and Ed answered every question Molly threw at him about the animals and their care. Even the less savory questions.

"I have heard that breaking horses for ranch life is a high-paying job, usually reserved for heavy-handed cowboys. Is that accurate?" She leaned against an empty stall when she asked that question, and one of her hands drifted to the pocket where she kept her notebook.

He recognized the itch to write. He'd felt it himself more times than he could count. But his writing always waited until he was alone.

"On a lot of ranches, yes. It's accurate." He hung up the lariat rope he'd shown her a moment before as he'd described roping a cow from the back of a horse. "It's work that bosses want done quick. A cowboy usually has somewhere between six and ten horses on his string. All of us are in charge of a couple of green-broke horses as well as the animals we ride for work. We're expected to finish their training, make them ridable and profitable for the ranch. Some men make a name for themselves, breaking the meanest horses. Or the most stubborn. But their methods would make your heart crack in two if you saw them in action."

Those fingers twitched again. "What are their methods?"

Ed tugged off his gloves, keeping his eyes on the dust-covered ground between them. "I suppose to understand it, you've got to think about a horse the way you would anything you love. Not everyone does. They see a horse the same way they see a wagon wheel. It's just a tool. Something necessary for travel. Easily discarded when it stops being useful."

Her fingers stopped fiddling with her vest pocket. "I have certainly seen such things in London. There are cabbies who work their horses to exhaustion."

"Right. Makes sense that there are cruel people everywhere, doesn't it?" Ed crossed to where she stood and leaned both elbows on the stall wall. He nodded upward at the rafters. "See that beam up there? Some people believe that the best way to start working with a spirited colt is to hang him there. All night. They'd use a rope or a chain attached to the halter, or even around the neck, and pull it up until the horse's head is stretched so they have to stand nearly on their toes to keep from harming themselves. They can't reach food. Water. Can't even move."

"That's awful." Her face had gone pale. "How does torturing an animal that way help anything?"

"When the cowboy comes out in the morning, he finds himself a horse that is sore, tired, and dispirited. A horse more likely to do what the cowboy wants, because it's easier than putting up a fight. It's called hang-tying." He nodded to her vest pocket, suppressing his grin. Might as well let her scratch her writing itch. "You can jot that down if you want."

She didn't need to be told twice. Pencil and paper in hand, she made several quick notations. "This doesn't happen at KB Ranch, surely."

"No. We've had a few who've tried it, but King takes exception to anyone hurting an animal. We had a cowboy a while back who'd use glass bottles on a horse. He'd hit the poor creatures on the head, breaking the bottle and making the critter obey. It was a good day when King forced him off the property."

She made more notes. "I suppose I never stopped to think how people 'broke' horses."

Ed lowered his gaze to the stall floor. "It's rarely a gentle process. You've got cowboys who use their spurs too much. Some think you have to ride a horse until it's near-ready to fall over, exhausting it, to get good results. Withholding food or water happens too. Anything that weakens an animal."

Molly turned, so she faced inward, like he did, and her shoulder was near to brushing his. "It's a wonder the horses aren't terrified."

"Maybe they are." He released a sigh. "We do things a little differently here. King and Abram are experts. Not too long ago, Abram said that you have to be an old man before you're a real horseman."

"Because of wisdom?"

"Nope." Ed grinned sideways at her. "Because you lose all your muscle. You can't strong arm a horse anymore, so you have to figure out better ways of training him. No more wrestling competitions."

She laughed, and the sound broke the solemn tension that all his talk of abusive practices had built up. Her shoulders slumped, and she dropped her head forward, her whole body loose and limp. "I hear stories from all sorts of people about things that aren't right or fair. Most of the time, there isn't anything I can do about them. Newspapers want stories that will sell. Telling people children are starving in London's streets isn't newsworthy. Anyone who wants to see such a thing can do so for themselves. Papers are all about politicians, faraway wars, and scandals that make for interesting gossip. Not things that people can change by walking out their front doors and doing something kind."

Her words, tinged as they were with heaviness and disappointment, softened his heart. He'd seen all that and more in his brief time in the world. "I grew up in a place where people cared too much. At least, they pretended to care. Instead of helping the children to live and prosper within their families, the children were taken away. Unless their family made special agreements, offered bribes, or hid their kids before the Indian agents came."

Thinking of home, of the problems plaguing the people he'd grown up with, Ed remembered the letter his mother had sent. Asking him to schedule a visit. He hadn't given it another thought after tucking it away in the box beneath his bunk. Guilt twisted his guts. His mother deserved better than that from him.

Molly appeared much more solemn when he met her gaze again, and her eyes had darkened. "What do you mean? Who takes the children? And where?"

"People appointed by the U.S. Government. They're called Indian Agents. They claim they take children to boarding schools, to give them medical treatment and education so they fit better in White society."

Ed glanced at the notebook still clutched in her hand, and he hesitated. It wasn't only his story to tell. What if he gave the wrong details? What if she wrote what he said in an article?

"I am only a quarter Cherokee," he said quietly. "And most of the time, the Cherokee ran their own schools. They're a little luckier in that way. Because of my mother and my father's mixed race, I doubt I would've been enough of a threat to the government to send me away."

"How are children a threat to the government?" she asked, her eyebrows drawing together in her confusion. "In London, they say that children living on the streets are nuisances. That they breed crime and disease. Taking them to schools and teaching them trades is the only way to save them from a short life lived in the gutter."

"Maybe that's how it is in large cities, where everyone is English." Ed took off his hat and rubbed at his forehead with his other hand. Considering. How much did he say? "All Indians are threats to the United States Government. A year ago, a man spit on my boots and said that the only good Indian was a dead Indian."

Her sharp intake of breath drew his eyes back to her. She looked paler than before. Her eyes filled with shock. "He said that to your face?"

"It's a common sentiment. And I've heard worse, Molly."

"But—but you're only a quarter Indian."

"People can't really tell that from looking. And the fractions don't make a difference. I look Indian. If I don't look Indian, I look Mexican. There are more than enough people in the Territory who hate both. That's why the government started up the boarding school, when my grandfather was young. He remembers friends disappearing. There one day and gone the next. An Indian Agent had come for them. Sometimes, with an armed soldier to enforce whatever rules they'd made up. They took the children away. And a lot of times, the children never came back."

His mother had been fortunate that the way she raised her children, and her sending them to the Indian public school the Cherokee had established, kept the Indian Agents happy. Even at a quarter Indian, Ed and his sisters could have suffered the same fate as the vanished children if the wrong person had a whim to do such a thing.

Molly's expression changed from interest to pain, and she turned around, leaning her back against the stall. "How long did such a horrible thing last?"

"You misunderstand." His gut clenched, but he kept his eyes on hers. "This isn't something left in the past. It's still happening."

Her jaw fell open. She looked the picture of dismay. "The government steals Indian children *to this day*? They never go back to their families?"

"The Cherokee, the Five Civilized Tribes, every tribe I've ever heard of, write letters to the government. To congress, the president, their local governors, begging for answers. They've gone to Washington, D.C. They've been to the schools themselves, where they are turned away or forced to leave by sheriffs, policemen, or armed soldiers. I've heard of fathers being imprisoned for fighting to keep their children home. No one cares."

"But *why*?" Her eyes blazed with an emotion that looked equal parts painful and angry. He understood. He had to fight feeling that way nearly every day of his life.

"Depends on who you ask. My grandfather says the tribes have more claim to the land than the Federal Government ever will. If they change the Indian, they change the rights to the land. And land is worth killing for. If you ask my mother, she says they want to assimilate people who aren't White into a more compliant culture."

He swallowed back more words and wished it was as easy to bury all the memories of the things he knew. The things he'd grown up hearing.

He shifted on his feet. His conversation with Molly had grown too painful and more personal than he wished. He didn't talk about his past. He didn't talk about how he wrestled with history and his identity if he stopped too long to think about his life.

And, quite honestly, keeping away from his family made it easier to *not* think about all the troubles the Cherokee and other Indian nations went through.

He stepped away from the stall. "It's not something I like talking about. And it's not something you'll be able to do anything about. Even if you write a dozen articles about the 'Plight of the American Indian.' People have tried. It's better to just let it go, Molly. Let's talk about horse training. And how to do it the right way."

She followed behind him, indignation in her tone as she tried to protest. "But Ed—"

He turned on his boot heel and fixed her with a hard stare. "If you want to write about Indians, get yourself to Oklahoma Territory and talk to the people there. Or head north and see if the Hopi Tribe's chief will talk to you, or west to the Navajo. If you want to write about the ranch, then let's stick to that topic. All right?"

The glare she sent his direction was full of outrage, and her chest heaved with an angry breath. When she bit out her answer, it was full of irritation. "Fine. If you don't want to talk about it, we won't talk about it."

Ed gave her one sharp nod. "Good. I think we both need to take a break. Hottest part of the day and all. I'll see you in a couple of hours." He didn't wait for her response this time. He simply turned and marched out of the barn.

When Frosty brought her back to work sometime later, Ed's temper had cooled. He was working with a calf while its mother watched from several feet away. He should've been the one to fetch her from the Morgan house, where she'd stormed off to after their last conversation.

Molly watched him over a fence rail. She stood on the outside of the paddock, watching him rub salve into the calf's hurt leg. He'd left his hat on the post beside her to make it easier to work on the animal. Frosty had exchanged a few words with her before leaving to attend to another matter.

Ed and Molly hadn't said a word to each other since her arrival. But as he released the calf to rejoin its mother, Molly said his name softly. "Ed? I'm sorry about before. It was inappropriate for me to push you on a subject of which I am so heartily ignorant. Will you forgive me?"

He wiped his brow with the back of his arm. He looked up at the oncoming clouds for the day's downpour. Then he sighed and met her gaze again. "Lady, you've got a tender heart and a strong sense of righteousness. That's what my *mamá* would say.

You're forgiven. But that doesn't mean I want to talk on the subject."

"I know." She fiddled with a loose splinter of wood on the rail, peeling it back. "Perhaps I will have to take that trip you suggested. To Oklahoma Territory. If I decide I want to know more, that is."

His shoulders relaxed. He climbed over the fence and hopped onto the ground beside her. "Can you forgive me for being hot-tempered about it?"

An uncertain tilt to her head preceded her slow nod. "So long as we're friends again."

"Sure thing." Dusting off his right hand, he held it out to her.

She put her hand in his, but they didn't shake on it. Not really. They merely stood there a moment, connected by that simple touch, staring at one another until she smiled. Ed smiled back, the expression tight on his face, then withdrew his hand and reached for his hat. It took another half hour or so before they found the same ease in each other's company they'd enjoyed before. All in all, Ed couldn't deny the relief he felt when he finally said something that made her laugh again.

CHAPTER 10

A desk didn't materialize out of nowhere. But when Molly requested a place to set up her typewriter, a spot with good light during the day and where she wouldn't disturb anyone at night, Frosty had brought a small table from the Steeles' home up to her room. He settled it beneath the window that faced the main part of the ranch, rather than the window that faced the rolling hills and mountains on the other side of her long, narrow room.

She quite preferred it there. She could look out over the buildings to enjoy the bustle of animals and men at work. When she took the cover off her 1894 Remington Typewriter, rolled a sheet of paper into place, and took her seat in a chair also brought up for her use, she stared out the window. Waiting for inspiration. Her mind a complete blank.

The partial history Ed had given her of his people, three days ago now, remained stuck at the forefront of her mind. He'd presented her with a page from a bleak horror story, worse than anything she'd read before. But it was a middle page. She didn't know the history that led up to the horror, nor did she know what came next. Or how it ended.

Though they'd agreed to drop the subject, she remained dissatisfied.

Molly leaned back in her chair and closed her eyes. She rubbed delicately at her eyelids. Try as she might, she couldn't coax any words from her tired mind onto the page. She'd taken the day off from ranch duties, with Ed and Frosty's agreement, to start work on her first Arizona report. The excitement in the Morgans' home, when she told them at breakfast what she was up to, had amused her.

"Will you write about me, Miss Molly?" Laura had asked, her eyes bright with hope.

Ben had chimed in, "Will you tell my story, about the time Tex saved me from a snake?" Molly had shuddered more than once at the telling of that little adventure.

Maddie, her British accent always stronger when she spoke to Molly, had been eager for a different reason. "May I read it when it's finished?"

For that, Molly had a ready answer. "I don't usually hand out my stories to others until I've sent them to my editor. Otherwise, people suggest a great many changes. I prefer to keep my work to myself until it's too late for people to give opinions."

That statement had let down all three children. In fact, Molly had nearly relented when their smiles turned to frowns and their eyes filled with disappointment.

But Evelyn had laughed. "Don't let them bully you with those innocent little expressions. We can wait to read what you've said. I admire your integrity as a writer. Think on it, children. It ensures that every word Miss Molly writes is all her own. No outside influence. No taking clever phrases from others. She depends on herself, and that is something to be admired."

At the moment, Molly didn't feel worthy of admiration at all.

The light-hearted account she meant to give of her arrival at the ranch seemed trite. Especially since there were bigger, more important stories in the world. In London, she hadn't sought after the tales that would stir the hearts of her readers so much as those stories which would open their minds or improve their imagination.

She had filled all her other stories about her time in the United States with adventure. How did a grocer become a tycoon in New York? How did the people of Philadelphia compare to their ancestors who had fought against the military might of England? What did people hope to find when they arrived at Independence, Missouri, and faced the so-called "Gateway to the West?"

Prepared to write the same sort of story for Arizona Territory, Molly had looked across the dusty plains and cactus-covered hills with a vague idea of typing out stories about cowboys, rustlers, Indians, and the fight to tame the American West.

Those ideas no longer sat well. Her stomach churned uncomfortably when she thought of writing the things the men at Fort Huachuca had told her about Indian battles of the past. All because of a short conversation with Ed Byrd.

Molly opened her eyes and stared out the window at the bright, clear blue sky that stretched forever in all directions.

Her notebook sat beside the typewriter, open to the page she had started when she arrived at the ranch. She hated to waste typewriter tape. Especially as far from civilization as she was. But when she had checked her supplies that morning, she had several rolls of the stuff. Maybe it wouldn't hurt, just this once, to transcribe her shorthand notes. Perhaps all she needed to get unblocked was to let a few words rattle out of her head and onto the page.

Placing her hands on the typewriter, her fingertips tingling with the familiarity of the raised keys, Molly released the breath she'd held tight in her lungs. And as the air left, she typed. Only her notes. Descriptions of the sky turning shades of orange and purple at night, the waves in the long grasses, the way the storms rolled in with thunder and lightning crackling across the mountains.

And the words of a story came at last.

Hours passed, and slowly the sheets of paper with ink formed a tidy stack beside the notebook. But it wasn't a short collection of words for publishing in a newspaper. There were too many words for that. Instead, she wrote *her* story. She could cobble something succinct for her editor later. The words she wrote now took her from her train ride across the desert to the moment she crossed a dusty military parade ground to meet a man with deep brown eyes and a smile she had come to enjoy perhaps more than was seemly.

A knock interrupted Molly's work as she finished writing about her impromptu tea party at the fort, and her delight at the unexpected meeting with one of her countrymen.

"Molly?" Evelyn called through the closed door when the clack of typewriter keys paused. "Are you hungry? We're having a luncheon with the ranch families, if you would like to join us."

Molly's heartbeat quickened, then slowed again with disappointment. The ranch families. Not the ranch employees. Ed wouldn't be there. He ate with the men in the bunkhouse. The ranch *families* included the Boltons, Steeles, Rounsevells, and Morgans. People with shares in the ranch and wives to care for.

Such arrangements made perfect sense. A newspaper editor wouldn't sit down at a table with his employees *and* his wife and children. It simply wasn't done. And among the ranch hands were men who would be uncomfortable at a table with women and children.

"Yes, of course. I'm coming."

She rolled the paper out from the typewriter and added it to her tidy pile of words. After covering her equipment with care, Molly went to the door. Evelyn waited for her, an eager smile on her face.

"It is so good to have you here with us. One new person makes quite a difference in conversation."

"I am happy to be of service, even if my conversation isn't nearly as stimulating as you say. How can I help prepare for the meal?" Molly followed Evelyn downstairs, only half listening to instructions for what they needed to carry to the main house.

Thus far, she had taken all her meals with the Morgans. Except for the one picnic-style meal with Ed and Clark on the day they had repaired fences. While she appreciated her hosts' kindness, an idea stirred in her mind.

Perhaps she could take dinner that evening elsewhere. How could she claim to understand the life of a ranch hand if an Englishwoman managed all her meals? Sampling the fare at the bunkhouse would enrich her experience and her writing, surely.

But how exactly would she get herself invited to eat with the cowboys?

When she arrived at the main ranch house, she hadn't come up with any ideas.

The main house had a dining room as well as an area to eat in the kitchen itself. Today, everyone younger than Clark would eat their meal in the kitchen. But the married couples, Molly, and Clark settled around the polished surface of a fine table for their meal. Even though everyone wore their usual clothes, which were made for work rather than formal occasions, it felt rather special to be gathered all in one place.

Mr. Bolton sat at one end of the table, Mrs. Bolton at the other —with a cradle nearby where her baby slept, oblivious to the noise.

"I've been wanting to gather like this for weeks now," Beth Bolton said after they finished a prayer over the meal. "It's been a busy season for us, hasn't it?"

"Indeed." Evelyn settled at her place, between her husband and Molly. "And we will have another flurry of activity before long." She placed her hand gently on her rounded stomach and exchanged a significant glance with Dannie Rounsevell across the table.

Dannie pushed her long braid back over her shoulder and put her hand over her husband's, where his rested on the table.

"We're looking forward to a little chaos. I can't believe how slowly the days go by, even while it seems like Evan and I met yesterday."

Clark groaned and leaned his head back against his chair. "As much as I like being a big brother and a future uncle, can we talk about something other than babies?"

Everyone at the table laughed, and King reached over to pat his son on the shoulder. "You'll be off to Baylor with your brother soon enough. Then you'll miss your mom's home cooking and your baby sister."

"True enough," Ruthie said from her place to the right of Mrs. Bolton. "And we'll all be missing you and your ornery ways."

Abram sat across from Ruthie. He'd taken the spot with a sweet remark on how it let him gaze at his pretty wife. The love the two had for one another was palpable, with all their kind looks and teasing words.

KB Ranch might have something in its well water to make for so many happy couples. And new children on the way, too. They were like something out of a fairy tale, though Molly couldn't think of one that started with the warmth and care of these people. That sort of thing was usually reserved for the end of a story, when lost children found their way home or the prince rescued the princess.

She almost envied them. Except, of course, in a single week she had seen every person sitting at that table do their share of work on the ranch. They cooked, cleaned, gardened, rode horses, tended cattle, taught their children, and dozens of other things. And while there was a dividing line between men and women for some of the work, she'd seen it crossed a few times, too. The men did the laundry for their expectant wives. Abram took his turn teaching the children about history and geography, two things he had a great passion for. Dannie spent time in the barn currying horses.

How would Molly explain such a phenomenon in her articles? Perhaps she would write something specifically for the women's magazine, using the ranch's culture as an example of how men and women's roles needn't be as strict as some suggested. She couldn't imagine a newspaper publishing her thoughts.

Just as she couldn't imagine why a London paper would run a story about American Indians losing children to boarding schools. Most of the stuffy politicians she knew would likely think the American government did everyone a favor by removing those poor children from their homes and families. Britannia, an empire with multiple colonies, saw no harm in conquering people and "civilizing" them.

The story wasn't hers to tell, anyway.

"You're mighty quiet, Molly," Frosty said, leaning forward to make eye contact around his wife. "Everything all right?"

"Perhaps all the work she's done has left her fatigued," Duke, the former Lord Evan, suggested from down the table. "My first week at the ranch nearly put me in the ground."

Ruthie chimed in. "You had a harder taskmaster than Molly."

"True enough," Dannie admitted. "I probably pushed Evan harder than Frosty's making you work, Molly. I didn't have a shred of mercy for him." The whole table laughed again, and Molly wondered when she'd have the full story of what had happened between those two. An English lord choosing to live on a desert ranch sounded absolutely absurd.

"I'm not the one bossing her around," Frosty said. "So no one can blame me if our lady reporter falls asleep before dessert. If that cowboy is pushing you too hard, Molly, I can have a word with him."

All eyes were on her at that point. Molly finally broke into the conversation with her polite excuses. "Ed is a considerate taskmaster, I promise. I am a little tired is all. And I am preoccupied. I started writing things out this morning to get my mind organized. It takes a lot of reflection to bend the words to my will. More often than not, they do not wish to comply and form the neat, orderly rows of a news article."

"Your words sound rather like unruly children," Evelyn said.

"Or stubborn cattle," Dannie added.

That started the group talking about the various disorderly aspects of their work. Children, cattle, chickens, and the like were discussed with merry indignation. Molly listened to the flow of conversation around her, watching the play of expressions on the faces of people who knew each other as well as family could.

King feigned offense when his wife commented that the men of the ranch would let their trousers stand on their own before they'd know to wash them. "I lived out here all on my own for two years, Beth. I managed just fine."

"I didn't want to say anything," Abram spoke up after he finished his last bite of pie. "But there were days I wanted to take you down to the river and throw you in."

Laughter flowed again, and the baby in the cradle made a sudden sound of impatience. Beth started to rise from her chair, but King was up before her. He motioned for her to stay seated. "I'll get her, honey. You enjoy your dessert."

He went to the cradle and lifted his baby girl with a happy grin. "How's daddy's little roper, hm?"

"Yesterday, she was your little sure-shooter," Dannie said with an amused smile. "You're going to spoil my baby sister."

"Only until my first grandchild arrives. Then I'll spoil 'em both." He winked at his eldest daughter, put the baby on his shoulder, and sauntered out of the room humming a cheerful tune.

Ruthie laid down her fork. "That baby girl brought new life to King, didn't she?"

"Children have a way of making us feel old and young all at once," Beth said, looking pointedly at the two expectant mothers at the table. "You both be sure to take care of yourselves as your time draws closer."

"Yes, ma'am," Dannie said. "Don't worry. We've got Ruthie checking on us every other moment, it seems."

"Midwifing is serious work." Ruthie rose and gathered up her plate with her husband's. "And I don't mean to have any trouble with you two or your little ones. Not on our ranch."

Dannie rested her hands against her middle and grinned at Molly. "What about you, Molly? Your life must be exciting, traveling the way you do, writing for newspapers. Do you think you'll ever settle down?"

Molly was quite used to that question. People had asked as kindly as Dannie, but they had also shouted at her in the street to go home where she belonged and make babies. "Maybe someday. If the right man comes along."

Unbidden, Ed's slow smile appeared in her mind's eye.

"They do that, you know." Evelyn smiled as her husband rose and gathered up her plate. "They come along, usually when you least expect it, and turn your world upside down."

Frosty chuckled. "I don't hear you complaining about it." He walked into the kitchen with his head held high and not a bit of worry in his expression.

"Do you plan to write more today, Molly?" Evan asked, arms crossed over his chest and his charming, lordly expression in place. "Is there anything with which we can help you?"

"Not presently, thank you. But yes. I do have more writing to do today. I think the Morgans would prefer I finish my work during daylight hours, so my typewriter doesn't keep them awake at night."

"Goodness." Evelyn's eyes widened. "You type at night?"

"Indeed. If the mood strikes." Molly had to laugh at the horrified expression on her hostess's face. "Never fear. I have lost roommates over the bad habit and learned my lesson. Now I confine myself to my notebook at night."

She rose from the table, taking her dish and cutlery with her. "Thank you for the company. It was lovely." She repeated the sentiment to those already in the kitchen washing up, then showed herself out.

There was more for her to write, of course. But she also had to puzzle out a way to eat her last meal of the day in the bunkhouse with a group of cowboys. The experience might be just what she needed to round out the next article she sent back to England.

CHAPTER 11

Despite Ed knowing that Molly wouldn't be working with him on Saturday, he kept expecting to see her at any moment. Every time he walked from one building to another, he looked over his shoulder for her. When he took his laundry out to the wash shed, he watched Frosty's house for any sign of the lady's coming or going. But the whole day passed with him only glimpsing her once, standing by the upstairs window, tapping a pencil against her lips and not seeing him at all.

He must be some kind of fool to think she'd give a moment's thought to him when he wasn't in sight. The possibility that she would still come say good morning had pulled him out of bed with a smile. And he'd had more than one grousing cowboy comment on his chipperness.

Whiskers even had the nerve to ask about it. "What brought back the old Ed? Haven't seen you smile like that in months."

"Only one thing has changed around here, *amigo*. It's that reporter." Dominó had still been in his bunk, so Ed had casually lifted one side of the mattress and dumped his friend onto the floor. The other cowboy took the hint and didn't say another word.

Cookie ruled the bunkhouse, and he'd slapped at the iron stove where he warmed the coffee. "That's enough out of all of you. If you're working, get to working. If you're leaving for your day off, get to leaving."

Ed, Whiskers, and Dominó were all working, since they'd run off the Saturday and Sunday before. Two vaqueros, Roberto and Rio, were already out sleeping at the far end of the ranch, at one of the little cabins they kept for that purpose. That left two cowboys to take off for whatever parts of the Territory they wished to cause trouble in.

Ace and Jimbo, as they'd introduced themselves when they'd hired up, didn't waste much daylight getting off the ranch. They kicked up a cloud of dust on their way to whatever entertainment they'd planned for themselves.

And Ed had wandered around the ranch, doing chores, looking over his shoulder for a pretty English lady.

Foolish. His *madre* would shake her head and despair of him. *"I have told you again and again, mi hijo. If you want a girl's attention, you must do more than smile at her."*

"I've done more than smile," he muttered to himself as he mucked out a stall. "We've talked. A lot."

He'd no idea what his mother would make of that. She'd probably raise her chin, look down her nose at him, and put a fist to her hip. Then she'd say something like, "Have you told her you admire her? That you want to know her better?"

Nope. And he'd do best to stop thinking about her before he tried. Sweet talking a woman who had no intention of being around long enough to learn his middle names was a bad idea.

That realization sobered him. And he finally stopped looking over his shoulder. But his mother's voice stayed with him. He could imagine her challenging him by asking: *"What do you feel when you look into her eyes?"* And the description of how she felt when she met his father for the first time was all too easy for him to remember. *"When I looked into your father's eyes, I saw my soul within them. That is when I knew everything would change."*

But nothing had changed for Ed. A pair of pretty brown eyes didn't have any power over his life or choices. Especially when their owner didn't bother to so much as say good morning.

He needed to think about something else.

The letter he still owed his mother entered his mind, but that wasn't any better than pining after Molly. . Yes, he needed to write a response. Eventually. When he'd had time to decide whether he ought to visit his family or stay put.

Staying put was easier. Something being easy didn't make it best, though. Ed brushed that line of thinking aside, too.

Instead of worrying about Molly or his mother's letter, he started thinking on his notebook, tucked in the lockbox beneath his bunk. He hadn't worked on his newest story idea in weeks. Not that it mattered, since no one but him would ever see it. And he knew how it ended. Still, there was satisfaction in writing it all out. Simple as it was.

He'd written several short stories over the years. Mostly stories wherein the Mexican wasn't the bandit, but the hero. Or a story in which an Indian saved a life rather than took part in a raid. It wasn't much. But it was better than what he'd read himself when he'd gone looking for books about cowboys and life in the west. The heroes in most of the books he'd found didn't look like him, or like most of the men he'd worked with either.

In their bunkhouse, they all looked as different from one another as a bee was from a butterfly. Ed was part Mexican, part Cherokee. Dominó's family had lived in Mexico for centuries, but he dressed more like an American cowboy than a *vaquero*. Whiskers turned red in the sun rather than brown, and his beard was such a pale blond it was almost white. Roberto wore the wide-brimmed hat popular in Venezuela, where he'd come from in search of new opportunities. Rio was half Black, half Mexican, descended from slaves who had fled Texas before the War Between the States, when Mexico had offered freedom to anyone who crossed the river. Ace and Jimboy were from Bisbee and Tucson, their heritage unknown but seemingly a mix of something other than White. They were orphans who'd grown up scrounging and worked their way out of the mining industry and into cowboying.

Cookie claimed his background didn't matter so long as people liked his food. Since he did things with beans and rice that made them taste like manna from heaven, no one questioned him or his origins.

When the sun descended toward the horizon, Ed wiped the sweat from his forehead with his bandana. He made his way to the large cistern where the cowboys washed the dust from their faces and hands, scrubbed the back of their necks, and then meandered back to the bunkhouse for dinner. It wasn't much, but it was better than a dust bath.

Ed unbuttoned his shirt to let the collar open a bit, and he used his bandana as a wash cloth to scrub his neck. He needed a good dunking, most likely. Or to take his turn in a bath.

"*Trying to smell sweeter for the lady reporter?*" Rio asked in Spanish. He stood on the opposite side of the cistern, a sly grin on his face.

Ed took off his hat and put it on a pole next to the cistern. "*What are you talking about?*" he answered in the same language.

Roberto stripped off his whole shirt and dunked it in the water, filling the already murky water with yet more debris. "*Dominó told us you like her.*"

"It's no fair when all of you start talking in Mexican," Whiskers complained. "Always makes me feel like I'm being left out."

"So learn *Spanish, amigo,*" Dominó instructed, slapping Whiskers on the back. "And don't worry. We don't talk about you. Much."

Whiskers stuck his whole face in the water and came up with his beard dripping. "I need a bath. But I guess that's what Sunday's for." Some of the cowboys only bothered to get a full wash once a week. Some less than that. Ed's father would've had a fit if he saw how much dust they accumulated in a single day. He'd been raised Cherokee, for the most part, and cleanliness was an important part of life. Indeed, certain rituals and sacred occasions were marked by bathing in cold streams and rivers, no matter the time of year.

There was a cold stream not far distant from the ranch. A place with cool water from a natural spring. There were trees, too, to block the sun. Frosty had shown the place to Ed once, years ago, after he'd stumbled across it himself. He'd shared the find with Ed specifically because of the Cherokee beliefs of purifying in running water.

Maybe it was time to pay that stream a visit.

Not because Ed really believed in all the things his ancestors did. But... he found peace in the rituals, in the connection to his family and his grandfather's people. And he sorely needed some of that peace.

A wave of lukewarm water hit Ed in the face, bringing his thoughts to a rude halt. He blinked and looked down at his soaked shirt, then up again at Whiskers. The man grinned at him. "Oops."

Before Ed decided whether or not to retaliate, Frosty appeared. The foreman dipped his bandana into the water and rubbed at the back of his neck. Since marriage, he'd taken to doing most of his wash-up at his home. Ed couldn't blame him one bit for that.

"How'd the day go? Anyone need to report on anything?" he asked his men. The real reason he came to the cistern at all was likely just to swap reports and let the men know their foreman stayed aware of the ranch work and the hired hands.

Rio and Roberto gave their report in heavily accented English with a mix of Spanish. Frosty understood enough of their language, especially when it came to the vaquero vocabulary. He didn't need any translation. Whiskers talked about the paddock work he'd done, breaking one of his green horses. Ed delivered a brief report on the state of the stables and barns, where he'd spent his day.

As the light faded in the sky, twilight turned the sky and desert purple and gray. With his reports taken, Frosty walked in a different direction from the men. Going to his house, where light already glowed from the downstairs windows and his adopted son waited on the porch with his dog. Ed didn't imagine the way his friend's gait changed as he neared his home. Frosty's legs stretched farther and moved faster, and when he called out to Ben, he sounded happy.

Frosty had needed those kids when they showed up, and his English wife and daughter had completed their family. Making Frosty happier than...well. Happier than he'd been as a bachelor cowboy.

In contrast to his friend's cheerful return to his house, Ed's steps slowed as he approached the adobe building that served as bunkhouse and storage room on the ranch. It was the first struc-ture to rise on the property, when only Abram and King worked the cattle and the land. Everything else had grown up around it. For a time, Abram and his wife and son had lived in one of the rooms, King and his wife and daughter had lived in another. Ruthie and the first Mrs. Bolton hadn't wanted to wait for a real house to join their husbands, but in time, their menfolk had built them comfortable homes.

Ed passed into the zaguán, the long, cool corridor that ran through the middle of the adobe building. Two long rooms on one side were used for storage and an office, of sorts, for Frosty. The two rooms on the opposite side were the bunk room and a rudimentary dining room and common area for the cowboys.

Ed went into the room that Cookie ruled over with an iron fist and wooden spoon. He hung his hat on one of the many hooks lining the wall. The others were already there, sitting on stools at the long table. Dominó had dumped the little rectangle pieces he'd taken his name from onto the table. His tiles were white, the dots on them a dark red, and he played a game he'd made up on his own. A sort of solitaire that he'd tried to teach Ed once.

He'd claimed he had to get inventive, since the usual game played with the tiles wasn't all that popular with cowboys. Likely because it was easier to travel with a deck of cards in hand than a box of clinking rectangles.

The stove in the corner had three pots on top of it, and Cookie stood over them like a mother hen watching her chicks. His face was always red from leaning over the steaming pots and pans. He wore a shirt he'd torn the sleeves from, his bandana tied around his forehead, and a canvas apron that was cleaner than most expected of a ranch cook.

Settled on a stool across from Dominó, Ed rubbed at the still-damp material of his shirt. "I know I need a bath, same as everyone else, but Whiskers probably needs it more."

"Next time, just throw him in," Dominó advised, not looking up from his tiles. "I have seen you teach larger men than Whiskers their place."

"I've no wish to humiliate him." Ed rubbed at the back of his neck. "Do you think—"

Dominó dropped his tile and jumped to his feet, and the others sitting at the table did the same. Ed, with his back to the door, followed suit without knowing why until he turned. Only two things would make men jump up from their chairs like that —King Bolton himself, or a lady.

And there she was. The lady reporter.

"Good evening, gentlemen. Please, do not get up on my account." Molly gestured for them to retake their seats, but no one moved. Her smile didn't falter. "I asked your foreman if I could join you for dinner. I would love to write about how cowboys spend their hours when they aren't in the saddle."

Someone behind Ed cleared his throat, but no one moved. Or spoke. Ed glanced at Cookie, whose normally florid face was somewhat pale. The man held his spoon at his side the way someone else might hold a weapon, his every muscle tense.

Ed stepped forward, to stand beside Molly. "Excuse our rudeness, Miss McKinney. We're not used to having such refined company in our dining room." And he couldn't quite believe that Frosty had been happy with this idea. If Frosty had even known about it, he'd have walked in with the reporter. Maybe she bent the truth in her favor. He lowered his voice so only she would hear. "You sure this is a good idea, ma'am?"

Her pretty eyelashes lowered, and her smile curled at the edges in a way that made his heart flip. "I think it's an excellent idea. I've looked forward to having dinner with you all day."

With him? No, he hadn't heard her right. Or she meant all the men. Not specifically him. Still, something pleasant uncurled in his chest and stretched, making his shoulders square and his chin come up. "Then we'd better get you dinner."

He didn't imagine the teasing twinkle in her eye, surely.

"Men." Ed turned to face them. "Let's show our new friend we've got better manners than a bunch of cattle. Stop gaping and get this lady a plate." Then he showed her to the stool he'd been using as though it was the finest chair in a big city restaurant. She took her seat, and Dominó immediately retook his.

"Molly, what a surprise," he said, his accent thicker and somehow—Ed wanted to grumble about it—more charming. "It is rare for us to break bread with one both as lovely and intelligent as you."

"Thank you, Dominó." She didn't seem the least bit flustered, or even flattered, by his compliments. Merely amused.

Rio had done as Ed said and found a plate, and Cookie filled it with rice, beans, and a beef stew as thick as gravy. The cook even put a spoon into the rice the way someone else might stick a shovel in the ground. Rio came to Dominó's side and reached across the table to lay the plate in front of the reporter.

Roberto brought her a heavy mug filled with coffee. But Cookie followed behind with a cup of water he'd poured out of a kettle. Probably something he'd boiled earlier to add to one of his pots.

"Corn biscuits are coming, too," Cookie grunted out, putting the cup down beside the coffee. "Would you like butter on yours, ma'am?"

Molly nodded with the regalness of a queen. "That would be wonderful, thank you."

"Butter?" Whiskers said from down the table. "You never give us butter on our biscuits."

"Guests are different," Cookie mumbled.

Molly looked about her at the men, her expression cheery, then tilted her head back to look at Ed, who still stood beside her stool. His head buzzed, but whether it was with confusion or due to her nearness, he didn't know. "Won't you join me, Ed? And Cookie, you must tell me all about the meals you prepare for these hard-working gentlemen."

By the time Ed pulled up a new stool and retrieved a plate of food for himself—because the men always served themselves— the other cowboys were eagerly taking turns telling Molly about life in the bunkhouse. And she sat there, taking it all in with her easy smile and dancing eyes.

Eyes he'd tried to dismiss from his mind all day, only to fall immediately under their spell again the second he saw them.

MOLLY HAD EXPECTED HER ARRIVAL WOULD DISRUPT THE MEN IN the bunkhouse. One woman in a place reserved for masculine activity always upended things. She'd once gained admittance to a board meeting in London where the only other woman nearby had been a secretary sitting outside the door. The men at that table had puffed out their chests and spoken to her as though she were a child incapable of understanding economics and such concepts as "supply and demand."

The cowboys didn't speak to her like that. No, they seemed far more interested in impressing her with their stories than with big words. They clearly saw her as a woman, though. A woman worth impressing. And they were certain she wanted to drink in everything they said.

Which was mostly true. She had even taken out her notebook to jot a few things down as she enjoyed her delicious, hearty dinner. The plate Rio and the cook had made for her had entirely too much food on it. She ate until she felt she might burst if she took one more bite, and said so, to Cookie's obvious delight.

Ed quietly removed the dish along with his empty plate. He returned to take his seat just as silently.

Why did the one man she most wished to hear from have to be the quietest in the room? Even Whiskers, with his shyness, had managed to tell her about the peach cobbler Cookie had made on the trail for them the year before. After welcoming her, Ed had hardly said a word.

Had she overstepped? Or was he still upset with her about their conversation in the stable? They moved past that, she'd thought.

"This has been such a wonderful meal," she told the men. "Now, you must act as though I am not even here. Go about your evening as you normally would. I am most curious about how you spend the hours between dinner and sleep."

They seemed reluctant to slip away from the table. At least until Dominó returned his tiles—which had disappeared into a box while he ate—to its surface. "Anyone wish to play a game with me? We can even wager for chores tomorrow."

"Sunday chores aren't worth wagering for," Whiskers said, leaving the table. He went to a chair against the wall. There wasn't a fireplace in the room. The stove provided enough heat in the winter, she guessed. At present, the windows were open, as was the door leading out to the corridor. A cool breeze came through from that direction, snaking around the room before finding its way out the windows.

Whiskers picked up a book. A well-worn book, given the yellowed pages and dog-eared cover.

Rio and Roberto agreed to a game, but only if Dominó

promised they could play cards after. Cookie clanged about with pots and pans, settling his kitchen down for the night. And Ed rose from his stool and left the room entirely.

Oh dear. Would he return?

What if he left to find Frosty and report on Molly's whereabouts? She hadn't exactly been honest when she'd left the Morgans' home that evening. She'd hinted heavily at having dinner with people she was most curious about, and when Frosty and Evelyn had assumed that meant Evan and Dannie, she hadn't corrected them. She supposed one might find it curious, that a marquess's son had left everything behind to live on a ranch. It would certainly make a good article in the paper, though she doubted anyone in England would believe it.

Why would a nobleman give up his birthright and place in Society to work on a dirty American ranch? The peerage would scoff at the idea and denounce anyone who wrote or printed such a thing as being out of touch with reality. Even if they all knew that the marquess's second son had mysteriously vanished in the wilds of the American west, making the tale quite true.

When Ed returned a few minutes later, Molly relaxed. He carried a shirt with him and a small tin box. He retook his seat beside her. The lantern hanging above the table gave the players enough light to see by, but it was soon evident that Ed needed the light more. The tin box he opened revealed a small sewing kit. No thimble. But a piece of wax paper with needles stuck through it and several small spools of thread were inside. And buttons. Lots of little white buttons.

"Are you sewing?" she asked, sounding more surprised than she wished.

"Who else would fix our shirts?" Dominó asked from down the table. He'd moved to the end with the two *vaqueros* to make it easier to play their game.

Ed took out a needle and one of the gray spools of thread. "Cowboys have to have all kinds of skills out here. We don't have our mamas to take care of us anymore." His easy smile made her heart stutter. "And it's not hard work. Sewing on a button. Just necessary."

She watched him lick the end of the thread, then carefully put it through the eye of the needle. "I confess, I didn't give much thought to clothing maintenance."

"You knew we did our own laundry."

"Yes. I've visited the laundry shed. I even helped Evelyn with bringing in the clothing today." She tapped her pencil against the notebook on the table. "What other skills do you employ? Do you cook?"

"Not as well as Cookie," Ed said. "But I can heat a can of beans on the trail, boil water, make coffee that keeps a man in his saddle for a few hours."

"His coffee is better than the foreman's," Dominó added without even looking their way. "But don't tell Frosty we said so." The other men in the room laughed, but not cruelly. This was a long-standing joke, she sensed. She'd seen that the men respected their foreman. He gave them all their orders, of course, but he'd always work alongside them.

She lowered her voice, only addressing Ed. Hoping for a moment or two of private conversation, rather like a silly girl enamored by a boy. "How did you learn these skills? I know there aren't any schools for your trade. Is it something you teach one another?"

"Or learn from home, if we're lucky," Ed said, voice lowered to match hers. "My family has a farm. My father keeps pecan orchards. I have younger sisters, but that didn't stop my mother from teaching me how to care for my clothing." His expression softened when he spoke of his mother, and his lips turned up at the corners with fondness. "She used to say '*Hijo*, you cannot expect a woman to do everything for you. Women have too much to do as it is, without looking after men who act like little boys.'"

"That seems contrary to what most women teach their sons." And she quite liked that Ed didn't seem perturbed by it. "Why was she so different?"

"I think she knew, even when I was young, that I didn't intend to stay on the farm where she could look after me." He shrugged, and his smile faded somewhat. "And she believes everyone ought to have the skills to take care of themselves. She writes me letters, sometimes, and she always reminds me to keep learning. To look after myself and others."

Molly put her elbow on the table and rested her chin in her palm, keeping her gaze on Ed. "She sounds wise. I think I would like her. If we met."

"Most people do." Ed didn't say that he thought his mother would like Molly, too. Instead, he finished the button repair and held it out to her. "See? Good as new."

She admired his work with a grin. "Excellent. If I have any loose buttons while I am here, should I bring them to you?" she teased.

"My mother would expect you to know how to repair them yourself." He sighed deeply, theatrically put-upon. "But she'd also say that a man should never refuse to help a woman."

"It seems I have put you in a difficult situation." She leaned closer and whispered, "What would your mother advise?"

Did she imagine the way his throat tightened as he swallowed? Had he blushed, or was the way his ears darkened simply an effect of the lamplight? Either way, his smile remained easy and relaxed. "Probably that I make sure you get back to your house safe and sound. If you've had enough of the bunkhouse for one evening."

"It isn't at all as rowdy as I expected," she admitted, glancing around at the men. Cookie had finished his work and sat in a chair near the window *knitting* socks, of all things.

Ed spoke with obvious amusement. "Come back when all the men are here, during a storm. That's when we play music. Sometimes, we get lucky, and Ace will sing. Things are rowdier then. When it's cool outside and we won't bother anyone with all our noise."

"What a thoughtful group of cowboys." She faced him again.

"I think I'll take your advice. And your escort back to the Morgans' home."

He closed up his sewing kit and left his shirt on the table. "Let me get a lantern." He disappeared out the door again.

Molly tucked her notebook away and stood, bringing all eyes back to her. "Thank you for a lovely evening, gentlemen. Perhaps I might stop by again?"

"Sure, Miss McKinney."

"You're always welcome, ma'am."

She walked out the door and waited in the cool *zaguán* corridor for Ed. She'd accomplished her purpose in speaking with the men and seeing Ed in a different setting. She liked him. More than she could remember liking a man before. Perhaps more than was wise.

Oh, she had been courted before. Handsome reporters. Men she met through friends. But she'd quickly lost interest in those men, or found she had no desire to make the time to get to know them as they deserved. She'd always busied herself with work, and happily so.

Something about Ed, about how she felt around him, was...special.

"Ready when you are."

She turned to find Ed exiting the bunkroom, a gun at his hip, hat on his head, and lamp in hand. The men of the ranch had all told her, at different times, how important it was that she always be with someone who had a weapon or else keep one on herself. For rattlesnakes or other predators. On her second morning, Frosty had admonished her about putting her boots on without checking them first. Creatures liked to crawl in boots during the night.

Really, one always had to be on the lookout for flora and fauna alike in Arizona Territory.

Ed walked alongside her on the outside of the paddock, going around where they kept stock horses. He kept the lantern high in his left hand. His right swung freely near the holstered weapon.

Molly walked on his left side with her hands tucked behind her back.

"I am glad you brought me to the ranch, Ed."

"Are you?" His steps slowed and he tilted his head to better study her. "It seemed the right thing to do. You are mighty interested in learning about cowboys and cattle."

"Mostly the cowboys. People are what make interesting newspaper articles, you know. The choices they make, how they see the world, that's what starts an adventure in the first place. I enjoy learning why people do what they do."

"Seems you're in the right line of work then."

"I suppose. I do love storytelling."

"Me, too."

The admission surprised her enough that she stopped in her tracks. He did, too, and held the lantern up higher, revealing a curious expression on his handsome face. She studied the soft glow of his eyes in the lantern light. "I didn't know you liked telling stories. Given how reticent you've been about giving an interview, it rather surprises me."

He shrugged. "I like *stories*. I don't enjoy talking about myself." He stood so close, she could almost make out her reflection in his eyes. Her chest grew warm, and her heartbeat picked up in speed, and she lowered her gaze to fight against the odd sensations.

"Oh. That makes you rather odd, you know." She tapped a finger against his chest. Upon a button he had likely affixed to his shirt himself. What a fascinating thought. "Most men, I find, enjoy telling me all about themselves."

He caught her wrist gently in his right hand, holding it there, her finger pressed to the little white circle. His voice lowered. "I'll tell you anything you want to know if you ask as yourself and not a reporter."

Why had her thoughts turned fuzzy all at once? She stared at his larger, warm hand where his fingers encircled her wrist. She swallowed. "A reporter *is* who I am."

"Part of who you are," he countered, his voice deep and soft, unlikely to carry beyond their little circle of light. "You're part reporter. Part English. Part woman. Part adventurer. There's more to you than any single word could explain."

Her heart fluttered and then beat harder, sending a blush into her cheeks as she lifted her eyes to meet Ed's again. They stood closer together than before, though she didn't think either of them had moved. How had this happened? What were they even speaking of before this moment? Molly couldn't recall.

"What about you?" she asked, voice hushed. She licked her lips and saw his gaze dip momentarily away from hers, to her mouth, then back up again. He smiled.

"What about me?"

"You must be more than a cowboy," she answered softly. "More than a Cherokee. More than a Catholic. More than a son to a lovely mother. More than Ed. What else are you?"

His hold on her wrist relaxed, and her fingers spread where they were against his chest until her palm lay flat upon his shirt. His hand moved up to cover hers. She could feel each breath he took against her fingertips and the callouses from his hard work against her skin.

"I don't know," he answered, after several heartbeats. "I am many things. More than I have words for. Like you. You are..." A soft chuckle escaped him, and he leaned closer. "I speak three languages, but none of them have the right word for you, Molly McKinney. Beautiful and intelligent." Then he grinned. "Fascinating and irresistible..."

Those silly spelling words. How had he remembered that in a moment like this?

She tipped her chin up, trying and failing to ignore the warmth from his chest, the softness of his breath against her throat. "They are lovely words."

Ed's eyes were warm in the lamplight. "*Where words fail, men must take action.*"

Her eyebrows raised. "And whom, may I ask, said such a bold thing?"

"My father. About something completely unrelated to this." Ed's hand left hers, his fingertips finding her cheek where they tucked a loose curl of hair behind her ear. His thumb grazed her chin, guiding her closer. "May I show you what I think, Molly? What I feel when I'm near you?"

Her lips parted as she whispered her eager permission. "Yes. Please."

Molly had been kissed before. Twice, actually. While she stood on the doorstep of her boarding house. Both times, she'd found the experience lacking. She hadn't understood why people spoke of first kisses with such doe-eyed expressions and wistful sighs.

Not until the moment Ed's lips touched hers. First in a gentle press, the sensation soft and sweet. The kiss a mere token of admiration. And then the touch changed as subtly as a sigh. The hand upon her cheek moved to her waist, pulling her into a close embrace. And his head tilted to better capture her lips in a kiss that sent electric currents from her mouth all the way to her fingertips, her toes, and her heart.

Her hands slid from his chest to his shoulders and then around the back of his neck as she leaned into the embrace. One kiss became two, then three, each one deepening as her heart raced. His right hand splayed across her lower back, holding her steady, keeping her close. She didn't mind in the slightest.

Their lips parted, and his next kiss was upon her cheek. Then at the top of her forehead, lingering against her skin. Her lips felt soft and swollen as she ran her tongue gently across them, testing to be sure they were whole and still hers. She slowly met his gaze and the softness in his dark brown eyes.

"That was..." She took in a shaky breath. "Words fail me."

His smile returned. "That's what started this in the first place."

"Mmhm." She couldn't resist tilting her chin up again. "I find I don't mind in the slightest." This time, she kissed him. When she pressed her lips to his, he released a soft hum that made her melt against him.

"Molly," he murmured against her lips. "Molly, the lamp."

"Put it down then," she said, pulling away enough to look at his left arm holding the lamp low.

"That isn't what I meant." He chuckled and his right arm, fully around her waist, gave her a gentle squeeze. "Anyone looking will see us. Your reputation…"

"Oh." Heat filled her neck and cheeks. The flames licked her conscience, too. "*You* might get in trouble." She stepped back and his arm fell away from her. "Ed, you don't think anyone noticed?" She looked across the paddock to the main house, where light poured from the kitchen window. Then to the Steeles' house, and the Morgans', farther away.

"Don't worry about me, Molly." He switched the lantern to his right hand and shook his left arm that had born its weight for the entirety of their interrupted journey from the bunkhouse. "Most I'd get is a lecture."

"In that case, I'm not worried at all." She leaned her head to the side and studied him. The fog lifted slowly from her mind, and she found herself presented with an interesting puzzle and a tangle of unlooked-for emotions. "You kissed me."

Ed had no intention of denying it, given his rather pleased grin. "I'm pretty sure you kissed me back."

"Yes." She studied the line of his jaw, the handsome shape of his face, the dark eyelashes framing his beautiful eyes. She couldn't deny her attraction to him. Nor did she wish to. But what did it mean, to have such a strong pull toward a man she had no hope of keeping? "And you can be certain I'd be happy to do it again," she murmured.

Ed sighed before saying, "I'm not sure that's wise." His answer deflated her somewhat, until he said, "At least, not until we've talked about this."

He wanted to talk? "I will happily listen to anything you have to say." Listening was what a reporter did best.

"We'd better get you back to the house first." He offered his hand rather than his arm, which she took with an inward sigh of delight. She hadn't counted on something so wonderful as their kiss. And, so long as she lived in the moment, she couldn't be bothered to worry about what it might mean for her future.

CHAPTER 12

E d woke up almost as tired as he'd been the night before. He'd left Molly on the Morgans' porch without saying more than good night, and he'd somehow made it to his bunk, where he'd collapsed with a groan. He hadn't gone back to get his shirt or sewing kit from the other room. He'd not been in the mood for the teasing or questions from his friends about walking Molly home.

He'd rolled over so his back faced the room and tried to sleep. Instead, he'd lain awake and heard as each man entered the room and searched out their own bunk. He'd listened as breathing deepened and turned to snores. He'd lain there, the rumbles of his fellow cowboys all around him, and hadn't been able to quiet his mind.

It seemed like hours before he slept. Hours of thinking about Molly, of reliving the way her lips felt against his, how soft the skin of her cheeks and hands were, and the way his hand fit so perfectly at the curve of her waist.

He needed to get her out of his head long enough to think clearly about what had happened. And what hadn't happened. Molly hadn't seemed to regret their kisses for even a moment. She'd almost seemed eager to continue the activity.

But Ed hadn't ever been the type to give his affection away so freely. He didn't go around kissing every pretty girl he encountered. And he hadn't ever shown interest, openly, in a White woman. Sure, the laws might permit those of Spanish descent to court and marry White Americans, but more people than not frowned on the mixing of cultures and skin colors. Especially if it was the man who possessed darker skin.

In Arizona Territory, as in most of the United States, there were laws against unions between certain races. In every state Ed knew of, a Black person could never marry outside of their race without incurring legal action, imprisonment, or worse, if the community took things into their own hands.

That's why he didn't dance with the ranchers' daughters in Sonoita. While no law officially prohibited someone like him from loving a woman of any race, he wasn't about to give anyone a reason to dislike him for "overstepping." He knew his place, and he kept to it. He'd long-since come to terms with the idea of marrying a woman whose skin matched his own in its shade. He just figured he had to meet her. Meet someone who made his heart pound and his head swim the way Molly did.

Not that he gave any thought to *marrying* Molly. They barely knew each other. She was a stranger. Better educated than he was. Anyone could tell that just by listening to her. Her clothes were fancy, her manners precise and impeccable. He lived in a bunkhouse and had been raised on a farm in Indian Territory. He was no more a match for her than his red bandana was for her lacey white handkerchiefs.

And she would go back to England, eventually.

Which made the kissing something his mother—well, both his parents—wouldn't approve of. Even if the lady involved was happy to enjoy the moment without asking for any sort of promise in return.

But there had been that moment when they first met—first laid eyes on each other—that he couldn't forget. No matter how he tried. He'd felt deep down in his soul that life would never be the same, and he'd spent all the time since then trying to dismiss that notion.

Ugh. He needed to think before he saw her. To make a plan of some kind, to ensure kissing Molly didn't happen again. Even if he wanted it to. No matter how much he enjoyed her company or the sweet taste of her lips.

Ed dressed in a rush and left the bunkhouse before the sun came up. The faster he saw to his Sunday chores, the sooner he could get away from his thoughts. Sunday meant visiting day for the ranching families. For the cowboys, it meant fewer chores and time to themselves.

Ed had every intention of taking that time to visit the canyon spring. Maybe being near the water that reminded him so much of home would help clear his head. He'd see to his chores, take a bath, and go to the stream instead of church. Nature was its own kind of church, wasn't it?

He had nearly finished his work in the stable when someone nearby cleared their throat. Another man. Ed tightened his grip on the shovel he'd been hanging up, then finished the action and turned around.

Duke stood in the middle of the walkway between the stalls. He was dressed in his Sunday best. "Good morning, Ed."

"Duke." Ed brushed his hands on his pants. "You're dressed a might nice for the stables."

"Dannie wants to visit a friend today. She wants to get out as much as possible before her confinement." The Englishman came a few steps closer, his expression serious. "I thought I'd check the horses and wagon ahead of time. Just to be sure everything is ready."

"Right." Ed shifted, sensing there was something the former English lord wasn't saying. "Is there anything I can help you with?"

"Perhaps." Duke came another step closer and appeared uncomfortable. "I am quite relieved to find you here, to tell the truth. You see, last night, after dinner, Dannie sent me to the

Morgans' house to borrow some tea." He waved a hand in front of his face. "And when I arrived there, Frosty said he'd wished they'd known. They could have merely sent some to our house with Miss McKinney."

Ed's insides twisted. As he'd suspected, Molly hadn't told her hosts where she was going when she came to the bunkhouse. The deception wouldn't please anyone. Nor was it safe for anyone on the ranch to be somewhere other than where they said they would be. People got lost, hurt, and in other types of trouble all the time in the desert. Folks had to know where their family was, where their employees had gone off to, so they could go looking in the right direction if anything bad happened.

"I can see by the look on your face that you have an idea of what happened."

Doubtless the Morgans had already had a conversation with Molly about it, too. Ed didn't see any point in continuing a deception he'd unknowingly become part of. "Miss McKinney came to the bunkhouse for dinner. I walked her home later."

"I know."

Ed blinked. "You know?"

"Dannie and I sat on our porch last night in the dark to enjoy the stars." Duke rubbed the back of his neck, his expression sheepish. "We saw you walk Molly back to the Morgans." Given Duke's furrowed brow and lack of eye contact, he'd seen more than the two of them walking. "I know you are an upstanding man, Ed. I am certain you did nothing wrong. But as your friend I thought I should advise you to be careful, for your sake as well as hers."

The warning, despite the kindly way Duke gave it, put Ed on the defensive. "You're right. We didn't do anything wrong. And we're not going to. I know she's leaving as soon as she's got what she wants for her newspaper, and I'm not about to risk my reputation or hers."

The horses shifted in the stalls. For an uncomfortable, short stretch of time, the only sound in the building was that of the animals eating and the buzz of flies the horses whisked away with their tails.

Duke studied Ed, then slid his hands into his pockets. "I consider you a friend. And you know how it was when Dannie and I met, with every expectation that I would one day leave. That knowledge didn't stop us from growing closer, though it made things difficult. I have no wish to come across as a hypocrite."

The stiffness in Ed's shoulders lessened. He directed his gaze upward at the rafters. "You aren't a hypocrite, Duke. I know Molly isn't going to stick around here for a cowboy." Even if she saw him as more than that, as she had said the evening before. "I don't want either of us to get hurt. What happened last night..."

Ed wanted to say it wouldn't happen again, but he couldn't force the words out. Mostly because he wanted it to. Feeling the soft press of Molly's lips against his and then never experiencing the sensation again? It hurt to think about.

Duke's commiserating smile made it clear he understood. "You are more than your vocation, Ed. Someday, the right lady will see that." He didn't say that Molly was the right lady. The Englishman didn't even hint that such a thing was possible. Maybe that made him a better friend than if he'd tried to give Ed hope. Duke clapped his hands together in front of him. "Now. I had better get to work on the buggy."

They didn't talk any further, instead working together in companionable silence. When the buggy was prepared, Ed excused himself to finish getting himself in order for the day. His plans included riding to the far reaches of the ranch, northward, to check the fences on his way to the spring.

After seeing to his chores and taking a cowboy-bath, Ed couldn't help feeling somewhat better. But it'd be nice to visit the spring, surrounded by shady trees and birdsong. The spring far outshone the bunkhouse when it came to finding a place to think. When he sat on the rocks and listened to the quiet of water and the rustle of leaves, he felt more at home there than anywhere else on the ranch.

Maybe he needed home right now.

His mother's letter pricked at his conscience again. He still hadn't answered her.

Instead of worrying over it, he prepared for his afternoon away from the ranch. He packed up a small bag with biscuits, a canteen, and his notebook, along with a novel Frosty had loaned him a while back. Then he went out to the barn. All the while, trying not to think about Molly and that if he stayed on the ranch, he might contrive a way to spend time with her.

Except not thinking about her was impossible.

Especially when she showed up in the barn as he was saddling up a horse.

"Where are you off to?" Her voice surprised him, coming from the other side of the stall. He froze, midway through cinching up the strap beneath the gelding's belly. Then he finished the adjustment with haste before turning around.

"Heading on a ride. I'm checking fences and then enjoying the day."

"Oh." She had to have stood on her toes to rest her arms along the top of the stall wall. Today, her long brown hair was done in two braids, one on each shoulder. The style looked childish on most, but Ed found himself admiring her lovely face the way he always did. "That sounds like a lovely way to spend the day. It seems like everyone here has plans to be off somewhere."

Ed swept off his hat and looked up at his horse again before meeting her gaze. "What about you? Are you off to interview more ranchers? Or staying here with the Boltons to meet their visitors? There's always lots of coming and going on Sundays, since there isn't a permanent preacher in Sonoita."

Her easy smile, warm and soft as it was, went straight to his heart. "So I've been told." She took hold of the wall with both hands and leaned back. "This is the first day I haven't wanted to fill my time with stories and writing. I thought I would find something more enjoyable to do, to occupy myself. Evelyn suggested a walk but reminded me to take a sharp instrument with me for fending off wild animals." She shivered theatrically and grinned at him. "That made the idea far less pleasant than it originally sounded."

He stepped closer, but several feet and the half-wall made the distance between them significant still. "You won't be working away at your typewriter?"

"It's Sunday." She leaned in close again. "The one day on the ranch, as I understand it, that no one is expected to do more than absolutely necessary. I know I haven't worked nearly so hard as you, cowboy, but I think I've earned a break."

"You won't get any argument from me, lady." He looked back at his horse, considering. Then watched her from the corner of his eye. "Did you get an earful from Frosty or Evelyn about last evening?"

"You mean for joining the men for dinner?" She batted her eyelashes at him with feigned innocence, then sighed deeply and deflated. "Not really. They were most kind. Frosty told me he didn't at all mind where I had gone, but he wished he'd known so he could have walked in first to make sure everyone was decent. You all were, of course. But Evelyn said, for safety's sake, to be clearer about where I spend my time. In case of emergencies."

His gut twisted. "The last time you disappeared without warning, a flash flood nearly swept you away. I guess that's reason enough to be cautious."

She shuddered and looked away. "I am daily grateful you came in search of me. Yes. I understand the practicality and safety of keeping people apprised of my whereabouts."

"That's just how it is on a ranch." Ed replaced his hat. "You never know when you'll need to gather folks up. I'm glad their concern didn't offend you."

"Not in the least. It made perfect sense. What if there had been a fire? Or a wild animal attack? Everyone would need to be accounted for." She shrugged and lowered herself from her toes to stand flat-footed. Only her eyes peeked over the edge of the divide then. "I suppose I will see you another time. I hope you enjoy your ride."

She hadn't gone more than two steps before he came out of the stall. "Molly, wait." His heart pounded in his chest, as fearful of rejection as excited by the invitation he extended. "Do you want to come with me?"

The two of them, off riding alone, weren't going to raise too many eyebrows. In more civilized parts of the world, where manners and etiquette held people in a firmer grip, things would be different. Asking a lady to accompany him alone anywhere would give matrons a reason to gossip and frown if not shock them altogether. But here, with nothing but desert grass and blue sky surrounding them, people didn't hold to the rules as strictly.

Duke's warning fluttered through Ed's mind, but he mentally brushed it aside. He wasn't going to do anything inappropriate. His parents raised him better than that. The only thing that actually worried him was that she might say no.

"I wouldn't want to intrude. It sounds as though your plan hinged on being alone." She laughed and brushed one of her braids back over her shoulder. "I can find a way to entertain myself without pestering you."

Ed looked down the stalls to where her mule had his head hung over the wall, watching his mistress with his long ears perked forward. "What about Chaucer? He'd probably enjoy the exercise."

Had Ed sounded too desperate? Of course he had. And he wanted to kick himself.

"Would he?" She looked down the row, and her mule bleated out a greeting. They both had to laugh at that, then Molly fiddled with the end of her other braid. "I have no wish to intrude on your time, Ed. Not if you want to be alone. Please, don't think that last evening—" She blushed and lowered her eyes. "Don't think that what happened means I have expectations for us other than friendship. We are still friends, first and foremost."

"It didn't even cross my mind when I asked you to join me," he promised. And it hadn't. All he cared about, he realized with some relief, was spending time in her company. He didn't have any wish to put words to what was happening between them or to rope her up with things that could never be. "And I don't have expectations of you, either."

What kind of a man would he be if he thought of nothing else but pulling her close and kissing her again? Sure, he'd enjoy the opportunity if it ever came by, but he wasn't about to force anything on her or their relationship.

Strangely, the reassurance seemed to dim her good mood. "I suppose it was only a kiss or two." She nibbled on her bottom lip, forcing him to remember and try to count exactly how many kisses they had exchanged.

The line he walked required delicate steps. "Only?" he repeated, trying not to grin. "Best kisses I've ever had. But that's not the point, Molly."

Her cheeks turned pink. "Really? The best?"

He scrubbed at his chin to hide his grin. "I find you attractive in all the ways that matter. But like you said, we're friends first. And I know you've got places to be when you finish up at the ranch. That means we're not making each other any promises. So I'm not about to dwell on kissing a lady like you when nothing else can come of it. That's not who I am."

"I see." She studied him with those intelligent brown eyes of hers. Trying to read him. "I suppose the temptation was too strong to resist last evening?"

"Something like that," he admitted. "Like I said. You're an attractive lady."

"And you do not intend to kiss me if I come with you today?"

"Nope. Wouldn't dream of it." Maybe that wasn't all the way true. He'd certainly dream about it. But he wouldn't act on it. Not unless she—nope. He couldn't go on thinking like that. Except... "No intentions at all."

"Hm." Molly tapped her bottom lip with her forefinger,

considering him and his words carefully before saying, "I would enjoy riding with you today, Ed. If you truly don't mind."

"I don't. I'd like your company, in fact."

"Very well. Then I accept your invitation." She spun on her heel and walked at double her usual speed toward the exit. "Let me tell Evelyn where I'm going, and I'll pack some lunch. Will you prepare Chaucer for me? Just so I don't delay your plans too much."

"Sure," he called after her. "No need to rush."

She waved and disappeared out the door.

Despite everything he'd said to her, Ed's heart beat a little harder, and his mood was a little brighter, as he adjusted to the thought of spending his day in Molly's company. And showing her the spring.

Evelyn Morgan hadn't disapproved of Molly's outing. Not precisely. But she had offered a word of caution. "I trust Ed, of course. He's always conducted himself as a gentleman. Only, if the two of you continue to spend time together alone, I worry that it may make it more difficult when the time comes to say goodbye. For the both of you."

"We are friends, Evelyn. Nothing more. I promise, I am not in the habit of leaving a string of broken hearts behind me everywhere I go." She'd kept her voice light, even teasing, but as she walked out the door with a satchel of food and a canteen of water, her heart had betrayed her by skipping a beat when she laid eyes on Ed coming toward her, leading his horse and Chaucer along behind him.

A grin stretched across his handsome face at the sight of her. "No chaperone?"

"You had better mind your suggestive words, Mr. Byrd, or I'll begin to think a chaperone is necessary." She handed him the satchel, and he tucked it inside his saddlebags with whatever else he'd brought along.

"I'll mind my manners," he promised, offering his cupped hands for her to step up and mount the mule. She placed her hand on his shoulder, boot on his hands, then vaulted up into the saddle.

From her height atop the mule, she looked down into his eyes. "Thank you, kind sir."

He wasn't an especially tall man. Especially when compared to Frosty, Evan, and even King Bolton. But he moved with a confidence and innate ability that she couldn't help admiring. He made her feel safe when he was with her. And looked after. Though she didn't need looking after, and hadn't since her fifteenth birthday.

Still. Ed's steadiness gave her yet more confidence in herself.

They rode away from the ranch buildings and made their journey across the open spread of land. Small streams ran between low-lying hills. Cattle dotted the landscape in clusters of ten or twenty. The long grasses had faded from true green to something lighter.

The late morning sun didn't press upon them heavily. Ed checked the northern fences, pronounced them in good repair, then turned her east, toward the mountains. "We're not going too far, but there's a place I'd like to show you."

"I am always ready for an adventure."

He gave her an approving look that went straight to her heart. "I know. I figured that out the first time we met and haven't forgotten it since."

Her stomach flipped happily. So he *did* think about that first conversation at the fort.

He led her along until they came to the mouth of a shallow canyon. Water trickled through the middle of it, likely from the rain they'd had the day before. A few more bends in the canyon brought the walls higher, and the water lower, trickling in from the sides. And then they emerged into a grove of thin, spindly trees. And through the grove, Molly caught sight of a pool of water reflecting back the blue of the sky above. Water flowed from the rock wall surrounding the hidden oasis, and the air around them was notably cooler than anywhere else she had been since coming to Arizona Territory.

"Oh my," she breathed in wonder. She dismounted Chaucer and led him forward, passing Ed as he did the same. She came to the edge of the water and looked down, finding it clear and clean, and not very deep. "This place...it's beautiful."

"I thought you'd like it. Even if you have seen Niagara Falls." She'd told him about that first adventure, seeing the falls from both the Canadian and the New York side. "There's something special about a hidden oasis like this. Not everyone at the ranch knows about it. Abram found it first, I think. Years ago. The Boltons know, too. Then Frosty stumbled across it on his own and told me about it after a time."

"It's incredible." She watched Chaucer drink at the water's edge, his long donkey ears perked up and forward. "Would it be all right to put my toes in, do you think?"

"I plan on it. Don't see why I'd keep you from enjoying the same thing."

In no time, they had the animals grazing on the bits of weeds beneath the trees. Ed dropped the saddlebags in the shade, then sat and pulled off his boots while she did the same. He rolled up his pants and went wading into the water, pulling his hat off as he went.

Molly's split skirts had a higher hem than her usual clothing, except a pair of bicycle pantaloons she'd tried once for a story. She didn't have to hold up the edges too high to avoid getting them wet, but after a few minutes of enjoying the cold water, she simply let the hem drop.

"This is delightful," she admitted, then put her foot down on a smooth and slippery rock. She barely managed a shout of surprise before her tailbone hit the bottom of the pool.

Ed whirled around, then sloshed toward her in a hurry.

"Molly, are you hurt?" He reached for her with one hand. "I should've warned you that the rocks can be slippery."

"I'm quite all right. No harm done." She grasped his hand and let him haul her up to her feet again. It was the first time they had touched since he'd bid her goodnight the evening before. Something she became acutely aware of when his strength pulled her closer than either of them anticipated.

Her hand landed flat against his chest, dampening his shirt. She looked up at him, her eyes searching his as her breath caught in her lungs and froze. And she forgot every promise she'd made to herself about remaining mere friends with the handsome cowboy.

All that mattered in that moment was how close they stood. She stopped thinking about everything outside of the two of them, standing in the stream, holding one another. His eyes darkened, and Molly closed the distance between them, standing on her toes and trusting him to keep her balanced. She met his lips with hers.

The kiss improved upon her experience from the night before and reassured her; she hadn't imagined the swirl of emotions she'd felt the first time they kissed. Nor had they abated. If anything, there was *more* to feel. More curiosity. More pleasure. More...hope.

Ed drew back, his chest rising and falling steadily as he breathed. Molly, her cheeks warm and her heart racing, leaned into him. She laid her cheek atop his shoulder and closed her eyes, catching his scent. He smelled of clean, sun-warmed cotton, leather, and everything wonderful. She wanted to bury her nose in his collar, but she refrained. Barely.

"Molly," he said in a whisper. "We can't—"

"I know." But she kissed his cheek anyway before she took a careful step back, the cool water and rocks beneath her reminding her how she'd found herself in that position. Her stumble. His assistance. And then she'd kissed him like some desperate heroine in a theatrical production.

At least he'd kissed her back.

He cleared his throat and took a step away. "If you're all right..." He looked her over. "You'd better find some sunshine to sit in to get dried up. The day's not cold enough to worry over being wet, but I doubt you'll enjoy dripping everywhere."

She looked down at her sopping clothes. "Yes. You're likely right." She walked around him, toward the rocks at the other side of the pool. Sunlight warmed them and would keep her from shivering. The springs supplying the pool with water brought it all in quite cold. She lowered herself to the warm rock but kept her feet in the water.

Ed returned to her side a few minutes later, this time with the saddlebags. He dropped them on the rock next to her. "Hungry?"

Pretending nothing had happened might be for the best, she supposed.

"Yes, starving." He handed her a leather bag for her to open while he went through the other, laying out the supplies he'd brought as careful as a hostess laid out a feast on a table. As she sorted out two sandwiches from wax-coated cloths, her hand brushed the spine of a book.

"Forgot my canteen," Ed muttered. "I'll be right back." He left her there and made his way to his horse and Chaucer again.

"No need to hurry," Molly murmured, barely raising her voice as she withdrew the book. It wasn't a novel, or something hard-backed from a publisher. The soft leather binding had no text or title anywhere on its cover.

A notebook, perhaps?

She opened it to the first page, curious about what sort of things her cowboy companion would jot down on its pages.

The first page didn't contain information about where to return the book if it was lost, as she expected. Instead, it had a date in the corner, and written at the top as though squeezed in later, was a title. *The Mexican Blanket.*

Her eyes read the first several lines without even thinking on it. Though she ought to have known better, Molly's curiosity overtook her. It was a story, and it began with a beautiful young woman weaving a blanket of blues, whites, and black under the direction of her mother, while her father spoke about the hardships of the coming winter.

Molly turned the page as the mother and father fell silent, and a noise in their small yard drew their attention. The young woman seemed to know who had come before her parents did. A young man, dressed like a *Gringo*, even though he had grown up in the same community as this family.

He'd come to see the blanket-weaver.

"Molly," Ed said, his voice unnecessarily sharp.

She snapped the book shut and looked up at him, sheepish and repentant. "Oh, Ed. I'm sorry. I didn't mean to pry."

He stood several paces away, staring at her with wide eyes and his mouth gaping open. His ears had turned a dark shade of red, too. Whatever she had stumbled upon, it wasn't something he'd meant for her to see. She hugged the book to her chest, whether to shield it or herself from his next words she couldn't say.

As Ed approached, his shoulders tight and his steps slow, he explained in a quiet, desperate way with each word enunciated carefully. "I know you did not. I should not have left it where anyone would find it. It is only that—my words are private. I do not mean for anyone to read them." He held his hand out. "May I have it back, please?"

"Of course." She held the notebook out to him with both hands. "I only read the first page."

He took it from her and then walked around the rock. He opened one of the now-empty bags and tucked it carefully inside. "I packed it when I thought I would be up here alone," he admitted, not looking at her. "And it's not—I'm not upset with you. You couldn't know. But I've never let anyone read them before."

"Read *them*?" she repeated. "The stories in that book? Are there more?"

He nodded slowly. "And more notebooks, too. It is only something I do to pass the time."

Her mind pieced together what he hadn't yet said, and Molly leaned across the stone to put her hand on his arm, bringing his attention back to her. As she looked him in the eye, she said, "You write stories?"

"To pass the time," he repeated firmly. "They aren't any good. A long time ago, I grew tired of reading other people's stories when I had so many of my own in my head."

Molly's mouth opened and closed as she tried to form words that would both reassure him and somehow communicate her surprise, without offering insult. "Frosty told me that most cowboys read, both to themselves and one another, on cattle drives and around fires at night. I suppose it stands to reason that cowboys would write their own stories, too."

"Maybe." He handed her one of the sandwiches. "Which means it's not all that interesting that I write."

"Oh, but I think it is." She accepted the food but didn't take a bite. She pulled her legs up beneath her and faced him fully. "I find it remarkable. You said you have stories in your head? Do you write things down that really happened, or do you make everything up?"

"Most of it is made up," he admitted, turning an apple over in his hands and lowering his gaze again. "At first, I rewrote stories I'd read elsewhere. Not word for word. I'd change details, maybe. Or I'd tell a story from someone else's perspective. There was this one story about *El Dorado*, with the *conquistadores* as heroes who fought an army to gain admittance to the city of gold. I wrote about one of the soldiers they faced, no more than a boy, trying to protect his home."

Her heart squeezed, and she put her hand on his arm. "That is an incredible idea, Ed. So many stories are told from the perspective of the conquerors, not often the conquered. Did you ever think to have it published?"

"Who would publish a story like that?" he asked, raising his apple to his lips and taking an aggressive bite.

Molly blinked at him. "Anyone, I should think. Magazines

156

with adventure stories. Even a catalog that sells supplies for mountaineering or exploring."

Ed swallowed his bite of apple. "The first problem with publishing anything is that I'd have to write well enough to make the story interesting." He shook his head, a heavy sigh escaping him. "I barely finished the seventh grade, at a Cherokee school."

"But you're well read, it seems. And you're intelligent. Really, though I only read one page, I was enthralled. I would have kept reading if you hadn't brought me out of the story like that." She gave him her most encouraging smile, but Ed only shrugged, and her hand slipped off his arm.

"The second problem is who I am. Mexican. Cherokee. People like me don't get published. Especially when some of the heroes in my stories"—he laid a hand over the closed bag—"look like me."

"That cannot be true. Why, there's a German novelist who has written dozens of stories about Indians, and they are always honorable and true. Evan—Duke—and I were discussing them at luncheon yesterday. He was quite enamored with those stories."

"He's talked to me about them, too." Ed shook his head. "I don't think the author has ever even been to America. Let alone met an Indian from *any* tribe."

"Oh dear." Molly sat back, easily seeing the stubborn set of his jaw. She would make no headway on the subject that day. "I suppose that would be rather discouraging. Though perhaps because it hasn't been done often, or done well enough, there would be an interest in your stories precisely because of the new perspective you could give."

He said nothing. He took another bite of his apple and studied the water.

"I really shouldn't pry any more, of course. If I promise to stop, perhaps you would let me read one of your stories?" When he looked up at her, eyes narrowed, she gave him her most coaxing smile. "Please? Or at least tell me more about them. *The Mexican Blanket.* What happens in that story?"

"Nothing important," he muttered, finishing off his apple in his next bite.

Molly let the subject drop. Though she didn't want to. Every instinct she'd honed in her time as a reporter screamed that she couldn't give up on digging deeper. She wanted, *needed*, to understand Ed's story. First, his passionate explanation about his people's missing children had stirred her sympathy and her righteous indignation. And he'd refused to speak about what people like her might do to help. Now she had stumbled upon a secret passion, his writing, and he refused to share it with her. His past and present called to her, and maybe...maybe his future did, too.

Molly squashed that thought, turning away from him to take a large bite from her sandwich. Silently, she berated herself. The future—his future, especially—wasn't hers to speculate over. Reporters dealt in facts. In things that had happened. Her only focus ought to be what she could get printed in black and white in a newspaper.

But she wasn't just a reporter, as Ed had told her. She was more than that. She was his friend, though they hadn't been acquainted long. Perhaps, when he came to know her better, he'd trust her enough for these conversations to continue. If she was lucky.

She had sensed there was something about Ed both remarkable and worth an interview. It seemed she was right. For more than one reason.

Molly spoke on other subjects until she drew Ed out once more. She tried to regain the camaraderie they'd had before she'd stumbled upon his notebook, and sure enough, by the time they had finished their lunch, they'd regained the easiness between them. She also refrained from kissing him again.

Perhaps if they both pretended like neither event had ever happened, they would succeed in preventing uncomfortable breaches in their conduct.

When they mounted up to return to the ranch, Molly even made Ed laugh with a joke about Chaucer's charm.

They accomplished the ride back in companionable silence. Molly's mind whirled with possibilities, and she wondered several times what Ed was thinking every time he looked over his shoulder at her and smiled.

Despite all her attempts to dismiss the interlude at the stream, Molly couldn't help remembering the feel of his hand on her waist and the touch of his lips against her own.

"We can't—" Ed had said.

But...what if they *could*?

CHAPTER 13

Laying in his bunk Sunday night, Ed couldn't sleep. Long after the other men were snoring, he stared into the darkness. Trying to make sense of things. Or at least talk some sense into himself.

Kissing Molly the first time had been a revelation to Ed, though he'd promised he wouldn't do such a thing again. When she'd kissed him again—at the stream—it shook him to the foundation of his soul. In the few moments they'd had, standing there and holding one another, he'd forgotten all the reasons he shouldn't kiss her.

His education, or lack of it, for one. Molly had obviously undergone a more formal upbringing and education than he had. She was intelligent and quick-witted. For another thing, she had more experiences than he had. The woman had traveled across an ocean and half the United States. He'd made it from Tulsa, Oklahoma to Sonoita, Arizona. And he'd only ever been a farmer's son or a cowboy. She had met important people on two continents.

She had so much more she wanted to see, so many stories to tell, and Ed.... He had a job to do. He rode a horse. Mended fences. Herded cattle. And maybe, sooner than he liked, he'd have to head back to his father's farm.

He'd read his mother's letter again before Whiskers put out the bunkhouse light. Nothing in it had sounded urgent. Yet he felt guilty for not having answered it yet. He always wrote back right away. But with every day that had passed, Ed had avoided what had usually been a simple task.

In the darkness, only his own thoughts for company, he finally admitted why. It was partly because he knew if he went back to Oklahoma now, he might stay. He wasn't as young as most cowboys. His mother would remind him of that. And she'd remind him that a cowboy didn't settle down. They weren't paid enough to support a family, for one thing. And concessions weren't made for cowboys with families. Frosty had a house on the ranch because he was the foreman. Ed couldn't expect the same.

Though Ed had denied it when his friends asked if he'd developed "itchy feet," as other cowboys did, he'd felt stagnant. No, he didn't want to go looking for another cowboying job. And while he might have enough saved to buy his own small spread somewhere, that hadn't felt right either. Not yet.

He puffed out an exasperated breath and rolled over.

He didn't want to go back to farming, though seeing his family would be good. But there wasn't anything for him in Oklahoma besides the people he loved. For some people, that would be enough. But Ed...he'd lived between his grandfather and father's world and arguments for too long. If he stayed in Indian Territory, he feared he'd feel just as stuck as he did in Arizona.

Sleep continued to elude him.

Quiet as the fox he'd been named after, Ed left his bunk with boots in one hand and his notebook in the other. As was his habit when he couldn't sleep. And out he went into the night. Above him, the stars glittered and gleamed in their paths.

He didn't go far. Just to the paddock, where he leaned against the rail and stared upward. The horses slept. Tex trotted over, gave Ed a sniff, then disappeared when he realized Ed wasn't a threat but someone who belonged.

Belonging. It was such an odd concept. He felt like he belonged in the place he'd made for himself on the ranch. But that didn't stop him from feeling restless, too. Would things be better or worse with his family? Could he settle in to a life of pecan orchards and raising corn? Somehow, he didn't think so.

He loved his family. All parts of it. He loved his grandfather, who worshiped God yet kept the old ways alive, too. He loved his parents, especially his mother, who taught him how to pray and look after others. He missed his sisters, and he wanted to see their children.

But he didn't want that life for himself.

An owl hooted from the direction of the barn, adding to the soft sounds of the night. At his parents' home, he'd often lain awake listening to crickets and night birds and the wind in the leaves of the pecan trees closest to his house. The sounds were so different there. He'd come to love the quieter desert nights, too.

The past and present wrestled for a place in his heart. And then there was one thing more—Molly. A woman he'd known for such a short time, yet her presence filled his mind in his every waking hour.

Ed slumped forward, his head hanging low. He had to get through her time on the ranch without losing more of himself to her. His heart was divided enough without giving a piece of it to a woman who would leave, likely without a backward glance. Because whatever she felt for Ed, she wanted her adventure more. He felt sure of that.

No one would give up a life like hers for a cowboy as uncertain of his future as Eduardo Byrd. He couldn't compete with the excitement that came into her eyes when she talked of her work.

When Ed had seen Molly holding his notebook at the spring, panic had seized him. His handwriting looked like chicken scratch. His words were too simple. His stories would seem childish, he knew, when someone who wrote for a living read them.

And he'd break—he knew he would—if Molly teased him about it.

Except she hadn't. She'd wanted to read more. And that had frightened him even more.

Ed groaned, and a horse snorted in reply. "Sorry to wake you," he muttered derisively. "No reason to burden the livestock with my troubles." He left the paddock, heading back to the bunkhouse. He didn't go back to bed, though. Instead, he entered the common room and lit a lamp. He settled in with his notebook and tried to lose himself in writing.

And he didn't think about Molly. Most of the time. But if he named the mule in his story Chaucer, well...she'd never know. And it would make him smile every time he thought about it.

CHAPTER 14

The second week Molly spent at the ranch passed by much as the first had. She worked mostly with Ed, at all sorts of chores, but also spent time with the ladies. Ruthie had taken an entire day with her to walk through gardens and along creek beds to show Molly what would grow in the dry Arizona soil. They discussed medicines and remedies for dozens of illnesses Ruthie had seen and cured over the years.

"How did you learn all of this?" Molly asked late that afternoon. She looked down at her notes, where she'd sketched a this-tle-like plant with fever-curing abilities. "If you don't have any of these plants where you're originally from, how did you know what to try?"

"Abram was a soldier first," Ruthie reminded her. "And I'd follow him from one camp to another. I did the laundry for the officers who didn't have wives or servants with them," she said, tucking the plant in her basket. "But when I had a moment to myself, I'd find the Indian scouts and *their* wives." She led the way across the flattened grass from the low-lying creek back toward the ranch buildings. "We didn't have too much in common, of course. Not even our languages. The main reason we got along was because I was kind to them. I shared my knowledge about the army's ways with them, and they shared some of their ways with me. I memorized as much as I could, and I wrote down things when I had paper and ink to spare."

"That is most impressive."

"Not really. That's just being a good neighbor."

Molly turned that thought over in her head for hours afterward. She knew medical doctors in England had mostly displaced the apothecaries who had mixed medicine for centuries. Now university-trained chemists mixed powders and tonics.

When one group replaced another, whether in a modern society or in places like the American west, how much knowledge disappeared forever? Molly jotted the question down in her notebook, though she knew well enough it wouldn't work for any of the stories she had planned. There was that travel book she meant to write, of course. And perhaps she could discuss the idea with Ed at some point. He hadn't opened up about his heritage any more than before, but if she approached topics from a rhetorical point, he sometimes let things slip.

Getting those tiny glimpses of his past didn't satiate her curiosity at all. She wanted to know more about him, and his family, and where he came from. And not because she was a reporter. Or a nosy friend. Because she wanted to know *him*.

But it would take longer than a fortnight, and time wasn't something Molly had in infinite supply.

She tried not to think about that too much. Especially when she was with Ed.

Friday afternoon, Ed brought her to the paddock to watch Abram train the young cattle dogs.

Frosty, his son Ben, Clark Bolton, and Lee Steele stood along the fence with them. Everyone focused on Abram. Only a handful of cattle were inside, along with Abram and Tex. Abram stood near the gate with Tex sitting beside him, watching him.

Another dog, the same size and age as Tex, sat next to Lee. His name was Scout. The dogs were brothers, and they were taking turns practicing their jobs on the ranch.

Abram whistled, and from outside of the paddock came Gus. Molly had the pleasure of seeing him every evening on the Morgans' front porch.

"Gus has been doing this for years," Ed said quietly. "He learned from his parents."

"They're beautiful dogs." Molly watched as Abram gave a command that Gus obeyed, going in toward the herd low on his stomach and waiting. Tex watched his sire with interest. Then Abram gave Tex the same command and the younger dog leaped forward with excitement before seeming to remember himself. He crouched low to the ground and approached the cattle the same way Gus had. "They look rather like English shepherds. Or collies."

The cattle were paying attention to the dogs, too. They'd all turned to face the canines, lowering their heads, as though sensing a threat.

"With notable differences," Frosty said from his place at the fence. "They're lower to the ground, which makes them a good fit for cattle as well as sheep." He turned his attention to his son. "All right, Ben. Go on in with Abram."

Ben ducked his head and slipped between the rails of the fence. He walked slow, so as not to frighten the cattle. The boy stood next to Abram and listened intently as he received instructions that Molly couldn't hear, but a moment later he started commanding the dogs.

"Gus," the boy shouted, and the dog's ears twitched. "Come by, boy." The dog edged to the left of the small herd. "Tex, away to me—" The smaller dog kept low and moved in the opposite direction from his sire. With Ben giving commands, the dogs slowly moved behind the cattle and started to nudge them away from the back fence.

The instructions were the same words she'd heard shepherds in England give their sheepdogs.

Abram gave commands with whistles, and the dogs separated one cow from the rest and slowly—through intimidation, it appeared—edged the animal into a corner. Then Tex kept that cow where it was while Gus received commands from Abram to move the other four animals to the gate, which Abram opened for them to leave.

Ben kept reassuring Tex while the young dog held the fifth animal back until the others were out of the gate. Then he called, "That'll do, Tex!"

The dog jumped up, turned in a circle, and raced back to Ben with undeniable joy. Ben knelt to receive his dog and showered praise on the animal, while Gus sat next to Abram, looking on with a tilt to his head.

"Fascinating that such a small animal can make the cattle do as it pleases." Molly leaned against the fence and put her chin in her palm. "One sees it all the time with sheep, of course. But cattle are so large. Do they ever refuse to obey?"

"All the time. That's why you don't stop training a dog until they're a couple of years old." Frosty climbed over the fence, and when his boots hit the other side he added, "We've had one dog killed since I've been on this ranch. It didn't get out of the way fast enough, and a cow's horn caught it. Men get hurt and killed all the time, too. Usually when they're behaving foolishly. Excuse me, Molly." He tipped his hat to her and climbed the fence into the paddock to speak to Abram and Ben.

"What exactly does that mean?" Molly asked, looking up at Ed. "Behaving foolishly?"

"It means you can't let your guard down out here." Ed gestured to the surrounding land, and his eyes lingered on the mountains. "Scorpions. Cougars. Rattlers. Cattle. Just about anything will take a bite out of you if you're not careful."

Lee Steele, Abram and Ruthie's grandson, looked down at the dog sitting next to him. "That's another reason we like our dogs so much. They won't let anything hurt us or the livestock if they can help it. Right, Scout?" He rubbed his dog behind the ears.

Molly stepped away from the fence. "They seem like intelligent creatures. I enjoyed the demonstration immensely."

"You should see Gus and Fable when they're helping with a hundred head of cattle." Lee pushed his hat up on his forehead, a gesture Molly had seen every man on the ranch hold in common when they wore an easy grin. "They practically fly across the ground, and I've seen Fable jump clean over a cow once to get where she needed to go. They're the best cattle dogs I've ever seen."

Ed gave a nod of agreement. "We're more efficient when we work with the dogs. We'll be moving the herd south in a few days. Rounding up as many as we can and getting them to greener pastures. If Miss Molly wants to come, she'll see them in action then."

The boy looked up at Molly. "Are you going to come?"

She hesitated. She could probably justify more time on the ranch if she participated in a cattle drive. Even a short one. "Of course. I am here to learn, and that sounds like a perfect opportunity. You'll have to tell me what to expect."

"Sure." The boy looked up when his grandfather called. "I've gotta go. See you later, Ed. Miss Molly." He darted away, his dog at his side.

"Two weeks on a ranch," Molly murmured, crossing her arms over her chest. "And I'm still learning new things every day. It seems there is never a moment's pause, either. From the moment you wake until you go to sleep, there is work to do, or to plan." She looked up at Ed. "Do you enjoy this lifestyle more than farming?" She knew enough about his past to know he'd grown up on his father's farm and orchard.

"I'd say it's just as exhausting." He grinned with the admission. "But maybe a little more exciting. When you're farming, you don't expect the beans to try to trample you the way the cattle will."

She shivered. "I had much rather take my chances with the beans."

Ed laughed and started walking, and she fell into step beside him. "I can't imagine you picking beans, Molly."

Keeping pace with Ed had become quite natural, following him everywhere as she did. This time, he led her to one of the outbuildings they used as a smithy. Ed promised to show her where they kept tools for various jobs she hadn't seen performed yet. Maybe not the most exciting thing to see, but even details that didn't make it into her stories could help her create the right feel for them.

They entered the building. The moment they stepped into the shade Molly heaved a sigh of relief. The sun overhead wasn't unbearable, but being out of it was far preferable. She took off her hat and fanned herself with it, looking about with interest. She hadn't been inside this building yet.

Shelves with small, square pigeonholes covered one wall. Boxes of nails were slotted into some of the holes, tools in others. Hanging overhead were hooks that held even more tools, some of which she could only guess at their uses. There were work benches along one wall, carpentry things laid out all about, and the smell of sawdust tickled her nose.

Ed spent a few minutes showing her how they'd organized the building into a makeshift blacksmith shop. They kept everything for shoeing horses, mending hinges, and other small metal work in the large shed. After the brief tour, Ed remembered a loose gate he needed to fix.

Ed brought their conversation back to farming. "You say you'd rather have beans than cattle to deal with." Ed had crossed to the boxes of nails. He removed several slender bits of iron, then crossed the room to the carpentry table. "Yet here you are, in the desert, learning about cattle, instead of back in England taking tea with a politician's wife."

"Those things are hardly comparable. Wanting to see the world isn't the same as wanting to work with cows." Molly walked over to a shelf laden with horseshoes and laid her hat down. She picked one up that had been worn smooth and turned it over in her hands. "Adventure is entirely different."

They were alone together for the first time since they'd ridden to the spring. Avoiding the subject of his writing and their shared kisses had been easy in the company of others. With it being just Ed and Molly, however, it was wiser for her to keep her distance. Even if she already imagined herself crossing the dirt floor to stand in the circle of his arms again.

Her cheeks flushed with warmth and she cleared her throat. "Has it been an adventure for you? To work out here?"

"Maybe." Ed had found a hammer. He put it on the table, next to his nails. If he felt what she did, he hid it better. "That's what my father thought I was after when I came west. He didn't argue with me about it. Much. He asked me, right before I left, if being a farmer was too boring for me."

Across the room from him, Molly tried not to sound too interested in the personal turn of the conversation. Every time he let something of his life slip, she swept it up and treasured it the way another might secret away a dropped coin. It was ridiculous. She knew that. Yet she couldn't help asking, "What did you tell him?"

Ed leaned back against the table and crossed his arms. He kept his gaze on the ground. "I told him I loved farming. I still do. I love the simplicity of putting seeds in the ground and watching things grow. When I was a kid, my *mamá* would take me out and show me the first little shoots of green coming up. And the orchards—my grandfather planted them and raised them alongside his children." The warmth in his voice assured her of his sincerity. He had loved where he'd grown up. He loved it still.

"Then why leave if you valued that way of living?"

He shrugged and tilted his head back. "I wanted to see what else there was." He released a sigh, both long and deep. "And getting away from home seemed like a good idea at the time."

Molly made her way toward him, moving slowly across the dirt floor. Maybe she needn't keep her distance. She could conduct herself like a lady. Especially while having an important conversation. "Most men likely have that feeling. At least, most of the men I have interviewed usually have something to say about striking out on their own. It's a rite of passage, perhaps."

"It wasn't that." He smirked and lowered his gaze to hers as she approached. And oh, how that tilt to his lips made her stomach flip. "Or not entirely that, anyway. Things were..." He paused and frowned before coming up with the word. "...tense. Between my father and grandfather."

That brought things back into focus for Molly. Here she'd been looking at him, thinking about the kiss she'd stolen at the spring, when he was trying to share a part of himself with her. Why did she have so much trouble focusing when he was speaking of the very things she most wanted to hear? Molly tilted her head to the side, asking for him to share more with nothing other than her eyes as she stopped in front of him.

"My grandfather is full Cherokee," Ed reminded her, his expression more somber than before. "He married a woman from Texas, with Spanish heritage. By doing that, he made life hard on his kids within the tribe. Cherokee trace their ancestry through their mothers. That's where all their rights come from. But he really loved my grandmother, and maybe he didn't care when he was young."

Molly softened her voice along with her smile. "That sounds rather like Romeo and Juliet. Except decidedly more romantic, given that your grandparents lived to tell their love story to their children."

Though brief, his lips quirked upward. "Maybe it's romantic. And not everyone objected to his choice of a wife. But my grandmother is gone now. My father, my aunts and uncle, they're all grown up. So my grandfather's focus has changed to the Cherokee people. Not that he'd ever stopped caring about them. How could he? And my father is proud of his heritage, too. It's complicated to explain." His eyebrows pulled tightly together. And he released another one of those sighs that held a hundred years of history.

Molly put her hand on his forearm. "You don't have to explain your family to me, Ed. But I will listen, if you wish. I *am* wildly curious."

"I guess that's the reporter in you." He grinned, but the cheerful expression melted away. "You won't publish this?"

"I won't." She moved to stand next to him, her shoulder against his, the two of them leaning against the carpentry table. "I will listen as a friend, not a reporter."

She held her breath after saying so. She waited for the man with the open smile and closed past to decide the course of their conversation. Something about Ed drew her in, and maybe, once she knew his story, it would be easier to walk away when the time came.

It would be like the final period on one of her columns.

"A friend," he murmured, not sounding entirely satisfied. Or was that merely her wishful thinking? "All right then. Friend." He nudged her with his elbow and smiled. "About a year after my grandmother died, my grandfather said he wanted his grandchildren—all of us still around—to learn more about our heritage. I thought I knew enough. He'd told me stories growing up. So had my father. I lived in a Cherokee farming community; my father had his own farm there. But that was one of the problems, for my grandfather. The allotment. He said the government had taken too much Cherokee land and divided it out, and divided the people, too. Making it impossible for the Cherokee to stay united as a community. My father, half-Cherokee, argued that it would be better to fall in line with the government. Conform. He said the Cherokee way of life was dying, and the government would keep taking things away until the Cherokee were nothing more than a memory."

Molly shuddered, then leaned her head against his shoulder. That connection, small though it was, felt right. She hoped Ed understood what she meant by it. That she offered him her support and her compassion, her caring for him. "That sounds awful. From what I've seen, your father is likely right."

"He doesn't want to be right," Ed said, his voice quiet. He leaned his head toward hers, and his cheek brushed her forehead. "When I left, the two of them were arguing all the time about what was best for not just the Cherokee people, but for our family. I left when they started dragging me into it."

They stood there in the quiet as Molly sorted through his words, standing closer than they had since their day at the spring. A dozen thoughts came into her head, but she cast most of them aside as unhelpful. Ed didn't want her to solve his problems. He wanted to talk to a friend. It wasn't her place to do or be more than that. "I'm sorry for what your grandfather's people face. And the discord in your family."

It felt like a weak response to what he'd told her. When his arm came around her shoulders in a brief embrace, she relaxed.

"I think everyone has a little discord. Now and then."

"Not me." The words slipped out without her meaning to say them, and then of course, she had to explain. "I grew up without a family." She shrugged and his arm fell from her shoulders, his hand going to the table behind her as he leaned back.

"I've wondered what that was like." When she raised her head, Ed was looking down at her, curiosity brightening his eyes. "Not that I mean to pry. I've known plenty of cowboys who don't know their parents or came from rotten families. But I haven't met many women in the same circumstances."

"I imagine I had a better experience than most, since I grew up in a girls' boarding school. I am one of those with an unknown benefactor," she informed him with the false smile she'd perfected when speaking of her past. "They paid the school to look after me until I was fifteen. Then I took a job as an assistant to the headmistress when the money stopped. I taught grammar and literature, and I dared to submit my own writing to magazines for ladies."

"And so became the journalist you are today." Ed held her gaze. "That can't be easy. Growing up and figuring out your path all on your own."

"No. It wasn't." She leaned into him a little more, craving the contact of another person. Something she rarely had, given a woman's place in polite society. Ed didn't seem to mind, though. In fact, most of the people on the ranch seemed quite at ease when it came to affectionate touches. Whether it was Evelyn kissing her children before sending them out to do their chores, or Duke and Dannie walking with their arms around one another, or Abram putting his hand on Frosty's shoulder when they greeted one another.

"Isn't there anybody in your life you'd run to if you were in trouble?" Ed asked. "Someone as close as family, even if they aren't yours by blood?"

She thought of the editors she had worked with, including Mr. Gilchrist. Then about the other reporters she knew. Even the other women at the boarding house where she lived. "Not really. I have several acquaintances and people I consider friends. But it always seems easier not to form attachments and to handle things myself."

The few beaux she'd entertained hadn't admired that independent streak, either.

Ed's shoulder stiffened beneath her cheek, but then his arm came back around her before she could worry that he felt the same as those other men had.

"That sounds like a hard way to live, Molly." He gave her one last, gentle squeeze before releasing her. Much to her disappointment. "I hope it isn't always like that for you. People need each other sometimes."

Molly smoothed her skirt and avoided his gaze. "What about you?"

He picked up the hammer and gathered the nails. "What about me?"

"Do you think you'll go back to your family someday? To the farm?"

He let the hammer slide through his grip, catching it on the end before he dropped it, then shrugged. His tone changed, more

175

casual than before. "To visit? For certain. To stay? Maybe. Maybe not. But I know I'm not going anywhere today. I've got a gate to fix. You should probably head back to the house. Evie's likely to have dinner on the table soon."

The dismissal stung. She thought they'd grown closer in those minutes alone. But Ed was pushing her away again. While a smarter woman might think it for the best, Molly couldn't help the feeling of disappointment snuffing her hope for something more.

"Yes. You are quite right." She gestured to the door. "You go on ahead. I don't wish to keep you. I'll be on my way, too." She walked across the room to retrieve her hat, and when she turned around, Ed remained where he had been before. Staring at her with a furrowed brow and his lips turned downward in a frown.

"Molly?"

She turned the brim of her hat in her hand. "Hm? Was there something else?"

He looked at the door, the frown still in place, then at her again. He crossed the distance between them in a few quick strides. Her eyes widened, but before she could think of anything to say or do he was bending toward her.

He placed a kiss, soft and sweet, on her forehead. "Thank you for caring."

She gulped. Maybe he wasn't trying to dismiss her after all. "You're welcome."

What an inane thing to say. Before she could think of something better, Ed had gone.

Sometimes, talking to him reminded her of the complicated steps of an old-fashioned waltz. Except she only knew half the required movements, and the orchestra stopped playing just when she thought she understood the rhythm of the music. Despite the awkward lurches in the wrong direction, she found herself desperately wanting to understand the underlying patterns.

She wanted to understand Ed. She wanted his trust. She

wanted to know him, and maybe it wasn't fair because someday, sooner than she liked, she'd have to leave. Molly wasn't certain she would have the whole picture before she did.

As much as she enjoyed the ranch, she couldn't stay forever. There was a whole world to see, and more stories to tell.

Why, then, did Ed's story feel so very important? Even more overwhelming, why was *he* so important to her? The thought of leaving did more than raise her ire. It hurt her heart. And she wanted more than a gentle kiss on her forehead. More than his words.

In the solitude of that building, with dust motes floating in the quiet air, Molly realized at last that what she wanted most, what she could never have, was Ed himself.

"Oh, no," she whispered, covering her heart with one hand. As though that would keep her feelings at bay. "Heaven help me. I think I've fallen in love."

Her secret stayed there in the workshop, floating in the sunbeams, unheard by anyone but her own two ears. And that was how it had to stay.

CHAPTER 15

S aturday came again, which meant Molly sat in front of her typewriter with her notebook open on the table. The machine waited for her to interpret her jotted notes into something worthy of publication. She'd found herself stuck on the explanation of the way animal life on the ranch interacted with people. She hadn't met with any truly wild creatures. She'd been told the ranch was too high in elevation to worry about scorpions and that it was the wrong season to find tarantulas roaming about. While this relieved Molly, readers often enjoyed the mention of dangerous encounters with creatures. Even small things that made them squeamish.

Though not one to give up, Molly knew when to take a step back and try something else. She rolled the sheet of paper out of her typewriter and tucked it into the bottom of her stack. She gave the pile of paper a pat and reminded herself she'd already written quite a lot that morning.

Encouraged that she might yet do more, Molly selected another blank sheet.

She rolled it into the machine and stared at the page, giving herself over to deep contemplation. Her fingers grazed the keys of her typewriter. She took in a breath. Turned the page in her notebook and read what she had written about the way the ranch communicated with the outside world.

Letters, retrieved by neighbors. Messages of importance brought by a courier. Considering how frequent and with what speed the Royal Post delivered mail in London, her readers in England would find the system used in Arizona antiquated.

She lowered her hands to the table and tapped her fingers against the wood. What else could she include in this particular report? Mail delivery was a rather dull subject. Unless she included a story of what such a delay could mean to a person living in the far reaches of the desert hills, what did it matter?

She hadn't run out of things to say about the ranch or the people in it. But she'd certainly found it difficult to make her experiences relevant to her readers in England. Perhaps she could consult with someone on the ranch. Maybe Evelyn. Or Frosty. Or her favorite of them all, Ed.

Without meaning to, she conjured up an image of the cowboy on the day they'd ridden out to the hidden springs. He'd charmed her quite easily with his easy smile and warm brown eyes.

Could she really be in love? Only a day had passed since she'd spoken the words aloud. A day and night of trying not to think on it. Then denying it to herself.

A fortnight wasn't long enough to fall in love, surely.

They had grown close since their initial meeting, of course. Even their shared kisses, which she'd worried would ruin their budding friendship, hadn't hurt the easy companionship she found with him. And friendship didn't seem an adequate word for what she felt for him.

But love?

Maybe she'd been sitting still too long.

Molly rose from her chair and stretched, hands overhead and then out to the sides. She'd once written a report on calisthenics and its place among both elite sportsmen and school children. Perhaps she needed to go through a few of the drills she'd learned.

Or maybe she needed some fresh air. That was more appealing than exercise. The room had grown quite still and stale. Yes, fresh air was the ticket.

She opened the window above her makeshift desk and leaned out to draw in a deep breath. She let her eyes sweep across her now-familiar view of the ranch. The Morgans' house, though enough apart from the others to give the family some privacy, commanded an excellent view of the outbuildings and animal pens. It was the perfect house for a foreman to keep watch even on days when he sat on his porch.

Which Frosty didn't seem to do all that often, actually. The man certainly worked hard.

A breeze caressed Molly's cheek, and she sighed happily. Yes, fresh air. That was all she needed. But when she drew back into the room, it was as still and warm as before.

Her eye caught the window on the other end of her quarters. Opening that one, she'd be more likely to catch a cross breeze that would cool everything down. She strode across the wood floors, came to the other window, and pushed it open. Immediately, a gust of cool air rushed by her and into the house.

Molly closed her eyes and let the wind brush across her features, tease at her hair, and dance past her. She opened her eyes to smile up at the distant mountains and the sky dotted with tiny white clouds. Though she wouldn't want to stay in the desert forever, Molly well understood the people who loved it enough to live out their lives beneath the vivid blue sky.

A rustle of paper caught her ear. Frowning, Molly turned to see what had caused the noise—

The wind picked up paper from her carefully piled stack, several sheets at a time, and propelled them out the window like stringless kites. Out they went, one after another, as she ran across the room, shouting at the objects as though they might develop the ability to heed her commands.

"No! No, no. Come back! Stop that!" She tripped over the woven rug, stumbling several steps, until she caught herself on the edge of the table and sent the remainder of her work scattering onto the floor.

On the floor was better than out the window.

She slammed the window shut, then ran out of her room as fast as she could. Down the steps, past a startled Laura and Maddie, through the parlor room—where Evelyn stepped out of her way with a startled yelp and hand to her abdomen—then out the front door.

She shouted over her shoulder an inadequate, "Sorry!"

A better apology would come later. At the moment, she had to save her work.

ED TRUDGED TOWARD THE MORGAN HOUSE, THEN TURNED TO WALK back to the adobe bunkhouse. Then changed his mind again, turning on his boot heel so sharply he left a hole in the ground. Then stumbled when that hole tried to keep him in it.

Anyone watching would've thought him a fool for certain. But it wasn't entirely his fault if his thoughts were addled of late. He couldn't stop thinking about a certain lady journalist living in the foreman's house.

Every time Ed got within arm's length of Molly McKinney, he wanted to scoop her up in his arms and hold her there, where she'd be safe and snug with him. The ridiculous urge meant he tried to stay at least six feet away from her as they went about the ranch.

That plan didn't always work out. It couldn't, when so much of the work they did required close quarters. He'd hold a calf for her to inspect. They'd both bend over a dry creek bed to note animal tracks, and he'd trace the line of a coyote's paw print while she sketched exactly what it looked like in her notebook.

At least they had other people around, most of the time. That kept him from making too big a fool out of himself. But yesterday, in the shed, he'd nearly wrapped her in his arms and kissed her senseless. It had taken more restraint than he liked to limit himself to the single kiss on her brow.

His chest warmed thinking about that innocent brush of his lips against her skin.

He started forward again, this time clutching the book he held in both hands. It wasn't a very large book, or an important one, but it was the reason for his hesitation. He'd brought the book with him to share it with Molly. He wanted to make a friendly gesture. Nothing more.

Well. Maybe he wanted an excuse to speak to her on a day he otherwise didn't expect to see much of her. Even if she had asked to come to dinner in the bunkhouse again that evening.

A meal he both looked forward to and dreaded. The convoluted thoughts made him stop in his tracks again, but this time, he growled at himself and kept going.

"I'm making more out of this than what it is," he muttered. He raised his head to look up at her open window, where he could see the black rectangular shape of her typewriter. But he didn't hear the clatter of the keys from this distance, nor did he glimpse her at work.

Maybe she was taking a break. Which meant he wouldn't be interrupting anything if he asked her to speak with him a moment. Just long enough to remind her about dinner. And show her his work. Or at least offer to show her.

But what if she didn't like it?

He stopped walking again and took a deep breath.

He could handle a rejection of his writing. He'd shored himself up against it over time. But...he really wanted her to like it. To see something in his words, in him, that would maybe make it difficult to forget him when she went away.

He wouldn't forget her.

Every time their arms brushed, their fingers collided over the work, or he helped her onto the back of her mule, he experienced a fizzle of electricity. It would shoot straight from the place where they had connected directly to his heart and make his stomach flip and his head grow light. Or some combination of those things.

If she felt the same, he couldn't say for certain. She blushed, sometimes, when he stood near. But he could reasonably blame that on the heat.

With each passing day, he cared for her more. Telling himself over and over that they were friends, that they could only ever be friends, was his only defense against feeling a world full of pain when she finally left.

He glanced up at the window when he sensed movement from it—a flash of white. But it wasn't Molly returning to work.

It was a cascade of paper flying out of the second-story window and into the desert air, fluttering like a flock of birds intent on escape.

Ed tucked his book into the back of his trousers, counting on the belt he wore to keep it in place, then ran as fast as he could to snatch the papers before they could fly south for the winter. He went after the closest piece first, snatching it from the grass, then went after the other tumbling sheets as they danced farther and farther from reach.

As he raced along the ground after the typewritten pages, he hoped someone closed the window before too many of them escaped. Molly appeared beside him, as though from nowhere, her hands snatching up her work quickly. They didn't say a word to one another until they'd gathered up all the paper in sight.

Panting, Molly held her rumpled work to her chest and looked up at him with wide eyes. "Did we get them all?"

He stretched as tall as he could to look around, then back to the house. The window looked shut. The two of them had run at least a hundred and fifty feet from the front door of the place. "Looks like it."

He looked down at her, noting her flushed cheeks and the tendrils of hair dancing along her neck in the breeze. She grinned at him. "Thank goodness you were here. I would've had to run a lot farther if you hadn't caught most of them already."

Ed held the sheaf of paper out to her, and the air licked at the edges as though threatening to take them on another ride through the field. Molly accepted his bundle and added it to hers, both arms wrapped tightly around the haphazard stack.

"I'm glad I came along when I did." Ed suddenly didn't know what to do with his hands, so he hooked his thumbs through his belt loops. Then pulled them out again to cross his arms over his chest. "Do you want help carrying it back?"

"No, I think I have it now. Thank you." She looked to the house, then to the rest of the ranch's buildings. "What are you doing all the way out here, anyway? Looking for Frosty?"

"No, ma'am. I came looking for you." And once more, he doubted his reason for coming. "I wanted to—" Her put his hand back to where his leather notebook ought to press, only to realize it was gone. He nearly swore, then turned and started searching the dirt for the book. "I must've dropped it while we chased the paper."

"Oh dear. What did you lose?" She walked ahead of him, her gaze sweeping the dirt and grass. "I'll help you find it."

"A book." He took in a deep breath. "Shouldn't be too hard to spot. Anything with a straight edge sticks out in the desert. I just wish it wasn't brown. That'd make things easier." He sent her a grin, then let his eyes pick through the grass and ground ahead of him. "It'll be easiest if you follow behind me and keep an eye out. I can retrace my steps."

"How?" she asked, sounding curious rather than disbelieving. "There was no rhyme or reason to our running about like a pair of mother hens." She glared briefly down at her armful of paper, rather as though they were unruly chicks.

She was adorable. But he couldn't let himself admire her overlong. That made things dangerous.

"My grandfather and father taught me about tracking. Then I met a Hopi scout a few years after I came to the ranch. He helped fill in the gaps for the desert. But the principles of tracking are pretty much the same wherever you go. And finding a man's boot print—" He pointed down at his footwear. "—is easier than finding a squirrel in the snow."

"Fascinating. Have you had much reason to track men instead of animals?"

"Nope. Usually, I'm looking for animals." He found his heel prints easily in the dirt, and the grass he'd stepped on was severely crushed. His grandfather would shake his head at the ease with which a cowboy boot could be traced through the landscape. But when Ed found his notebook slipped sideways between tall stalks of grass, he was grateful.

He scooped up the book and turned around, holding it out in triumph.

"Bravo." Molly grinned at him and tried to shuffle her papers at the same time. "What sort of book is it?"

"My notebook."

Her eyebrows shot upward, and she gave him her full attention. She tilted her head the way she did when she had a question but thought it polite not to ask for more. Her eyes glowed with curiosity. It was a familiar expression by now. And he found it charming.

He looked at the papers still sticking out of her arms at odd angles. "Are you sure you don't need help carrying those?"

"I think it best I don't release them until I am safely indoors. Although I would appreciate your assistance with something." She looked down at the sheaf in her hands and sighed. "It will be rather like putting a puzzle back together. I don't number my pages until I am ready to send them in, so everything will be jumbled together. If I read through them, it will be much easier to return this mess to order. Do you think you have time to help with that?"

"Sure." Ed looked back at the Morgans' house. "If Evelyn doesn't mind my intrusion."

Molly's nose wrinkled, and she nudged him playfully with her elbow. "You know quite well she is an angel. I am willing to wager she will ply you with biscuits and lemonade, or tea, or whatever drink you prefer."

They walked the rest of the way back to the house together. Molly explained how her desire to clear the air had led to the unexpected exercise of chasing her work down, and he couldn't help but laugh as she recounted her flight through the house to save the escaped paper. She grinned right along with him, cheerful as ever. They were both in good humor when they walked through the front door.

Evelyn Morgan was seated in a rocking chair near the window, embroidering a piece of clothing that looked too tiny for even the tiniest of humans to wear. Did babies really come in such a small size? Ed hadn't had much call to be around little ones. Even Mr. Bolton's new baby, though the proud father had shown her off to his men one evening about a week after she came into the world.

She'd been as small as a doll, with a round little face, all wrapped up in blankets. The first sight of her had made Ed think of the nieces and nephews he'd yet to meet back in Oklahoma. Had they been that small when his sisters had brought them into the world?

He needed to return his mother's letter with one of his own. But his heart had started to tug him in two directions. Back to his family's farm and here. At the ranch. But not entirely because of his job.

After Molly explained her situation to Evelyn, her words leaning heavily into the difficulty of putting everything back in order, she asked if Ed might stay to help her organize her work.

"Of course." Evelyn didn't even hesitate to answer. "Ask the girls to bring their game in here, so you can have the kitchen table to yourself. I imagine that would be better than trying to work anywhere else." Her well-educated accent always made it easy for Ed to picture her as a fine lady. Even when she talked about kitchen tables.

They settled at the table in short order, and Molly laid out the mess of crumpled papers on its surface. She sighed and started spreading them out. "I don't put different stories on the same pages. That will be somewhat to our advantage. I think there are three here. One about the children on the ranch, so anything that mentions children and their family we can put in one stack. There's another about the way women out here do and do not keep up with fashion. And the third is about the way young men enter the cowboy trade."

"I'm not sure I'd call it a trade." Ed sat down in the chair next to hers and took up a piece of paper. "It's more of a temporary career."

Molly shot him a teasing smile. "May I quote you on that?" She picked up a sheet of paper, and he watched as her lips silently moved, reading what she'd written. "Cowboys." She put the paper in between them.

Ed picked up another, skimmed through the words. "Children." He put it down, starting a new pile, above the first. They both read another and, at the same time, said, "Fashion."

Molly smirked and placed her sheet down first. "Thank you for your help, Ed."

"You're most welcome." He winked at her, then kept going through the half of the pile on his side of the table. They had it all sorted into the three categories quickly, then Molly assigned him the cowboy article.

"See if you can make sense of the order, won't you? It's about ten pages. I always start the new page on a new sentence, so broken up phrases won't be of any help."

For the first time, Ed was able to read her actual work. Even if he could only get snatches of it, reading the first and last paragraphs on each page. The paper she'd used was quite thin. If he held it up to the light, he could easily see through it. That probably made it easier to send stacks of it through the mail.

"It's called onion-skin paper."

He looked at Molly to find her watching him. She smiled and turned back to the paper in her hand. "All the newspaper reporters I met in New York City use it, so I decided I must as well."

"Do you like typing things out instead of writing your stories by hand?" He'd heard the noisy apparatus just like everyone else who came within twenty feet of the Morgans' house when she was using it. "I think the sound would drown out my thoughts while I wrote."

"It was certainly distracting the first time I tried one. But I was so excited to use it, I grew used to it. Now I find the typing almost soothing." She lowered the paper in her hand to meet his gaze, her eyebrows drawn together. "Sometimes I still write my thoughts out by hand, when the typewriter isn't nearby. Would you like to try my typewriter?"

Ed picked up another thin sheet of paper and shook his head. "That's not necessary. I'm sure I'd never need to use one. The way I write suits me fine." He glanced at the book he'd put on the corner of the table. Her gaze followed his, but she didn't mention his book. Though he could guess her curiosity was bubbling like a pot ready to boil over.

"If you change your mind, I'd be happy to let you use it. I quite love my typewriter." She gave her attention back to her work.

Ed made it through another couple of pages before he mounted up enough nerve to tell her the real reason he'd come with the book in hand. He needed to get it out before he talked himself out of showing her what he'd written. He cleared his throat.

Molly's hand stilled before it reached a new sheet of paper. "Do you need something to drink? I'm afraid I overestimated Evelyn's desire to serve you refreshments." Her eyes twinkled merrily. Neither of them had any intention of giving the expectant mother more work to do.

"No. Thank you." He tried on a smile, but given the way she tilted her head at him, he didn't look as relaxed as he meant to. "I wanted to tell you something."

Her eyebrows raised. "I'm listening."

If she had any idea how much her expressions spoke to him, she'd run the opposite direction. Ed felt like running sometimes. One look at a person shouldn't make a man go weak in the knees. "I brought my notebook because you seemed interested in reading it. Before. At the spring."

Her eyes rounded, and her lips parted as though she meant to say something, but she pressed them closed again. He could guess well enough that she'd swallowed whatever she'd wanted to say in favor of thinking her words through.

After a few quick blinks, she managed to say, "If you are comfortable sharing your stories, I would be delighted to read them. Even that single page I read intrigued me. But you needn't feel obligated to share."

"I'd like you to read it," he said quickly. Then he picked up the book and held it out to her, not willing to give either of them time to change their minds. "I'd like to know what you think of the whole story. What you think about any of them. You're the only writer I've ever met. Even though I don't intend to do anything with my stories, even though they're just for me, I'm curious if they're any good. If anyone else might ever think they're good."

The way her eyes brightened as she accepted the soft leather book made his heart turn over. "Thank you." Then she held the book to her chest, placing it over her heart as she met his gaze. "I know it takes a lot of courage to share this sort of thing with someone. Especially the first time. Thank you for trusting me. I truly look forward to reading anything you've written, Ed."

His ears warmed up, as did his chest, and he wanted to kiss her again. Instead, he turned quickly back to the papers on the table. "You're letting me read your work right now. Fair's fair, I s'pose."

"I suppose," she repeated, a touch of humor in her tone. Then she went back to work beside him. The two of them worked together in the quiet, and Ed felt happier than he had in a very long time.

DINNER IN THE BUNKHOUSE HAD BEEN QUITE THE OCCASION. MOLLY sat across the table from Ed, and Dominó dealt her into a game of poker. She'd never played before, and it seemed the cowboys had a secondary game going on of discovering who could help her the most without outright cheating.

They'd also told her about a mine Abram Steele and King Bolton had started during the early days of the ranch, but soon gave up on it when they realized their time was better spent on cattle. The defunct mine was situated two miles to the north, in the hills.

"May we go and see it?" she asked, looking at Ed with some excitement.

He considered the question. "It's not much more than a hole in the ground."

"If he won't take you, *Señorita*, I will." Dominó grinned and laid down his hand. He was the only one not interested in helping her win. When the other men saw his cards, they all groaned and slapped their own on the table.

"It's like you don't even want to give the lady a chance," Whiskers whined. He'd warmed up to her and didn't seem as shy as he had before.

Ed shot Dominó a glare, but whether it was over the cards or Dominó's invitation, Molly couldn't guess. She'd noticed Ed seemed more protective of her when she spent time with the other cowboys. Maybe Dominó had picked up on that, too, and meant to tease him. She didn't mind all that much, either, when Ed answered.

"Of course I'll take her. I've shown you everything else you wanted to see, Molly. I just don't think you'll find this trip all that interesting."

She picked up the new hand Dominó dealt in time to hide her smile behind it. Because the truth was that anything she saw or did with Ed in her company was interesting.

He walked her back to the Morgans' house with a lantern in hand. This time, they didn't stop to look at the stars. Or to exchange a kiss. Though she found herself wishing they would. All the way to the porch steps.

Frosty and Evelyn had left a lantern hanging on a hook by the front door, making it easier for her to navigate the steps in the semi-darkness. There wasn't any light in the front room, though she'd glimpsed a soft glow from the couple's bedroom window. She'd stayed out late enough that they'd put the children to bed and retired for the evening.

Which meant she didn't mind lingering on the porch steps, facing Ed and holding her shawl around her shoulders as they talked. "You really don't have to take me out to the mine. If you don't want to."

Every moment spent with him made it more difficult to deny the connection she felt between them. Her former headmistress would think Molly had lost all her sense, falling head over heels for a man she'd barely met. But she'd never met anyone like Ed. She'd never wanted anything the way she wanted his company. If he knew how she felt, would he run in the opposite direction? Warn her away?

Nothing about how she felt was ordinary. Nothing about *him* was ordinary.

He put his lantern down on the step, and he leaned against the porch rail as he answered. "I don't mind the ride out there. I'm happy to show it to you."

Gus had been sleeping on the porch when they arrived. The dog rose and went down the steps, yawning but demanding attention all the same. Ed reached down to scratch the dog behind his ears.

"You have been an excellent guide. And instructor." She watched his eyes as she spoke, taking in everything about him. She'd never met anyone who affected her the way Ed did. Every-thing about him, though not something that might stand out for others, made her lean into their friendship with greater trust. But it made her want more than friendship, too.

"I don't know about that. Just about anyone would've been the same, or better. Even Duke might've been more fun to follow around. He's got more enthusiasm for the work than people born to it, that's for sure." His easy grin made it easy to laugh, but she hastily smothered the sound with her hand over her mouth. She'd no wish to disturb any of the family in the house.

The dog huffed as though he wanted to remind her to keep her voice down, then went back up the steps to collapse again on the porch. Protecting his family.

"Lord Evan is rather enthralled by the life he leads here. Of course, I do think Dannie has something to do with that."

"Likely so." Ed leaned a little closer and lowered his voice. "I hear they're crazy for each other."

"It is rather delightful to see the two of them together. He tries so hard to dote on her, and she's always insisting on doing everything herself." Molly looked in the direction of their home, seeing nothing but dark shadows where she knew their house was situated. "They seem happy."

Ed spoke softly, matching her tone. "That sounded a touch wistful, Miss McKinney."

"Did it?" She released a sigh, then a soft laugh. "Oh dear. I do sound rather maudlin. I assure you, I am happy for them both. They are an inspiration for anyone who hopes to find love. Perhaps, someday, I'll find that too." Her heart squeezed painfully at her slant on the truth.

She had found love. But too quickly. In too strange a place. Far from England and in the middle of an important moment in her career. Could she give everything up for love, the way Duke had? Could she take a leap of faith like the former countess who had married a stranger?

Ed's next words he said softer still. "Someday might come sooner than you think, Molly."

She swallowed. Was it wrong that she hoped for another kiss?

Did it make her a bad person to crave something like that from him when she knew she must leave him behind? She hadn't any right to Eduardo Byrd. He had a life outside her visit, and a visit was all it could be.

Despite her troublesome thoughts, Molly leaned closer to him. "It might come for you too, cowboy. Any day now, some rancher's daughter might sweep you off your feet."

He chuckled. "Maybe. But I don't see it happening. Not with the ladies around here. They're too old, too young, too in love with someone else, or their parents would be upset if they so much as smiled at me."

They sounded like excuses to her. Excuses to not even try. And she didn't exactly mind, either. Jealousy was an unbecoming shade on anyone, and she certainly had no intention of wearing it.

"I think you could charm just about anyone you wished. Even a sweetheart's parents." Molly sighed and leaned back on her heels. All the talk of his imaginary sweetheart made it difficult to continue hoping for a kiss. "You have never said... is it possible you left someone to pine for you in Oklahoma? Perhaps that's the real reason none of the ranchers' daughters hold any appeal."

Though she couldn't imagine how a woman could let Ed go. Not any woman who had a real chance with him.

"I didn't leave any sweethearts behind," he said, expression sober. "Broken-hearted or otherwise." Ed offered a small shrug. "I was too young when I left to be thinking that direction. I wanted freedom and adventure. I want those things still." He turned his head away from her, working his jaw and allowing her an excellent view of his profile. "I had a letter from home. From my mother. She asked me to come for a visit."

The change in subject piqued her interest. "Oh? When does she want you to come?"

"She didn't say precisely. Just said they all missed me." Ed rubbed at his temple. "I haven't written back yet. That probably doesn't make me the best of sons." He shrugged, then grinned at her, the topic dismissed with that one expression that made her stomach forget it was a vital organ and not a butterfly net. "I'll take you to the mine on Monday, after chores. So we can both relax and rest up tomorrow. Maybe do some reading."

"Oh, I'll certainly be reading." Molly intended to read his stories. She would take the lantern up to bed and start that evening. "Thank you for your help earlier, with my papers. And for tonight, in the bunkhouse. And your book. And...well. Everything else."

"I'm always happy to help you, Molly. In any way I can." He spoke with such an earnest look on his face that Molly almost dismissed her earlier misgivings. He cared for her. She knew he did. Despite the differences in their stations and cultures.

He cared. But could he love?

She leaned in close and whispered, "You're a wonderful man, Eduardo Ramirez." Then she kissed him on the cheek. Not too quickly. She couldn't let him miss the deliberateness with which she placed the token of her affection on his work-roughened cheek.

Molly didn't wait for a response. She turned and marched up the steps, picked up the lantern from its hook, and went inside. She turned as she stepped into the house and caught him looking at her with something like awe upon his face.

She nearly ran back to him to do a more thorough job of wishing him goodnight. But good sense prevailed, and she closed the door between them.

When she climbed into bed, the lantern already placed on the small bedside table, she propped herself up with a pillow and opened Ed's notebook. Just a few pages before sleep. That's what she promised herself.

Yet as she read, his words drew her in, just as his soft smile and kind eyes did. Then the words took on a life of their own, pulling her deeper and deeper into each character. Molly knew what it was to be swept up in a novel, but this was different. In the stories she read, one spilling into another, she found something different. A mingling of hope and resignation. Heroes who existed in small and simple ways, yet stood tall when the time came to protect and act for what was good and just. The hours passed as she met and loved the people Ed had created and filled with life, and Molly didn't feel tired at all.

In truth, she had never felt more awake in her life.

CHAPTER 16

S unday, Ed kept away from Molly. In part because he dreaded hearing that she disliked his writing. Or, worse, that she'd tried too hard to like it when he had no talent for it. He also figured it wasn't the best idea to be near her while he struggled with the temptation to return her kiss, innocent as it was, from the night before.

Every time they touched, he wanted more.

That meant he was sitting in the bunkhouse, pretending to be absorbed in his book, when Cookie came in with mail he'd picked up the day before, in Tombstone. He'd taken his two days away from the ranch to enjoy the town and pick up supplies for the bunkhouse. When he walked in waving envelopes, Ed hunkered back down in his chair and ignored the others asking for news.

Which meant he nearly jumped out of his skin when Cookie slammed a letter against his book. "This came for you, Ed."

Having already received one letter from home that month, Ed hadn't expected another. Not unless it was bad news. Really bad news.

He snapped his book closed and tugged the letter out of its

pages. Then ripped it open. It was from his mother. And her words were brief.

Eduardo, your grandfather is ill. He has asked you to come to speak with him, as he wishes to see all his grandchildren. This is the third time he has had such an attack to his health in the year. Each time an illness like this comes, then passes, he is left weaker. Please come home for a visit. There may not be much time left to see him.

She hadn't sent a telegram. That meant something. She'd trusted he'd have time to receive a letter and make the journey home without arriving too late. But he couldn't delay more than a day.

And that was the moment he made his decision. He was going home. For how long, he didn't know. But he felt, deep in his heart, that he wouldn't return to KB Ranch anytime soon.

"Ed?" Dominó sat nearest, and when Ed looked up, his friend was watching him with a frown. "*¿Hay algo mal?*"

"*Sí. Es mi familia.*" Ed explained the situation quietly, and in Spanish. Dominó listened, but said nothing until Ed had finished telling him what the letter said. "I have to leave. Soon."

Dominó didn't even hesitate to nod. "When family calls, you go."

Ed rose from his chair. "I need to speak to the foreman."

"Frosty isn't going to stop you," Dominó said. "He will hurry you along your way."

"I know." And if Ed asked, Frosty would let him leave immediately. But...there was one more thing he wanted to do before he went away. He needed one last afternoon with Molly. One more moment, between just the two of them, before they said goodbye forever.

His heart cracked down the middle, and Ed rubbed at his chest in an attempt to soothe the pain. Then he released a sad chuckle. Strange. He'd thought she'd be the one to leave first.

He left the bunkhouse, only Dominó aware of the reason why. The others were busy. Reading. Playing games. Laughing. When Ed walked out the door, leaving the normal sounds of his life behind, he stopped in the dark shadows of the *zaguán* and leaned against the wall.

Five years. He'd spent five years on this ranch, working with Frosty, watching as cowboys came and went. He'd helped fight off rustlers, and he'd driven cattle to market for King Bolton. The KB Ranch had become his home.

And with his mother's request, he might not see it again. Ever.

Because the feeling in his gut told him he'd never be a cowboy again.

Ed gathered his thoughts and tucked them away. He'd worry about what Oklahoma meant for him later. Right now, he needed to speak to Frosty. Needed to get his plans ironed out.

He crossed the stable yard, then made his way to the Morgans' house. He tried not to look at the second-story window where Molly's papers had flown free the day before.

Only the day before? How had he spent so much time with her, how did he know her so well, when he could easily count the days since they had met?

He kept his head down and his eyes on the path his boots had to take to arrive at the front door. It'd be easier if he didn't let himself think about Molly.

He knocked, and then he waited.

Frosty himself answered, looking relaxed and happy. Happier than he'd ever been before Evelyn and the children had entered his life. The tall, lanky cowboy had everything a man could want. "Afternoon, Ed. Want me to fetch Molly for you?"

The foreman made the offer so easily, and Ed had a moment of chagrin. Everyone had to know how he felt about the English reporter. Even if they'd all cautioned him against developing feelings for her. When he shook his head in the negative, Frosty's welcoming expression faded.

"Is something wrong?" Frosty asked as he stepped onto the porch. He closed the door behind him. "You don't look so happy."

"I've had a letter from home." Ed shifted uncomfortably and lowered his gaze. "They're asking me to come back. My grandfather is sick, and he wishes to speak to me. They think this will be the last time I see him."

"I see." Frosty's hand abruptly grasped Ed's shoulder, startling him into looking up. "I'm sorry to hear that, Ed. You're a good friend, and I hate to see you upset. If you've got to go, you go. I'll make sure your pay for the month is ready for you first thing in the morning. I imagine you'll want to leave right away?" The blue-eyed cowboy had such an open, earnest expression that Ed couldn't doubt the sincerity of his friendship. "We won't hold you back for anything, Ed. But I promise, you'll always have a place on this ranch, so long as I'm foreman."

Gratitude tightened Ed's throat, and he had to swallow twice before he could speak. "I promised Molly I'd show her the mine tomorrow. I'd like to do that, if that's still all right with you. Then I'll leave in time to get to Tucson by sunset. It's only a small delay—"

"And you want to say goodbye as a man of your word." Frosty smiled with a knowing tip of his head. "We'll make it as easy on you as we can. Why don't you take the day off to prepare your things, say goodbye, and take Molly out to the mine? I'll help in whatever way you need."

"Could you not say anything about this to her yet?" Ed asked. "I'd like to tell her myself. Tomorrow."

"Sure." Frosty held his hand out, and Ed took it to receive a firm handshake. "You're a good man, Ed. And a good friend. This place won't be the same without you."

Ed nodded his thanks, his throat closing again. He backed up a step. "Working with you has been an honor. Thank you, Frosty. I'll always be grateful for your friendship, whether or not I'm cowboying for you."

When he arrived back at the bunkhouse, Ed didn't go into the main room. Instead, he went to the bunkroom. He had things to get in order before his departure. Laundry. Personal belongings to sort through. And if he focused on those tasks, he could forget, for just a minute, that he wasn't merely saying goodbye to his home. But also to the people he cared about, like a second family.

MOLLY TURNED THE LAST PAGE IN ED'S NOTEBOOK WITH A HEAVY sigh. In the one hundred pages of the book, he'd written seven beautiful stories. In each one, the hero had been an unlikely individual. A Mexican girl, an aimless drifter, a former slave, an Indian scout, an old Cherokee chief, a mother running a roadside inn, and a stable boy. They were all people with only one thing in common. They had good hearts. And in each tale, they overcame a hardship unique to them, with talents and goodness.

She closed the book and looked at the mantel clock. It was late. She'd had to take breaks between each story to think on them. To take meals. To see to her own needs. But she'd picked up the book with eagerness each time she came back to it.

"Was it a good story?" Evelyn asked from her place on the couch beside her husband. The two of them sat side by side, each holding a book. The children had gone to bed an hour before.

"Yes. Quite good." She hadn't told them where the book had come from. Only that a friend had gifted her some of their work. She'd been vague, to protect Ed's secret talent. Though now, she wondered if that was best.

Chris yawned and brought his fist up to muffle the sound. "Forgive me, ladies." He snapped his book closed. "Guess it's about time for me to turn in. What about you, Evie?" His arm went around his wife in a gentle hug. "You ladies going to burn the midnight oil? I can cook breakfast if you're up late."

The easy way Evelyn smiled at her husband made Molly's heart twinge with the smallest bit of envy. The two of them were obviously devoted to one another. Anyone with eyes could see their affection, and even more—their respect for each other.

"I think I need to turn in, too. The more rest I get now, the better." Evelyn's hand fluttered to her abdomen. She didn't need to tell them that there'd be no rest for her soon enough. "If you don't mind, Molly."

Molly rose and resisted the urge to stretch her arms above her head to work out the kinks that settled while she'd read Ed's book. "Not at all. I think I've stayed up late enough. And tomorrow promises to be a full day of work." She sent a grin at Chris, and the foreman's smile flickered in response.

He must be more tired than usual. He never neglected to offer a word of advice or tease her about her place as the new ranch hand. "Goodnight then, Molly."

She left the room first, Ed's book tucked up close against her chest. As she climbed the steps to the second floor of the little house, Molly turned over the words that had occupied most of her day.

The stories had touched her heart. They had made her consider the lives of people she otherwise had never given much thought to. For a short time, she had seen the world through the eyes of a Mexican girl weaving a blanket, and a Cherokee chief watching the world he knew change around him. She'd learned what it felt like to have people look upon her with suspicion, merely for the color of her skin. And more. So much more.

Ed had a gift with words. A gift that she might have envied once. She wrote facts. She told the truth and often had her words edited to make her stories more succinct. More interesting to the public. She gave information to her readers to know more about the world as it existed at that moment.

And Ed? He did something different. Something almost magical. His words, his fictitious tales of men, women, and children, would show people the truth in their own hearts and present to them what the world could be.

If he'd let others read them.

She closed the door behind her and looked about her room, her eyes lingering briefly on the shadow of her covered typewriter. The stack of paper beside it, weighed down with an old horseshoe Ed had given her, was quite small again. She'd bundled up most of her work and put it in a thick envelope, addressed to the New York newspaper that partnered with her London office.

There weren't many things left for her to do on the ranch. And she hated knowing the day to leave approached far sooner than she wished.

Molly placed Ed's book carefully on her makeshift desk, between her typewriter and the papers. Giving the cover a pat, Molly readied herself for bed. Her thoughts turned to the man she'd befriended. To Ed—Eduardo. It was a pity he didn't use his full name often.

As the one person who had read his work, the responsibility of encouraging him to share his talent and insight with the rest of the world weighed heavily on her shoulders. The world of publication was daunting and difficult, but Ed wasn't faint of heart. He had courage and determination. And so much talent.

If anyone could face the gatekeepers of the press, it was Eduardo Byrd.

Regret plagued her heart for leaving with the knowledge that she must leave him behind soon. What choice did she have? Her soul wasn't ready to settle, her feet planted in the dirt, when there were still so many adventures on the horizon. There was still so much world to see.

Someday, she would put her trunks in an attic and let them collect dust. She'd have a garden to tend and a cat to curl up at her feet while she read novels and newspapers. And she hoped someone would be there with her. Someone like Ed.

Her heart gave a painful throb, and she realized she had started crying when a tear ran down her cheek. She had let herself fall in love with him. If the thought of leaving him behind hurt this much, what would the actual moment feel like?

Molly sat on the edge of the bed to plait her long brown hair, and she imagined what it would be like to have a home like this one. To sit the way the Morgans did, curled up together with books and a fire in the hearth. Children sleeping in the next room. It was a pretty daydream. And it was all too easy to picture Ed as the one beside her, writing in one of his books.

Turning down the lamp and sliding beneath the quilt, Molly tried to put everything from her mind. Especially her dwindling time at the ranch. It was better to think only on the next day and no further. How she wished he would kiss her one more time, but such a thing was unlikely.

At least she had him all to herself in her dreams.

CHAPTER 17

I t didn't matter that the sky promised a beautiful start to the day. Storm clouds hovered in the back of Ed's mind. Because Ed knew by the end of the day, he'd be gone from the ranch. Leaving Arizona Territory and friendships he'd made in his time as a cowboy wouldn't be easy, but he'd manage. That was just the way of things. He'd said goodbye to a lot of people over the years, and sometimes it was easier than others.

What might have made it worse that morning was that only one person knew he'd be pulling up stakes before sunset. Frosty had promised to keep it quiet. Ed didn't feel like going through any fanfare. He'd say his goodbyes one at a time, nice and quiet, and then ride away. He'd only take one of his horses, and the ranch would buy the other two that were his from him.

And that would be the end of it.

The winds had changed for Ed, and he doubted they'd blow him back to KB Ranch anytime soon.

In the barn, he saddled up Chaucer first and then the horse he'd take back with him to his father's farm, Colonel. He'd keep his promise to Molly and show her the mine. He'd tell her goodbye while they were alone. Then he'd come back and say farewell to everyone else.

Colonel snorted as Ed cinched the belt running beneath the horse's belly. Ed gave the horse a pat. "I don't want to hear it from you today, boy. I've got enough on my mind." Molly's mule stamped impatiently from where he waited in the corridor of the stables. Ed smiled at the impatient creature. "We'll get going as soon as your Englishwoman comes out. I'm thinking she's enjoying her breakfast still."

He hadn't been able to eat anything that Cookie had put in front of him. But he'd packed up a fair bit of food in case he and Molly got hungry while they were out. Molly had praised the trail-cook's dinner two evenings before, which made it easy to get plenty of food out of the bunkhouse for a possible picnic.

"You make sure she gets all the corn muffins she wants, Ed," Cookie had said as he wrapped everything up in clean cloths. He'd sliced up smoked ham, cheese, and a large square of cake for them, too. "She works hard enough to have a good appetite on her. No use letting her waste away."

Molly had charmed all of the cowboys. Even Whiskers, who still blushed the moment she entered the room. Ed didn't blame them in the slightest. She listened to everyone with the same warm smile, eyes full of interest and responses thoughtful. She made people feel important when they talked to her. Like she really wanted to hear everything they had to say.

He loved that about her.

Just like he loved her smile, her pretty brown eyes, and her laugh. He'd do anything to make her laugh. He'd never hear that sound again after today.

Ed dropped his forehead onto his horse's saddle and closed his eyes. He took in several deep breaths, trying to sort out the familiar scents in an effort to calm himself. He couldn't start his ride with Molly, their last outing together, on such a rotten foot.

He smelled leather and horse. Hay and dirt. Scents that had been part of his life even before he left his father's farm. When he got home, a lot would be the same. There'd be more grass and trees, and wet earth instead of dry, but he'd be at home.

Nothing ever changed at home.

His heart squeezed painfully. He didn't want to go. But before Molly came, he'd not exactly wanted to stay in Arizona Territory, either.

Molly's sweet voice sang through the building. "Good morning, Ed."

A shudder went through him at the sound of her voice, along with a heat that started in his chest and worked its way quickly through the rest of him. He could smile. He'd focus his attention on her. Nothing existed outside of their time together.

He went to the stall door and leaned against it, folding his arms atop the wood. "Good morning, Miss Molly." He took in her sunny smile, the blue blouse she wore along with her split skirt and dust-covered boots. Her hair was in one long braid down her back, and she held her hat in both hands. "You ready to go look at a hole in the ground?"

She stopped in her tracks and raised her eyebrows at him. "This morning? I thought you'd make me do a whole list of chores before riding out there."

He grinned at her and tipped his hat farther back on his head. "I thought we'd have a little fun first. Chores can wait." Then he winked at her. "Chaucer's ready to go if you are."

Her eyes darted to her mule, then back to him. "Really? How clever of him, to get himself saddled and everything."

Ed chuckled and led Colonel out of the stall. "Mules are like that, I hear, when they're trying to impress a pretty girl." He caught her cheeks turning pink as he walked by her, and the sight made a new crack appear in his heart.

He shouldn't flirt. Not when he knew he'd be saying goodbye in a matter of hours. But knowing he had to leave—as much as it hurt—also set him free in a way. No one could say anything about him leading her on. Or acting in a way that was harmful to either of them. He'd leave. That would be the end.

He really hated endings.

Ed helped Molly mount after they'd left the barn. She

grinned up at him from Chaucer's back. "This is wonderful. I much prefer riding out before the sun is high overhead. It's far cooler at this time of day."

"Yep." He mounted Colonel. "And it's not a bad distance from here, either." He led them out through the adobe building's corridor and back out into the sun. The mine was at the north end of the valley.

"Thank you for this, Ed." Molly rode alongside him, her face turned up to the bright blue sky. "I know there are mines still in operation all over the Territory, but it will be interesting to see one that has been abandoned. I've been thinking of writing a piece about what the land looks like when people leave it behind."

Much like he was about to leave everyone behind. Including her.

Ed had to swallow back the taste of loss before he could respond. "People don't tend to leave a lot out here. There was a township that King and Abram started out at the mine. Did anyone tell you that?"

"No." Her eyebrows went high. "What happened to the people who lived there?"

"A couple of them bought ranches and still live nearby. Most just packed up their gear and went on to the next mine, card table, or saloon."

"Is there a ghost town there?" she asked with obvious eagerness.

"Nope. Wood is too precious in these parts. When people leave, if they don't take the wood with them, someone else comes along and picks a building apart. I think one of our barns is made from wood reclaimed from the site. Frosty came to work around the time they were pulling things down, and then I showed up a couple of years later."

"They just take whole houses apart?" Molly shook her head. "That seems like a lot of effort."

"It's cheaper than hauling new wood out from one of the

mills. Folks get mighty thrifty when they live far from civilization." He wouldn't be all that far from big cities, large townships,
and the like fairly soon. Kansas City wasn't far from his parents'
home, and Tulsa was even closer though not yet quite as large.
The roads were clear and wide, and trains ran several times a day
in that part of the world. People could get just about anywhere
they wanted in next to no time.

"That's fascinating. In England, even in cities with as many
modern adaptations as London, there are buildings that are
hundreds of years old that are never torn down. We merely
repurpose them. Take down old awnings, replace lost bricks. The
Tower of London still stands, and William the Conqueror built
that in the eleventh century."

"I hope someday people find things like that on this conti-
nent," Ed said quietly. "I've heard tell of cities carved into the
walls of canyons, but I've never been to see them myself. There
are mounds in Illinois that are laid out like city blocks, and some
people think they're what's left of ancient cities."

"Isn't it fascinating? I especially love places where the old and
the new come together."

For a time, they talked of history. She shared what she knew
of ancient European civilizations, things she had read in old
books, and discoveries that were made every time someone went
to dig in their back garden.

"Not every time," she insisted when Ed laughed about it. "But
it isn't all that unusual for someone to find Roman coins or old
pieces of pottery here and there."

"We find arrowheads all over my father's land," he told her.
"And old tools. Out here in the desert, sometimes we find old
wagons left where the wheels broke. People can't seem to help
leaving parts of their lives scattered everywhere."

"I always wish I knew the stories behind such things," she
admitted as she weaved Chaucer through a small patch of prickly
bushes. "Did the lost coins come from a king's immense wealth?
Were the arrows found from a battle or hunting expedition?

Perhaps a family had great hopes of coming west, and when their wagon broke, they disappeared and turned back."

Ed didn't even think before he said, "That's one reason I enjoy writing. I can tell the story the way I hope it actually happened."

Molly's eyes widened and her smile became enthusiastic. Her words tumbled from her lips at a speed he hadn't heard from her before. "Oh, Ed, I love your stories. I have been waiting for the right moment to bring them up. I know not everyone wishes to speak of their writing, but I absolutely must tell you how beautiful I found your words. Everything you wrote was incredible. The story of little Pedro saving his brother from a bandit? And the Mexican blanket! I wept right along with Maria. Then there was that chief—Silver Bear—I thought him so noble and brave, to stand up to his own people as he did. I completely agreed with him that the old ways ought to be saved even as new ways are learned."

He stared at her as she spoke, and their mounts slowed to a stop as neither of them pressed the animals up the rise in their path. Molly had gestured with one of her hands as she talked about each of the stories he had written with familiarity, as though she had memorized every detail. Hope built inside him. She couldn't mean it, surely.

Except Molly glowed with her honesty. "Ed, your writing is wonderful. I fell into each story and hated coming out again. You have a storyteller's gift, and it's incredible."

Nobody had read his stories before. He'd written things for school as a kid, of course. And he told his family and friends stories of things that had really happened. People said he had a knack for that kind of thing. For making people feel like they were actually present.

But this was different. This was Molly, a woman who made her living with words. Someone who had devoted her life to reading and writing. Ed watched her carefully, searching for any hint of insincerity. "You enjoyed them?"

"More than enjoyed them, Ed," she said immediately,

reaching across the open air between them to place her hand on his arm. "I loved them. After I finished each one, I had to think about them. Devouring them in my mind and heart to understand them fully. There was so much. If you don't mind, I would like to read them again. But if you need your book back—"

"No," he said immediately, shaking his head and covering her hand with his. "I don't need it back. Once I've written everything down, I don't go back to them. Not often, anyway. You can keep it."

She withdrew, her eyes large as dinner plates. "I couldn't! Ed, they're too wonderful. In fact, I think you should have them published."

Despite the growing heat of the morning, Ed's blood turned cold. "Published?" He shook his head. "I already told you. I've no interest in that." He looked away, to the hill in the distance. "We're nearly to the mine. We shouldn't stop." He nudged Colonel forward, and a moment later Molly and her mule had caught up.

"Are you angry with me?" she asked, voice small and uncertain.

"I couldn't be angry with you, Molly." He couldn't even imagine it. He cared for her too much. "But I'm not interested in letting anyone else read what I've written."

She was silent for a long moment, then asked the single-word question. "Why?"

Why, indeed. He'd written in notebooks for years. The need to fix old stories had started it, then the desire to write down the stories he wished existed in the world kept him going. They were for him. Stories he wanted to see told. But he didn't need anyone else to see them. Why would anybody else care?

"They aren't great stories, you know. They're not important, either. Not adventures, like Mark Twain or H.G. Wells writes. They aren't even like what other American authors write. Henry James, Herman Melville, Nathaniel Hawthorne. The closest thing I've found to them is the *Adventures of Joaquín Murieta*." He shook his head. "And they don't deserve to be mentioned in the same breath."

"I'm not familiar with that story," she admitted, sounding confused.

"It's about a bandit from Mexico, and a Cherokee wrote it." He remembered when his grandfather had handed him that book, proud to show him that Cherokees could have a voice. Even if it was only an old dime novel, the cover half-torn and the pages loose. Another truth escaped his lips. "It might've been reading that novel, over and over again as a kid, that made me want to come out west to begin with."

They had crested the last hill between them and the old mine, but Molly wasn't looking out at the view or the large hole in the side of the hill. She was staring at Ed, her whole body angled toward him, her brown eyes amber-colored as they burned with her thoughts.

"Words have power, don't they?" she said, her tone soothing. "They made me want to travel across an ocean, to find them and share them with others. They make people pack their bags and journey west to look for a new life. They bring hope to children who live in dark houses with few kind words. They set people free from drudgery and despair. Words educate, but they also give hope to so many. You have the ability to do that with your work, Ed. I know it. I felt it with every single page of that notebook."

He swallowed and shook his head. "They aren't for anyone else, Molly. I wrote them for myself."

"You shared them with me."

"Yes, but you're different. I could share anything with you." But he didn't say more or delay long enough for her to ask. He gave Colonel a good kick to his sides and his horse trotted down the hill, then lengthened his stride to gallop to the opening of the now defunct Coin Toss Mine.

Ed wouldn't outrun the explanation for long. Because Molly would want to know what he'd meant. And she deserved to know, too. But how did he tell her he'd fallen in love with her? Despite everything that stood between them—race, class, education, and the distance that must inevitably come between them. A cowboy from Indian Territory couldn't hope to be with a reporter from England. No matter how much his heart wanted her.

ABRAM STEELE HAD NAMED COIN TOSS MINE AFTER HE WON THE coin toss that determined where he and King would start digging. The two of them had hired miners and others to come out and continue the work while they raised their families and their cattle. They'd never made a fortune, but what they had pulled out of the ground had come in handy a few years later when the worst droughts anyone had ever seen nearly wiped out all the cattle in Arizona Territory. Ruthie had told Molly the story a few days before, while Molly helped her in the garden.

Ruthie had answered enough questions about the mine, and then Abram had confirmed the details, so Molly didn't have a lot to ask of Ed when they dismounted outside the yawning opening of the man-made caves.

Which meant her mind focused more on what Ed had almost said than it did on the timbers holding up both rock and dirt on either side of her.

Ed pulled a lantern out of his saddle bag and had it lit before they stepped inside. He held it up high and walked silently inside, with Molly behind him. Seeing him like that, leading the way with the light dancing across his handsome features, Molly could only think of one thing. The first time they'd kissed in the lantern-light.

She'd thought, when they first met, that Ed didn't want anything to do with her. Perhaps he'd even found her nosy and annoying. Then he'd saved her life, and Molly had been certain he'd think her unlucky and perhaps even a danger to herself and others. Instead, he'd taught her everything he knew about the ranch. He'd let her try her hand at anything she wished. He'd never mocked her when she made a mistake, only offered kind correction or advice.

And he'd grown to trust her. Enough to show her pieces of himself that no one else had ever seen. And she'd lost no time at all falling head over heels in love with him.

Perhaps it was time to tell him the truth of her feelings. She couldn't hold them back forever, could she? What would Ed think when she told him the truth? She hadn't any idea what might come next. Nor would she know, until she confessed her feelings and found out if Ed might feel the same.

Their footsteps echoed off the walls as they went deeper, and Molly forced herself to take note of the walls they passed. The mine didn't look like much. And her impatience with her situation grew. She looked over her shoulder, seeing the mine's entrance as a tiny bright spot in the dark behind him.

"Ed?" She pushed her hat off her head, letting it fall against her back while the leather strap around her neck kept it in place. She didn't exactly need it, given there was no need to shade her eyes from the sun in the mine.

He stopped walking, and she saw the shadows dance down his throat as he swallowed. "Is it everything you hoped it would be?" he asked, voice strangely hoarse.

"No," she admitted, the word hardly loud enough for her to hear. "What did you mean when you said I was different? You said you could share anything with me. Why?"

A timber in the side of the mine shaft protruded near his elbow, a long hook set inside it. He hung the lantern there. Then he turned and took off his hat, rolling the brim in his hands. He raised his gaze to look past her, over her shoulder, and into the darkness. "It doesn't matter what I meant. But there is something I have to tell you, Molly. And it's not easy to say."

A pounding rush filled her ears, so like the sound of the flash flood he'd saved her from that she put a hand over her heart to still the memory, only to realize it was her own heartbeat that made the sound. Whatever Ed was about to say, she knew it would sweep her up the way the flow of water nearly had.

"I'm listening," she whispered. The lamplight only revealed half his face, and she studied each line of him with hope. If he confessed his feelings for her were the same, nothing else would matter. They could sort everything out later.

"I'm going back to my family's farm."

Her heart stuttered, and the flood of hope stopped as though it had hit a canyon wall. "What?"

"My mother sent for me. My grandfather is sick. They've asked me to return, and I'm leaving tonight for Tucson. I'll take a train to Oklahoma Territory, to Tulsa, and then I'll be with my family. As long as they need me."

Molly sorted through his words, shaking her head slowly as she tried to find one good thing in them. "Tonight? But—does anyone else know?"

"Frosty. And King, by now. It's my family, Molly. I must go."

She could understand that much. But... "You're going to leave, just like that? Right now, today?" She looked around them at the darkness. "And you are telling me this in the middle of a *mine*?" She scoffed and stepped away, ready to leave him in the dark and find a better answer for her questions out in the light of day.

Ed caught her arm gently and tugged her back to him so they stood face-to-face and boot-tip to boot-tip. "I wish I didn't have to go." The light from the lantern shone gently on his face, and Molly saw new lines etched where she hadn't noticed them before. Lines of pain. "If I could stay here on this ranch with you, I would. But I can't, Molly. I've felt this coming for a long time. I knew I would leave, even if I didn't want to admit it to anyone. Especially myself. But it's time."

Tears blurred her vision, and Molly did her best to blink them away. He was telling her goodbye, when she'd been ready to confess her whole heart to him. It wasn't fair. Why had she met Ed only to lose him so soon? He was the beginning of the best story she'd never heard, and she wanted to know the ending.

But it wasn't to be.

Ed's hands drifted from her shoulders down her arms, to her wrists. With great care, he pulled her closer and wrapped his arms around her. Holding her close. Molly leaned into his embrace, though she kept her hands tucked against his chest. With her cheek against the buttons of his shirt, she inhaled deeply. Her whole body trembled with regret.

"I'm grateful I met you before this happened," Ed whispered into her hair, his lips brushing her forehead as he spoke. "You are like no one I've ever known before. I wish I had more time with you."

If only she could tell him how much she wished for the same. Were they always meant to part? If he hadn't needed to leave, she would have. Especially when they had no ties to one another. Only a few stolen kisses. A shared story or two.

"Oh, Ed," she whispered. She couldn't stop the tears from falling down her cheeks. "I know how important your family is to you. I wouldn't dream of saying anything against your going to them."

His arms tightened around her. Had she said the right thing?

"Thank you." He leaned back just enough for her to tip her chin up and meet his gaze. She'd been ready to march right out of the mine and leave him behind a moment before. Now, she wanted to linger as long as possible. The moment they stepped out of the mine and into the light, it would be over. Everything between them would fade away, like a quilt left too long in the Arizona sun.

"I should be the one to say that." She put her hand on his face, running her thumb along his well-defined cheekbone. "Thank you for teaching me so much and showing me everything. You made my time here quite wonderful."

One corner of his mouth went upward, and his eyes glittered down at her with emotion. "You weren't the best ranch hand I ever trained, but you're certainly the most intelligent. And the prettiest."

She laughed at his unexpected flirtation, then rose on her toes to kiss him. She'd only meant to press her lips near his, giving him a quick peck as a parting show of gratitude, but Ed had other ideas.

He wrapped his arms tight around her, pulling her so their bodies were flush against each other. And he met her lips with his own kiss—a long, lingering kiss that sent lightning bolts from the top of her head to her toes. Everything fizzled and grew hot. She closed her eyes and leaned into him, tasting him with full knowledge she would never do so again.

Molly needed enough moments with Ed to last a lifetime, yet she only had this one moment to get them. Because he hadn't said he loved her, and she wouldn't burden him with her admission. Not when he already had to lose so much, leaving one life for another.

Words were powerful. Even when they went unspoken.

CHAPTER 18

Goodbyes were never an easy thing to take part in. Ed and Molly returned to the ranch in a far more subdued fashion than how they'd left. She barely spoke to him. After he helped Molly see to Chaucer's comfort, she surprised him by throwing her arms around him in a last embrace. She'd squeezed tight, and Ed had wrapped his arms around her waist to return the gesture. If only he could hold on forever.

Molly stepped out of his arms with her gaze already averted. "I'll miss you," she said. And then she left the building at such a fast clip, he didn't dare call after her for fear it'd make her run all the faster.

Maybe he ought to be grateful that Molly stayed away as he said farewell to his oldest friends, especially when his heart broke the moment she disappeared from his sight. He accepted his last payment from Frosty, along with a letter of recommendation from him. Then he went to take leave of Ruthie and Abram. Ruthie insisted on packing him a basket of food for the train.

"I don't hold with the food they serve on those dust-boxes," she'd said as she wrapped bread in cloth for him. "And who knows what you'll find at those train-station restaurants. Food poisoning, most likely."

He accepted the basket along with her love, then went up to the main house to say farewell to Duke, Dannie, and the Boltons.

"What's the quickest way to Oklahoma Territory?" Duke asked as they shook hands. "How long will it take to get home?"

"Two days of train travel, I think. I'll sleep in Tucson tonight and board the train east in the morning." Ed accepted an embrace from Dannie.

"You're one of the best cowboys I've ever met, Ed." She stepped back and smiled at him. "Let us know when you've settled, or everyone here will fret about you."

"I'll send word," he promised.

Their kind wishes carried him out the door and to the bunkhouse, where he gathered what he didn't want to leave behind. He'd gifted most of his things to the other men, but had packed up a quilt his mother had made and his used notebooks.

Colonel didn't need his saddlebags loaded down with too much weight.

Ed mounted his horse and surveyed the ranch one last time. Five years of his life, he'd worked with the people and the animals on the land. He'd never forget any of it. And then he raised his gaze to the Morgans' second-story window.

He hadn't promised to write Molly. She hadn't made any promises either. And it was for the best. Why they crossed paths when nothing could come of it, he didn't know.

He should've asked her to wait for him, or to meet him some place in the future. That's what his heart wanted. But her dreams of traveling and adventure, her desire to write, were important to her. He'd never ask her to give that up to come with him. Or to be a farmer's wife. He didn't particularly want to be a farmer.

He'd liked being a cowboy, but that couldn't continue as he grew older and wanted more. Being near Molly had opened his eyes and his heart in ways he hadn't anticipated. And now he had to leave her behind.

His throat closed up, and he pulled his bandana up over his

nose and mouth. Then he rode out, not looking back. He kept his face forward, going to his family and an unknown future.

MOLLY HADN'T MUCH EXPERIENCE WITH THE CONCEPT OF BIDDING A permanent goodbye to anyone. There had been the headmistress of her boarding school when Molly left to find employment, but they had both been so excited that the occasion hadn't been marked with tears. Molly still wrote to old school chums, too. They left for marriages and family several years before Molly walked out the doors to become a writer for a woman's magazine.

When she'd arrived back at the barn with Ed, she'd seen to Chaucer's needs, given her cowboy one last embrace, and had dashed into the Morgan house before anyone could speak to her of the tears spilling from her eyes. She and Ed had said their goodbyes. She'd leave him to do the same with the others on the ranch.

She paced her room for what felt like ages. Then she tried to write, but wound up shutting her notebook and throwing it on her pillow. It landed with a hard *thunk*, hitting another book already at rest on the bed. Ed's book.

Molly lowered herself to the mattress and picked up the leather-bound notebook. She turned it over in her hands, then opened it to look at the looping handwriting. Her heart turned over, and her eyes prickled with unshed tears. Ed's words were beautiful. If only she could've made him see that before he left. Or talked him into publishing.

Or asked him to write to *her*.

What sort of a woman begged a man not to leave her behind, though? Molly hadn't ever begged a man for anything. Not even her job. Her stories, her words, stood on their own. And she wasn't about to wait for Eduardo Byrd or anyone else. Molly didn't wait on anyone. Because the news waited for no one.

She sniffled and tried to find her handkerchief in the top drawer of the little nightstand. Instead, she found the blue bandana Ed had given her the day they'd left Tombstone. She smoothed the fabric out in her lap. "This is ridiculous," she whispered. "We barely know each other."

But that wasn't true. They hadn't known each other for a long amount of time, but Molly knew Ed. She knew his heart.

She reached into the nightstand again, this time to take out the only possession she had kept with her all her life. The one thing she'd brought with her to the boarding house that had served as her home for most of her life. Her little golden locket.

She touched the delicately etched surface, then gently opened the heart.

Most people assumed lockets had pictures in them. Photographs, drawings, or even tiny paintings of people inside. But not Molly's. She had no image with which to remember her parents. Nor did she quite remember what they looked like. Her father had worn a large mustache. Her mother had brown hair and eyes like hers. But she remembered a far more important thing about her mother and father. She remembered how they had loved her.

She'd felt safe when they'd been near. Warm when her mother had embraced her. Happy when her father had tossed her in the air when he'd returned to their home—another blurred memory—at the end of the day. And she remembered her mother had gifted her this locket. Empty.

"Someday, you'll put the thing you love most inside," she had said.

The locket lay open in her hand. Empty. Without a story to tell.

She ran her thumb over the indent meant for a picture. Then she snapped it closed and put the locket around her neck. She hugged Ed's book to her one more time, then wrapped it up in the bandana.

A good reporter never left a story unfinished. They persisted until they had all the details. Until they knew the beginning, middle, and end.

And Molly prided herself on being the very *best* at her job.

CHAPTER 19

Ensuring that the porters loaded Colonel onto the train
properly didn't take long. The horse waited in a small
paddock with other animals taking the journey east with their
human counterparts. Ed had checked and double-checked the
tag on Colonel's lead to ensure it had all the right information on
it before he left, saddle bags over his shoulder and hat on his
head.

He went to the long, raised wooden platform where a handful
of others waited in the cool early morning air. The sun hadn't
risen high enough to make anyone uncomfortable. Yet. But Ed
shifted and felt like pacing anyway. He'd barely slept the night
before. All he'd thought about was a woman with brown eyes and
a smile that melted his heart.

He'd considered sending her a note. He'd written one out on
hotel stationary in his room, then crumpled it up into a ball.
Then he'd tried again. And again. And then he'd given up. He'd
need a whole book full of blank pages to explain himself to
Molly, ask her to forgive him, and ask her to maybe write him
back.

Better to leave. To let things stand as they had happened.
Even if it robbed him of sleep for years to come as he

wondered what life might've been like had he told her what was in his heart. Maybe she wouldn't think he'd gone crazy, falling for a woman he hadn't even known for a full month. Then again, she might laugh. He hadn't exactly considered that their exchanges didn't mean as much to her as they did to him.

If he had been the only one to fall in love, it was better this way.

A light touch to his shoulder pulled him from his heart-breaking thoughts. "I beg your pardon, sir. Is this the train to Oklahoma Territory?"

Time stood still, along with Ed's heart. His lungs tightened, and his mind raced. Everything in him said it was impossible. It couldn't be.

He slowly lowered his saddlebags from his shoulder to the ground, along with the small basket of food from Ruthie, and then turned around to see the most beautiful sight he'd ever beheld. A lady reporter stood behind him, wearing the same traveling costume he'd seen on her the first time they'd met at the fort, making her the very picture of an English lady. One corner of her mouth hitched upward, and her brown eyes glittered with mischief.

"Molly Elizabeth McKinney," he said, voice hoarse. "What are you doing here?" It wasn't what he wanted to say. He wanted to sweep her up in his arms and crush her to his chest and proclaim that he'd never, ever let her go again.

As though she sensed that, Molly's smile grew larger. "I'm following an important lead on a story, Eduardo Enoli Ramirez Byrd." She lifted her chin up and folded her hands in front of her. "I need to know how it ends."

Ed lowered his head a little, bringing them closer together. "What about the newspaper articles on the ranch? Do you know how those end?"

"Eduardo." She put her hands on her hips and batted her eyelashes at him. "I had everything I needed to write about the ranch after a week of being there. I stayed longer so I could get to know *you*, you ridiculous cowboy."

He didn't need to know more than that to swoop her up in his arms and kiss her. A kiss of hello and how are you, a kiss saying he'd missed her a year's worth in a single day. And she kissed him right back, even though they stood out in the open at a train station with a dozen others milling about.

Someone whistled, and good-natured laughter followed the sound. Train stations were a place of coming and going, of I-missed-you and don't-gos. When Ed stepped away, his gaze stayed glued to hers. "How did you get here?"

"Duke brought me in a wagon. I've already given the porter my trunk." She beamed up at him. "I left the ranch an hour after you did, but the wagon took longer than riding a horse, I suppose. I checked into a hotel so I could surprise you this morning, and Duke walked me to the station before he wished me luck and went back home. It was really quite sweet of him."

"I'll write him a thank you note later." He took her hand in his. "It's the best surprise I've ever had. But you can't really want to see Oklahoma, can you?"

"Of course I can. That's where your from, isn't it? Your family is there. Your home. I'd love to see all of it. Not that I expect you spend all your time with me," she rushed to add as her cheeks turned pink. "I know your family needs you first and foremost. I can keep myself busy until you have a moment free."

"How?" he asked, shaking his head. "There's not much for you to write about."

"I'll be fine," she insisted. "I can take care of myself. All that matters to me right at this moment is you."

That deserved another kiss, but after a quick glance around, Ed settled for tucking her hand in the crook of his arm. A distant whistle sounded, and they both turned to see the train coming toward them on the track. Steam hissed from the engine as it slowed to enter the station. "I guess we'll have lots of time to talk," he said, looking from the train to her. "It's a long way to

Tulsa. Then we take a spur line up to Claremore, and a short ride to my parents' home."

"I'm with you all the way." She squeezed his arm before leaning against his shoulder. "I couldn't imagine anywhere else I would rather be."

Ed didn't know if he was dreaming or not. She felt real. As he helped her step into the train, he didn't want to leave her. Not even long enough to grab their things where they'd dropped them. But he went back and nearly tripped all over himself, going down the train aisle to get back to her side. He tucked the bags and basket away, then sat down beside her and claimed her hand in his again.

Nothing about the two of them together made sense. But maybe they'd figure out a way around things together. Molly had a good head on her shoulders. And he loved her with his whole heart. He just needed to figure out if that was enough. If he was enough for her. And she'd given him the time and opportunity to put all the pieces together.

"I am so glad I'm with you," she said, her head on his shoulder, as the train pulled away from Tucson.

Ed's heart flipped and bucked like an unbroken stallion. "Me, too, Miss Molly." He kissed her temple. "Me, too."

Mrs. Byrd hadn't wasted a moment in welcoming Molly. She'd berated Ed for not warning them he had a lady with him, switching to Spanish while she told her son he needed to learn better manners, then back to softly accented English as she embraced Molly and led her away to a bedroom.

No one even questioned Molly's place among them, or why Ed had brought her to them. There were very few questions asked at all, which made Molly hesitate to voice her own.

They had arrived late at night, in a wagon Ed borrowed from the Claremore livery. Even if Colonel could comfortably carry them both to the farm, there were saddlebags and her trunk to see to. After two days of train travel, Molly sank gratefully into a bed that had belonged to one of Ed's sisters. The moment she closed her eyes, she slept deeply and comfortably until the next morning.

After Molly dressed, she left her room to walk down a narrow hallway toward the bustling sound of people starting a morning in a kitchen. As she walked along, her eyes took in details she hadn't noticed the evening before in her exhaustion. There were photographs hanging along the walls, interspersed with lovely bouquets of dried flowers, and an ornate crucifix which was itself a work of art.

Laughter erupted from the kitchen doorway, followed imme-diately by the sounds of several people hushing one another. Spanish words floated softly through the air, but Molly caught several of them, such as "la amiga bonita con Eduardo." *Eduardo's pretty friend.* Her cheeks warmed, but she didn't hide her smile.

The sun had only just turned the sky from pink to a gray-shade of blue. It was early, and the lamps around the kitchen made the room bright and warm.

"Good morning," she said as she crossed the threshold. "Mrs. Byrd, thank you so much for welcoming me into your home."

Ed's mother was possibly one of the most beautiful women Molly had ever seen. She'd thought so the night before, and thought it again when the woman turned from the hot stove with her arms spread in a welcoming gesture. "Oh, Miss McKinney, it is I who should thank you. You brought our Eduardo home safely."

Mrs. Selena Byrd could not have been over five feet in height, and she wore her long, shining black hair in a single braid down her back. Her eyes were warm and gentle, the same rich shade of brown as her son's, and she moved with an energy that women Molly's age would envy.

"I am afraid I cannot take the credit for that. I am more of a stowaway on this visit than I am a protector." She slipped closer to where Ed stood and wished she could slide directly into his arms to bid him good morning. But such a display of affection, with no understanding between them, wouldn't be appropriate in his family's home.

Ed and his father had been sitting at a little round table, but both rose when Molly came into the room. Ed's father was the tiniest bit taller than his son, but it was obvious at once that Ed took after him in nearly every way. John Byrd, half-Cherokee and half-Mexican by birth, dressed as every farmer she had met dressed. His black hair was shorter than Ed's, and his skin more coppery than tan. But they had the same cheekbones, the same nose, and the same sparkle to their eyes.

"A stowaway?" he said, slanting a look at his son, who smiled somewhat sheepishly. "I cannot think why anyone would want to follow this son of mine halfway across the country. Certainly not because of his looks. He takes too much after me."

His wife picked up a clean wooden spoon and shook it in his direction. "You know you are both too handsome for your own good, John Byrd. Stop teasing our guest."

"I don't mind in the slightest." Molly sidled up next to Ed, contenting herself with brushing her shoulder against his.

His eyes held warmth and a glitter of happiness in them as he whispered, "Good morning, Molly. I missed you."

Could a woman be so lucky as she felt in that moment?

"Pancakes all right for breakfast, Miss McKinney?" Mrs. Byrd's question kept Molly from responding to Ed's gentle admission.

"Yes, thank you. Please, call me Molly. May I do anything to help?"

"No, you are our guest, Molly." Mrs. Byrd waved her help away with the same spoon she'd shaken at her husband, then turned back to the stove. "Sit down. Tell us everything our son has been doing in Arizona. We can hardly get a word out of him."

Ed pulled a chair out for Molly to sit. "Mamá, I have given you all the answers I have. And I write to you all the time."

"A mother worries," Mr. Byrd said, a wide grin on his face. "Coffee, Molly?"

"Yes, please."

He walked over to a cupboard and took out a white mug, then swept a coffeepot off the stove. He kissed his wife before returning to pour Molly her coffee. "Honey or sugar? Milk?"

"A little milk, thank you." She held the steaming cup in both hands and looked around at the kitchen, marveling at how different and yet the same it was when compared to the kitchens she had sat in at the ranch. This kitchen was larger, with cupboards and shelves on every wall. There were cookbooks, pots, pans, and crockery everywhere. The walls were white-washed and spotless, the floors were wood-planked and polished to a shine. And—

"Is that an icebox?" she asked when Mr. Byrd opened one of the small cabinets.

"Sure is. Brought it home from the county fair last spring." He stepped aside to open the door fully to show her the shelves inside. "Butter, cream, and milk." He closed the door after retrieving the milk pitcher.

Only Ed seemed to realize that Molly was turning over a thought in her head that she didn't dare voice. He reached for her hand under the table and gave it a gentle squeeze. "I think Molly's wondering where you keep your tomahawk, Papá."

Molly gasped and gave Ed a sharp look. "I thought *nothing* of the sort!"

But Mr. Byrd and Ed were both grinning at her, and Mrs. Byrd came to the table to put a plate full of pancakes down with a hard *whack*. She put both hands on her hips. "You men are terrible. Pay no attention to them, Molly. This is one of their favorite games." She shook her head and muttered, "*Santos, líbrame de los hombres necios.*"

"Mamá, we are not that bad." Ed lowered his gaze to Molly's. "I'm sorry, Molly. It is a game, and I should've outgrown it by now. Sometimes, when people come to our home, they expect something that looks less like this. Less...civilized." He shrugged. "But the Cherokee have lived in Oklahoma for many years. We have the same farmhouses, the same businesses, the same schools as everyone else."

"Sometimes, I think your grandfather would have us all go back to living in lodges," Mr. Byrd muttered. "A house for winter and a house for summer." He served Molly first from the plate, then his wife, before filling Ed's plate and then his own.

"Are you and grandfather still feuding?" Ed asked, his smile disappearing. "I thought things were better."

"They were—they are," Mr. Byrd insisted. "You will see. After breakfast, we will go to his house. Which also isn't a lodge," he told Molly with a wink. "He lives in the cabin he built when he and my mother were married. It's on our land, on the other side of the creek."

Molly looked at Ed, then back to Mr. Byrd. "Thank you. I look forward to meeting him. But I promised Eduardo that I wouldn't be in the way while you tend to family matters, so my visit can wait. I know your father hasn't been well of late, Mr. Byrd."

"He was ill for a time," Mr. Byrd grew somewhat solemn. "He's on the mend now, and I know he would like to meet you, Molly. If Eduardo brought you all the way here, stowaway or not, you must be special to him. That makes you special to all of us, too."

Her cheeks must have been bright red, given how quickly she felt them fill with heat. "Thank you."

"We mean it, Molly." Mrs. Byrd put her hand on Molly's before taking her seat. They bowed their heads and said grace over the food, then ate. While Molly had kept her questions to herself, Ed's parents didn't mind peppering her with several. They asked about her purpose in their country, about her writing for a newspaper, then backtracked to her education and her family. Mrs. Byrd expressed her sorrow that Molly hadn't grown up with parents and siblings.

"It isn't all that terrible when you've known nothing else," she reassured the kind-hearted woman. "I never lacked for company or friendship, and my school teachers were kind. I can't imagine what it would be like to grow up in a home like this, with family."

"Sometimes, it was torture," Ed said with a heavy sigh.

"Eduardo." His mother narrowed her eyes at him. "I will tell your sisters you said that."

"Then the torture will really begin," his father said with an amused grin before he hid it behind his coffee cup.

When they had finished their meal, Molly again insisted on staying behind while Ed went to visit his grandfather, his own father with him. She went onto the back porch to bid them farewell and watched as he walked through the long green grass into a grove of trees, where she caught the barest glimmer of sunlight shining on water. Then he was gone from sight.

"Do not worry about him too much, *niña*." His mother came out onto the porch with her and gestured to the rocking chairs. "Would you like to finish your coffee out here in the fresh air?"

"That sounds delightful." Molly went back inside to bring her cup with her, settling into the chair as Mrs. Byrd took the one next to her. "You have a beautiful home."

"Thank you. We have worked hard to make it a comfortable place." Mrs. Byrd leaned back in her chair and set it to moving at a slow, steady rhythm. "My oldest daughter, Camila, has her own plans for the house when it is hers. I look forward to seeing how she makes it her own."

Molly stopped her chair mid-motion. "Your oldest daughter? Is she moving here?"

"Yes. Her house is smaller, and she has had her fourth child. We thought it best to trade. At Christmas time." Mrs. Byrd seemed cheerful until she saw the expression on Molly's face. "This confuses you, Molly?"

"Well. Yes. I thought—that is, Eduardo was so certain that you wanted him to come home to work on the farm. To live here, with you." He'd confided in Molly his concern about taking up farming, during their long train ride, and she'd listened with an aching heart. He'd spoken of the farm as though warning her, and perhaps he had been. He certainly hadn't seemed enthusiastic about the idea so much as determined. Perhaps even resigned.

Mrs. Byrd's forehead wrinkled, and she shook her head slowly. "No, we would not ask that of him. Eduardo has always been a good boy, a wonderful son. But he has never liked to farm. He is too adventurous of spirit. We know this." She looked up to the grove of trees where the men had gone. "I am certain his father and grandfather will set his mind right on the matter. Camila and her husband, they love the land and the farm. We thought to leave it to them someday."

"Eduardo thought he was coming here to stay," Molly said, her heart squeezing with concern. What would his reaction be when he realized that wasn't his family's intent? Would he return to KB Ranch and cowboying? Would she follow him again, if that was his choice?

Yes, her heart whispered. *The story isn't over yet.*

Molly said no more of her concerns. Ed and his family would talk. They would sort through things. And Molly would try her best to wait patiently. Because Eduardo was worth waiting for. Her newspaper editor might have to content himself with quite a few articles about Arizona and Oklahoma for a time.

"Mrs. Byrd, is there a place where I might set up my typewriter? I hate to be a bother, but my editor is expecting to hear from me soon."

CHAPTER 20

E noli Byrd, the first of his family to wed a woman not born to his people, looked smaller than Ed remembered. He stood to greet Ed and his father the moment they came within sight of his small porch. It really wasn't much more than a long overhang of roof and packed earth. And the older man had no reason to be outside, except that he enjoyed it.

He welcomed Ed with a warm embrace, and the old man's frame felt slight and delicate, even though he was still as tall as Ed. He spoke in his people's language—a tongue taught to Ed by his father and grandfather.

"Little Black Fox, you are here at last to visit. I have missed you."

"I missed you, Grandfather. I came when you asked." Ed sat down only after his grandfather retook his seat, searching the old man for signs of illness.

"I must seem very old with my gray hair. I walk with a cane now." He gestured to the doorway, where a long polished stick leaned against the wall. "I still believe I have many years left on the earth."

Ed's father chuckled. "You are stubborn enough to outlive us all, Father. But your illness worried us."

The wind came through the trees and danced across the porch, laughing along with the old Cherokee as he settled deeper into his chair. "It is good to keep the younger generation alert. I am well now. And I am glad you have come, Black Fox."

Enoli, the second name Ed's mother had given him, was an Anglicized version of his grandfather's Cherokee name, which meant Black Fox. His grandfather had chosen his name but consented to Ed receiving it as a gift at his birth.

"I am here as long as you need me, Grandfather," Ed promised with his whole heart, even though so much of it belonged to Molly. Their days together on the train had proven the best of his life. They had talked about everything. Books they'd read, the way they both wrote, how they came up with ideas, their favorite music, and history. The only thing Ed hadn't dared to bring up was what would happen when Molly had to leave him behind. And what he felt for her.

It wouldn't be fair to ask her to stay when his life hinged on what his family needed from him.

"As long as I need?" Black Fox repeated, a smile on his face. "Forever, then? Would you tie your young life to mine?"

"If that is what you want," Ed said without hesitation. "You and my parents have taught me that our family is the most important thing. Our home."

"And what if I live for twenty more years? Will you stay here, by my side?" his grandfather asked, raising his eyebrows.

"That is what we do. We care for our own."

"Sometimes. Little Black Fox, I have many people to care for me. I did not ask you to come so that you could nurse an old man." He chuckled and put one hand on each knee, then leaned toward Ed. "I asked you to come because I miss you. I was ill. And there is a concern that the next time I am ill, there will not be time for you to make a long journey to see me."

Ed's shoulders dropped. He studied first his grandfather's face, and then his father's. "You didn't mean for me to come back permanently?"

His father shook his head. "No, son. There was some urgency. We hadn't heard from you."

Ed needed to read the letter again. His mother had urged him to come home, he knew that. But had he imagined that they would also expect him to stay? He had expected it of himself. His time at the ranch was over. He felt that in his soul. But if not the ranch, and not the farm, what was he to do?

"You have the soul of a wanderer," his grandfather murmured. "A long time ago, you would have left your family to trade with other nations. To see the world. These days, our young people leave on the trains for the cities, and so many never come back. I feared you might be the same."

"I will always return home when my family needs me."

Black Fox nodded deeply, his expression more serious. "I know this now." He sighed and then switched to Spanish, the tongue his wife had taught him when he'd courted her. "You seem relieved. But still confused."

Making the switch to the same language easily, Ed explained, "I am not certain what I should do now. I thought I was here for a long stay."

"No one will make you leave, Enoli," his grandfather said. "We will keep you as long as you are here. But your spirit will sweep you away soon enough."

"Perhaps not," Father said. "He brought a woman with him."

"Oh?" His grandfather perked up at that. "A woman? Where is she? Why did you not bring her here to meet me?" Then he pushed himself to his feet. "Is she your wife?"

Ed stood up quickly and snatched up his grandfather's cane. "Not yet," he said, somewhat distractedly. "That is—I haven't asked her. I'm not sure I can—"

"Nonsense. I asked your grandmother to marry me before we even spoke the same tongue." Enoli accepted his cane and immediately started off in the direction of the large farm house.

Ed looked at his father with wide eyes. "What, he wants to meet her now?"

"Now is all any of us have," Enoli called over his shoulder, proving his hearing hadn't suffered with his age or illness. "The future is for the children."

Father chuckled. "Come along, Eduardo Enoli. Your English-woman needs a proper introduction."

Still reeling from the news that he wasn't expected to take up farming again, Ed hurried with his father to catch up to his grandfather. They crossed the stream and went up to the house. Ed's mother sat on the porch, sewing in her lap, and a familiar clack-clack came from inside the house.

"What is that noise? It sounds like a woodpecker in a tin can," Enoli said as he climbed the small rise, barely using his cane.

Ed couldn't stop his grin as he answered, "That's her type-writer. I think you'll like it, Grandfather."

A WEEK PASSED ON THE FARM, AND ED HAD THE PLEASURE OF introducing Molly to his sisters, his brothers-in-law, and the nieces and nephews that even he hadn't met yet. The whole family doted on Molly, teasing her relentlessly about her friend-ship with Ed. He almost wondered whose side they were on. But each of his sisters made a point of telling him in whispered asides, "I *like* her, Eduardo. Don't let her get away from you."

They spent their days roaming the countryside, or Molly would work while he helped his father on the farm. They visited his sisters' homes, and then they visited the Cherokee school and government buildings. Molly read his copy of *The Life and Adventures of Joaquín Murieta*. And every day, they grew closer than the day before.

Peace had entered Ed's soul in a way he'd never experienced before. With Molly there to bid him good evening each night, and sitting at the breakfast table with him each day, he found he wanted still more time with her. He wanted all the hours of the day and night in her presence. And his family sensed it, too.

He had to decide for himself what that meant for his future, and hers.

"Will you walk with me?" he asked after dinner on the eighth day of their stay. The sun had gone down, and his parents sat in the parlor together. His father read the newspaper aloud while his mother embroidered a gift for a friend. Neither of them even looked up when he extended the invitation.

"Oh—if it's all right with your parents. Mrs. Byrd?"

Mrs. Byrd smiled, her eyes gleaming from behind her spectacles. As if she knew a secret—one that Ed had barely admitted to himself. "Of course, Molly. Don't stay out too long."

They slipped out the door and down the path to the stream, where fireflies had begun their nightly dance. Ed took Molly's hand in his and drew her close beneath the shadows. He leaned back against a tree, and Molly came with him, rising on her toes to meet his lips with hers.

They hadn't kissed, and had barely touched, since their arrival on his family's farm. He savored the moment, drinking her in, cupping the back of her head with one hand and wrapping his other arm around her waist. She sighed as their lips parted, then shivered and leaned against him.

"I missed that," she admitted.

"Molly." He said her name with the same tenderness with which he'd kissed her. He couldn't wait any longer. He needed to tell her what he'd decided. "There is something I need to say to you."

She leaned back, and the faint glow from the moon showed him just enough of her expression for his heart to skip a beat. She was so beautiful. So wonderful. "You can tell me anything, Eduardo."

His lips tipped up, and he took in a deep breath to steady himself. "I have decided"—Would she think him foolish?—"that I want to publish my stories. I've spoken to my grandfather, to my father, my mother, and I have told them that I write. They all want to read my work now, of course." He shuddered and released a nervous chuckle. He said the rest in a rush, pouring out what had been on his mind for days, but that he hadn't known how to say. "But I forgot how much I love this place, and my people, and my grandfather's people. And I'm not sure how much good my work is, or what it could do, but if I could get my words into the world and they made even the smallest difference about how others think about Indians and Mexicans, if it could just show them that we are people with a rich history and a bright future, maybe it would help things to change." He sucked in another breath, his lungs having grown tight as he spoke without stopping. "Do you still think I could do it? You are the only person I know who writes. Your opinion means everything to me."

Molly had grown quite still in his arms, he realized. She stepped back, her hands falling from where they'd rested against his chest. Ed let his hands fall from her waist to his sides, confused, and suddenly concerned.

"Molly?"

ALL OF MOLLY'S HOPES HAD RISEN LIKE A WAVE, ONLY TO DASH against the rocks when Ed asked her opinion about his publishing.

It wasn't fair for her to be disappointed, of course. Even if he had just brought her out to a romantic spot, all alone, and kissed her nearly senseless. None of that meant that he was going to declare his feelings for her. She shifted her mind's course and forced herself to concentrate on the matter at hand, even while her heart stung with perceived rejection.

"Of course you can do it, Eduardo. Your writing is incredible." She forced herself to smile, to put cheer in her voice. Because, truly, she *wanted* this for him. She hadn't said a word about it, not since he had told her in Arizona he didn't want anyone to read what he had written. That sort of thing couldn't be persuaded. Not even by someone who loved him.

He had arrived at his conclusion on his own. And she couldn't be happier for him.

His laugh trembled. "I don't know the first thing about publishing."

"To be honest, I don't know much about it either. In regard to books, anyway." She wanted to learn it all, though. "I can help you, if you'd like, write letters of submission to magazines. Or perhaps to newspapers, for serial stories. That might be a good place to start. Oh, Eduardo." She stepped closer again, her excitement finally getting the better of her wounded pride. "Your words will mean so much to so many people. I am so glad you're going to try. I know you'll be a success. I can feel it."

"I'm glad you have such faith in me. That makes this next part easier." He took her hands and kissed one, then the other. Her heart jumped, as startled as a deer in a meadow. "I can't offer you much right now, Molly. And I want to give you everything. Because I love you."

Like the flash flood he had rescued her from, his confession came without warning. And just as she had then, Molly put her full faith in him and stepped into his arms. "I love *you*. And you are all that I need."

"Molly. Are you sure?"

"I'm sure. I love you with my whole heart. I think I've loved you since you saved me from that flood in the desert." She couldn't help but grin. "A once in a lifetime sign, one would think, that I belong with you."

He held her close and kissed her. Her forehead. Her cheeks. He grazed her lips with his. "The first time I saw you, I knew everything would change. I just didn't know how."

"You're going to marry me before we leave here," she said, pushing aside what little shyness threatened to silence her. Being bold had brought her this far in life. It could take her a little further, and get her precisely what she wanted most—to be Mrs.

Eduardo Enoli Ramirez Byrd. "I'm going to have to change my by-line," she muttered to herself.

He laughed, the sound rumbly and pleasant in his chest before it burst out into the night air. "Did you just ask me to marry you? And you're worried about how you'll sign your work? Molly. We haven't even had a courtship yet." He didn't sound like he minded the idea all that much.

"I didn't ask," she protested. "That's your job. I merely gave you a deadline. Those are quite common in the writing world. You should get used to it."

"Oh, I should? Anything else I should get used to, Miss Molly?"

"Yes. You should know that I will never, ever let you out of my sight again. That I love you with my whole heart. And I want to see the world, but only if you're the one by my side."

"That sounds absolutely perfect, actually." He bent his head toward hers. "Will you marry me then, Molly? Because I want all of those things, too."

She gave him a *most* enthusiastic *yes.*

EPILOGUE

SEPTEMBER 1911, 15 YEARS LATER

Τ he train rumbled slowly into the small Sonoita station. Only one car carried passengers. The rest were empty, ready to fill with cattle or carrying supplies out to the ranchers and farmers of the small Arizona Territory community. The conductor had complained to them about the tiny spur-route, but Molly had set about asking him a dozen flattering questions regarding his time on the railway.

"They say cars will be faster than trains someday," the grumpy conductor had said with an irritated twitch of his mustache. "I say who would want to travel in those rattly things when we've got the elegance and efficiency of trains?"

When the sun went down, the conductor wandered off to see to paperwork and chat with the engineer, leaving Ed's small family to themselves.

Eduardo Enoli Ramirez Byrd, known in literary circles as E.E. Byrd, gently nudged his wife so she would wake before the disturbing sounds of the steam-engine's brakes could rouse her from sleep. She blinked slowly and covered a yawn.

"Are we there already?"

"Nearly," he told her, then nodded to the seat across from hers. "And you're both too tired to be any fun."

Curled up on the seat across from her mother was their thirteen-year-old daughter, Selene Maria Byrd. She'd wrapped herself in a quilt her abuela had gifted her during their recent visit to the family farm, and she looked both far too young and too old for Ed's liking. The world she was growing up in was so different from what it had been during his childhood.

Molly always reminded him when he grew worried that they were making the world a good place, and a better one. Ed himself had been invited to present a paper to the Society of American Indians, a new organization with great hopes for promoting unity among American Indians regardless of tribal affiliation or assimilation. Their first meeting was in a month, at Ohio State University.

"I'm so proud of you, Eduardo." Molly had said those same words to him many times in their fifteen-year marriage. And he'd had every reason to feel the same for her. Together, they'd gone on many adventures.

She'd even taken him back to England to meet his English publisher, then on a tour through Europe. Their little Selene had been born in Paris, of all places. Perhaps the first ever Cherokee to have that city on her birth certificate.

"Do you think she'll like it here?" Ed asked quietly, wrapping his arm around his wife's shoulders. "A desert can't be all that impressive to someone who's seen—well. Everywhere else."

"You said the same thing about Oklahoma, and have you ever seen a happier little girl?" Oklahoma had won statehood years before, but Arizona was still waiting. Some promised it would happen the following year.

"That was different. She'd never been on a farm before." He idly raised his hand to trace the heart-shaped locket his wife almost never took off. Inside she had the tiniest photographs. One from their wedding day, and one of baby Selene.

"And she's never been on a ranch before, either," Molly reminded him. "And, I hate to bring it up, but we know there are quite a few handsome cowboys who live in the area."

Ed shivered with feigned dread. "That won't be a worry for a few more years, at least."

Molly chuckled and snuggled closer to him. "We should wake her up."

"I know. We will in a minute. Then she'll ask a thousand questions, just like her mother." He kissed his wife's forehead. "Thank you for coming all this way with me, Miss Molly."

"This is where it all started, my love. And I can't wait to see everyone again. KB Ranch is an important part of our story."

"Our story," he murmured, looking down into her soft brown eyes. "You know, out of all the stories we've read and told, ours is my favorite."

"Mine too. And I know precisely how it will end."

"Oh really?"

"Yes." She twined her fingers through his. "Happily ever after."

AUTHOR'S NOTES

The Society of American Indians was a real organization that existed from 1911-1923. Though it was short lived, the Society has a long legacy of fighting for fair treatment, equality, and justice for Native Americans. It was also founded by Native American artists, authors, and professionals. The Society was in many ways the forerunner of future American Indian organizations. Throughout history, Native Americans within the Arts have been advocates for their people. I imagine Ed would've been the same. First through his writing, and later through speaking engagements, and finally as an inspiration to others to take up the banners and continue the march for peace, hope, and equality.

Though the mention in this novel was brief, the so-called Indian Schools of the 19th and 20th century (yes, children were forcibly removed from their families into mid-way through the 1900s) did irreparable harm to the children and families affected. Many children never returned home, and in the last several years we have learned the horror of why as investigators have discovered mass-graves at these old school sites. My heart breaks more every time I think on it or see another mention in the news. As a romance author, and with this book, exploring those atrocities was not the focus of this book. There are many others out there who have written about this difficult subject. I would encourage my readers to seek out more information about this time in history. I truly believe if we do not educate ourselves, we are doomed to repeat the mistakes of the past.

Regarding female reporters: In 1891, Rachel Beer became the first female editor of a national newspaper in the UK when she became editor of *The Observer*. In 1893 she purchased the *Sunday Times* and became editor of that paper too. By 1894 the number of women journalists was large enough for the Society of Women Writers and Journalists to be founded. By 1896, the society had over 200 members.

The KB Ranch is loosely based on the Empire Ranch, which was founded by an Englishman and his Canadian partners in the 1870's and is a working ranch to this day. The letters written by the Englishman home are still available to the public today, and they were immensely helpful in writing this book. I had the opportunity to tour the working ranch and several original buildings, including the adobe structure that served as the bunkhouse in this book.

Notes on laws regarding interracial marriages: Arizona law in 1896, when this fictional story is set, did not allow several types of interracial marriages. Most of the United States had laws in place against interracial marriage. Arizona passed their anti-miscegenation law while still a territory, on December 19, 1865. This included white people marrying Blacks or Asians. In 1931, Filipinos and Indians (Hindus was how it appeared in the law) were added to the list. *There was no law against a white person marrying a Native American or person of Latin-American descent*, though that law existed in other states. On December 23, 1959, Pima County Superior Court Judge Herbert Krucker struck down the state's anti-miscegenation law as unconstitutional.

These have been heavy things to write about, even in brief. I know I did not do them justice. I tried my best. Perhaps in part because of all that I learned while writing this book, and for a few other reasons, I find I am not able to continue writing western romances at this time.

Of course, no period in history is without its heartbreak or its horrors. I acknowledge that. But writing this book was a struggle to me in multiple ways. So I thank you, reader, for taking a chance on a Regency author writing cowboy romances. I hope you enjoyed them.

I still have many stories to tell, in other time periods and even other worlds. I hope you'll keep me in mind when you're looking for a novel with honorable heroes and kind-hearted heroines.

Keep up with me and all my upcoming books by signing up for my newsletter on my website.

ACKNOWLEDGMENTS

Thank you to my incredible children, Lucy, Tarver, Jane, and Teague. They still tell people, with pride, that their mother is an author. I love their confidence in me. I love them. Thank you to my husband, who is also my best friend. He is the reason I write romance, because he daily works hard with me to make our happily ever after happen.

Many thanks to my editor, Jenny Proctor, for holding my hand and getting me through the many mistakes, edits, dry-spots, and encouraging me to let my characters "break the rules."

My dear friend Shaela Kay, who acts as a sounding board, cover designer, dear friend, peer, coworker, and fellow co-conspirator—she is truly the best. Honestly. She puts up with a lot from me. She deserves a plaque. "Most Patient Friend in the World."

Thank you to my assistant, Marilee Merrell, who keeps all the gears moving even when I have more than a few loose cogs or accidentally throw a wrench in the works. Her kindness cannot be overstated. She is awesome.

Thank you to the Sally Squad who helped me through a rough summer by being supportive, hilarious, and awesome.

And last but not least, thank you to my pets. My Aussies, who inspired the ranch dogs, Izzie and Frosty. My tabby-cat, Willow, who made certain to jump between the keyboard and my hands more than once. I'm certain she wanted to check in with my mental health just as much as she wanted scritches.

ALSO BY SALLY BRITTON

ABOUT THE AUTHOR

Hello Reader! I would love for you to sign up for my newsletter to keep up with my new releases!

Just a little about me: I, along with my husband, our four incredible children, and our house full of pets, live in Oklahoma. So far, we really like it there.

I wrote my first story on my mother's electric typewriter when I was fourteen years old. Reading my way through Jane Austen, Louisa May Alcott, and Lucy Maud Montgomery, I decided to write about the elegant, complex world of centuries past.

I graduated in 2007 with a bachelor's in English, my emphasis on British literature. I met and married her husband not long after and we've been building our happily ever after since that day.

Vincent Van Gogh is attributed with the quote, "What is done in love is done well." I love those words so much that I've taken them as my motto, for myself and my characters, writing stories where love is a choice.

All of my published works are available on Amazon.com and you can connect with me and sign up for my newsletter on my website, AuthorSallyBritton.com.